[Lure the Lie]

Cat Connor

9mm Press

For information regarding permission email the publisher at 9mmpressnz@gmail.com, subject line: Permission.

ISBN Print: 978-0-473-57154-2
ISBN ePub: 978-0-473-57155-9
ISBN Mobi: 978-0-463-57156-6
ISBN D2D: 978-1-7385851-6-8

Editor: Nicky Hurle
Cover and formatting: 9mm Press

Dedicated to all people who've enabled me!

Chapter 1
[Crockett: The package.]

If no one was watching, this is the story I would write.

The truth. The real story. My story. My emergence from an early retirement of sorts. There are many stories and near stories out there and none of them start with once upon a time and none of them end in happily ever after. That's not to say that people aren't happy, I'm sure there are plenty of happy people out there in the world. Happiness is subjective. What makes me happy doesn't necessarily make anyone else happy.

This is the story I need to tell before I cannot. It's only a matter of time before they come. Before they find me.

The most wonderful things about technology are also the aspects that trap us all. As the net closes in, the truth needs to be heard.

I am David Jason Crocker and I've done some shit. And no, that's not my real name.

Four years manning a desk, for my own good, and I'm suddenly back in the game.

My boss, William MacKinnon, asked me to step out of the shadows and take charge of something codenamed *Witcher*. I think he's watched too much *Netflix*.

But it is nice being out in the field again.

Let's get this shit done.

* * *

I eased off my Harley in the Mitre 10 carpark. Good that they had motorbike parking so I didn't risk damage from cars. There's always some idiot who wants to park right next to my bike. Sunlight bounced off the chrome on the mirrors and smacked me fair in the eyes as I took my sunnies off. Another stunner of a day. Squinting, I set them on the seat before removing my helmet and hanging it over a mirror and the throttle. With my sunnies back on, I locked the bike, dropped the key into my right jeans pocket, and shrugged off my heavy leather jacket. Sun beat down on me. I caught sight of myself in the shop windows nearby. Not too shabby for forty, pal. Still got plenty of hair, no sign of grey. Didn't lose much muscle being a pencil pusher thanks to a gym membership. I pushed my hair back off my face in an attempt to cool off. Maybe my usual black wardrobe choices weren't the best. Black jeans, black tee-shirt, black jacket, black boots. Perhaps I'd think about that next time I did a replacement shop. I smiled and turned away from my reflection; like I'd buy anything other than black.

Fairly confident that no one would touch my helmet, I flipped my jacket over my shoulder and walked away. Pretty warm for nine in the morning.

I adjusted my stride and walked across the car park; there were never many cars on a Monday. I crossed to the walkway that led around the carpark by Briscoes. The semi-shade was a welcome relief. The big skate park across the road was empty. By lunchtime it would be full of teens. Skateboarding. Smoking weed. Thinking they were cool. They weren't. They were young. Real cool takes years to acquire. One day.

Time was on my side as I walked down the ramp and into the subway. Murals by a local artist lined the walls. It was an interesting and colourful depiction of native birds. Commissioned street art. No one had tagged it yet.

At the other end of the subway, I turned left and took the ramp up to street level, not the stairs. I emerged by the railway station, and turned right to Bus Stop A. No buses around to block my view of this stretch of Fergusson Drive. To the south I could see the police station, and to the north the Countdown supermarket. Directly across from where I leant against the wall by the glass bus shelters, was Writers Plot Bookshop, nestled between Tommy's real estate office, some blank windows, a doorway, and a café called Cake and Kitchen.

I checked my watch. Deliberately early is better than late. I searched the footpath toward the police station; no sign of the woman who would be opening the shop. She lived close and walked to work on fine days. Good chance she'd walk today. The sun beat down on my head, little beads of sweat gathered on my brow. I wiped the sweat away with my fingers, ran my hand through my hair, and wished I'd brought a cap.

A few school kids biked past; they were late for school. People began to arrive for a train. Ten minutes of leaning on the low wall was about all I could stomach.

Antsy.

I sauntered along the front of the railway station, all the while watching the road near the police station. Then I saw her, a lone woman walking my way. There was something about her gait that drew my attention.

The woman walked with a slight limp. She favoured her right leg. Over her left shoulder she wore a light purple messenger bag. She had on purple sneakers, dark blue jeans, and a black short-sleeved tee-shirt. A long light brown ponytail hung through the back of her bright blue cap. Her ponytail swung as she walked. She stopped in front of the bookshop and fished around in her bag. She unlocked and slid the heavy door open. She stepped inside and closed the door behind her.

Looked like the lady I was supposed to see. I wandered back to my resting spot to give her a few minutes to do whatever needed to happen before she flipped the closed sign to open.

The lights flickered on. She disappeared from view for a few minutes, then returned and put something on the front counter. The door sign flipped to open, then she slid the door all the way back and put the sandwich boards outside.

I pushed off the wall, pulled my jacket back on, and made my way to the crossing, passing the strange bronze sculpture of stylised people, walking in single file, away from the station toward the town. I waited for a truck then crossed the last stretch of road. The café was closed. I turned right and walked to the bookshop. I slowed when

I passed the doorway that led up to Veronica Tracey's Private Investigation agency. The closed sign hung in the window, as I expected. The agency opened later on a Monday. Typical MacKinnon, using a courier and a dead drop instead of delivering directly to me. Seemed like a lot of effort and extra steps.

The bookshop window display caught my eye - military books. One large book about Australian and New Zealand Forces during WWII looked interesting. Something for later.

I strolled into the shop and sized up the interior. The counter was set mid-way down the left interior wall. The right and back wall were filled with shelves of new books. On the right of the counter, in the middle of the room, stood a big display stand of children's books. It had several levels and all the colourful picture books were outward facing. Nice. Pretty sure Mitch's girls would like some of the books. Probably should send some back home to the nephews as well. More things for later.

I switched my attention from kids' books to the woman on the other side of the counter.

She smiled. "Hello, welcome to Writers Plot."

I rocked on my left heel. She looked familiar, but not familiar enough. Didn't think I'd met her before. Stunner though. I steadied myself and forged ahead, "Thanks. It's my first time in here. I was hoping you could help me." Didn't see a name tag.

She glanced at the computer screen in front of her, a small frown crossed her brow, then she looked up at me.

"Sorry, checking for online orders." She smiled again, shut the laptop, and gave me her full attention. "This is your first time in Writers Plot, is that what you said? What can I help you with?"

"A courier package was left here for me ..." Saying it felt stupid. Why would someone courier something to a bookshop for someone else? Back in Oz, it was usual for people send things to their nearest newsagent if they weren't home for deliveries. Didn't know it was a thing here in New Zealand.

"I see. We have a few customers who use our address."

"You do?"

"Oh, yes. Several life-style block people use the bookshop address for Trade Me purchases rather than paying rural delivery. It is easy for people to pick parcels up on their way home from work." She smiled brightly. "What is the name on the parcel?"

"Dave Crocker."

She frowned at me for a split second. Then opened the laptop. "We just received an online order that is to be given to a Dave Crocker when he arrives."

Had to be MacKinnon. The guy can't help himself.

"Hope I like it," I said, with a grin.

She opened a curtain under the counter and lifted out a courier packet. She checked the name before handing it over. "Here is the parcel, one moment and I will get the book."

She checked the laptop again and wrote something on a post-it note. With the note in her hand, she turned around and took a small book from a shelf within arm's reach. She stuck the post-it to the cover and passed me the book. "And this is the book."

"Thanks." I looked at the note: *Time to move on from limericks*. It was a Poetry book. Bloody MacKinnon and his sense of humour. I looked up. "I didn't get your name."

"People call me Emily."

I grinned. Interesting way of talking. "People call me Crockett." I waited for a wisecrack and none came. Was rare for anyone to pass up the opportunity to link me to Davy Crockett, especially with my nuts Aussie-meets-American accent. "Nice to meet you Emily." I extended my hand.

"Nice meeting you, Crockett."

We shook. My oversized paw swallowed her tiddler of a hand.

"Could I buy you a coffee sometime?"

Emily's expression changed, the smile in her blue eyes faded, replaced by a quizzical look. "Do not think I like it much," she said, then added, "Milo is what I drink."

"Most people know if they like something or not," I said, with a soft laugh.

Emily shrugged. "Most people are not like me." Her smile returned.

That was when I noticed a long thin scar that ran down from her temple over her jaw and down her neck. I tried an age guesstimate, I'm not great at guessing the age of women. I went with somewhere between twenty-five and thirty-five. Wide band. It's not easy narrowing the band on a woman's age if they're over twenty and under forty.

"Have you worked here long?"

Emily looked thoughtful before answering. She nodded her head slightly. "Almost a year."

She moved out from behind the counter and around the side of the children's display. She straightened books on the picture book shelves. I watched her moving and noted I was correct that she favoured her right leg, leaning a little heavily on the left as she moved.

"Did you hurt your leg?" I asked, tucking the courier packet into my jacket, and pulling the zip up. Too warm a day for a zipped jacket, but at least my hands were free. She froze momentarily, her hands still above a book she was about to move. "Sorry, didn't mean to pry."

"You ask a lot of questions." Emily looked up from the bookshelf, her expression softened. "I did, but I think it was a long time ago." She moved closer to me, bent a little to lift her jeans away from her ankle. The fabric moved and revealed a prosthetic limb. Metal, rather than flesh-like. "I am a little bionic," she said, with a laugh. "From the knee down."

"Shit, sorry, that's rough." Good one, Crockett.

"It is fine. I am used to it. I can even walk normally. Most people do not notice."

"Maybe I'm a little more observant than ninety percent of the population, especially when a pretty girl is involved."

She laughed. "Is that flirting?"

I tipped my head to the side a bit. Definitely. "Maybe a little. I'd like to take you out for a Milo sometime or a hot chocolate, because I don't think too many cafés serve Milo?"

"I would like that."

I could feel the smile as it reached my eyes. "See you round, Emily the Milo drinker."

Her voice crackled, broken by her laugh. "Is that my name now?"

"Maybe I'll just call you Milo."

Emily's laugh flowed free and easy across the shop and over me. She had an effect, no doubt about it.

"I have a nickname," Emily said with delight. "No one has called me a nickname before."

I winked. "See ya round, Milo."

There was more traffic when I left the shop than when I'd arrived.

I waited for cars to stop at the pedestrian crossing, the sun cooking me slowly under my jacket, and made my way back to my Harley. As expected, my helmet was still hanging where I'd left it. I roared out of the car park and south down Park Street, enjoying the rush from the wind. I needed to see a man about getting tooled up. Being back in the field meant I could breathe again. Without a sidearm I felt vulnerable. There was a chance a few unsavoury characters with an axe to grind might surface. I hoped not. Four years should've been long enough to have the bounty on my head fade away. Should have, but who knows? Admittedly, I pissed off a lot of people and they're not the type to let shit go.

* * *

It was beer o'clock by the time I finished my errands and returned to the safety of home. It felt good to be out riding around, but better to be home. Baby steps.

I opened the courier packet from MacKinnon, removed folders from the inside, and chucked the packaging in the bin. I placed four manilla folders on the coffee table and lifted my beer, taking a generous swig. One thing about New Zealand, they know how to make a decent beer. I placed the drink on the table and picked up the first file.

The first page presented a picture of a man in his late forties sporting an impressive greying beard. Art Jefferey. Art was a carpenter. He had his own business and employed two other people. There was a note to see the other files enclosed. Art's reputation as a carpenter was impeccable; there was nothing he couldn't do. He was trustworthy, friendly, thorough. He had an up-to-date police background check. His regular clients ranged from the super wealthy to regular people. Everyone loved Art. His business was thriving. In fact, he was turning work away and had a list of people happy to wait for him to have time for them.

I closed the folder, took another long pull of my beer, then opened the next folder. Again, there was a photograph on the first page. Dink Heimowitz. Fifty-five, balding, one-seventy-nine centimetres tall, modicum of a beer gut. Dink was an electrician, who sub-contracted to Art Jefferey. Dink used to own his own business but was hit by poor management and a lack of acumen. The tax department took everything including his house. He started again but remained a small operation. I turned the page and saw a note; Dink was a drinker. He could down four beers with lunch and go back to work with no one any the wiser. I shut the folder and moved it aside. Dink sounded a potential problem. I didn't need problems like that.

The next folder was a bloke called William Bailey. He was a plumber and everyone called him Plunger. He was early fifties, one-eighty centimetres tall, wore his hair short with noticeable greying at the temples. Plunger sub-contracted to Jefferey as required. He also owned his own business, did well, then sold it and retired early.

The last folder contained the bio for a woman, Veronica Tracey, known as Ronnie. She was ex-New Zealand Security Intelligence Service and had owned her own PI firm with two friends for the last six years. I knew about the PI gig, and I'd walked past the door earlier. MacKinnon wanted me working with Ronnie. As I read, I discovered she owned the building the offices were in and the ground floor bookshop. Nice back up plan. Ronnie was late thirties, tall, slim, attractive. She was well-known in the area and people liked her. That might be helpful.

Four people all capable and about to become my charges or my new team, depending how you looked at it.

I needed to make some phone calls. I had two jobs on, because nothing is ever simple. Back in the field and back in the deep end. I already knew what Ronnie was working on, or about to be working on: she was part of *Witcher*. That brief came across my desk yesterday and MacKinnon mentioned Ronnie was going to be pulled into the job as he wanted us on it together. Said she had special skills, but he didn't stipulate what those skills were. MacKinnon used to work for the Americans then moved to Australia and went to work for the Australian Security Intelligence Organisation. He had a high opinion of Ronnie Tracey. After four years behind a desk working out of the Australian High Commission in Wellington, I was itching to be back in the field, doing something, anything, that meant life was returning to normal. Ronnie was part of *Witcher*, like it or not. I didn't have an opinion either way. Never met the woman, but a certain amount of curiosity brewed.

The other job was codenamed *Trojan Horse*. Perfect for my new team of tradies. I reviewed the other files once more. There was a renovation that needed specialist attention. The owner of the house was having a lot of trouble getting qualified tradesmen for the job. I smiled. That'd be because they were all told to back off, politely of course. The way was clear for me to send in a team and while doing the job, they would install state of the art surveillance equipment.

I finished my beer and found my cell phone under the papers on the coffee table. I rang the number for Ronnie

Tracey. She answered fast.

"Hello, Ronnie, this is Dave Crocker."

Ronnie didn't miss a beat. "Hope you picked up the package all right?"

"Yes, thanks. Can we meet?"

"Two o'clock tomorrow at my office?"

"Can we do it earlier?"

"No."

Didn't expect that.

"All right, see you at two."

Next, I called the phone number for Art Jefferey.

"Hello, Art speaking."

"Dave Crockett here, Art. I take it you've heard of me and know why I'm calling?"

"Yes."

"I've a job for you and your tradies. You'll be working on *Trojan Horse*. I'll text the address and the name of the homeowner. Sounds like they're getting a bit desperate."

"You want us to install the usual gear?"

"Please. One more thing. If you can get away without using Dink, that'd be great."

Silence.

"Mate, we're installing a fuck-ton of surveillance gear, we need our sparky."

Now that I did expect. "All right. Just keep an eye on him. No day drinking."

"Sure. Cheers, mate."

I placed the phone on the coffee table and leaned back into the couch. It took no effort to smile. I was back and life felt almost normal. It hands down beat running background checks for security clearances day in and day out.

Chapter 2
[Ronnie: Two jobs in one day.]

"Donald Henere-Tracey, you utterly magnificent moron," I muttered to the world beyond the windscreen of my Mustang. It felt like I was staring into the abyss that was about to become my so-called life. Donald's stupidity ripped tattered holes in my future. "I can't believe he'd do something so stupid." *Idiot.*

I gripped the steering wheel with both hands and imagined it was Donald's neck as my knuckles blanched. So much stupid. Angry didn't begin to describe how I felt after the phone call from our Nana.

Life was about to become insufferable. I screeched to a halt outside our house and jumped out of the car. I tried counting to ten but gave up at two. I'm pretty sure I was not overreacting.

"Donald! You plonker!" I yelled, as I stormed through the unlocked front door. "How bloody could you?"

A door closed ahead of me.

Oh no, you don't.

There'll be no sneaking away, you little shit.

I crept out the front door and waited by the corner of the house, out of sight. Huffing, puffing, and heeled boots on concrete drew closer. As tempting as it was to trip him, I resisted. He might royally piss me off at times, but he is my cousin, and we share a house, and, like it or not, we also share a grandmother. Nana really would not be impressed if I tripped Donald no matter how much he deserved it. Probably shouldn't punch him either. Instead of tripping him, I grabbed his arm as he levelled with my hiding place.

A high-pitched shriek filled the air. He batted wildly with his left hand, trying to either dislodge or kill my hand.

"Settle, petal," I said, as I tightened my grip on his forearm through the silky fabric of his shirt sleeve.

"Oh, it's you," Donald replied, dropping his left hand to his side. "I thought it was a spider." With a flick of his dark eyelashes, and an attempt at composure, he asked, "Did you want me for something?"

"You can drop the innocent act. You knew it was me. You know why I'm here." I squeezed and twisted his arm, digging my fingers into his flesh. I could probably get away with giving him a Chinese burn.

"Ronnie! You're pinching," he squeaked.

"Let's go back inside for a little chat about Nana, shall we?"

"I'm late ... for ... for an appointment," Donald said. "I'm late!"

He didn't look anything like a white rabbit but he was beginning to sound like one. I think Nana fancies herself the Queen of Hearts, so maybe Donald the plonker is the aforementioned vermin.

"Really? Late?"

He nodded. The wide blond streak in his dark brown hair flopped up and down.

"I have a new client at the salon. Don't want to make a bad impression."

I narrowed my eyes at him. Nice try, fool.

"You don't have your purse," I said, after a brief pause.

"It's not a purse. It's a man bag," Donald replied, with exaggerated patience and a head toss.

"You say man bag, I say purse. Wonder what Nana will call it." Donald flinched. "Shall we go ask her?"

"No need to trouble Nana, Ronnie." He squeezed out a smile. "It's a purse."

"I'm sure she'd be delighted to see us with or without your purse."

His smile changed. I sensed a creeping manifestation of bravery taking hold of dear Donald. I'd be putting an end to that.

"Are you sure you want to go there?" He flapped his free hand in the general direction of the retirement home. "Visit the Old One, I mean."

"Of course. I love to spend as much time with Nana and the *Cronies of Doom* as I can squeeze into my day."

Donald and I were the same age. Our fathers were brothers and raised us together from the age of ten. I knew every trick in Donald's dog-eared play book and wasn't in the mood for his games.

"Why don't we have a cuppa?" Donald said, trying to turn back to the house. "You look like you need a cuppa. You work too hard, Ronnie."

"With Nana?" I countered, ushering him toward the car. "It'll be fun."

His shoulders drooped. A long sigh escaped, and somewhere in the midst of the sigh, quiet words formed and fell over his pouty lips. "It was an accident."

"What was, Donald?" I squeezed his arm a little tighter and gave him a good pinch.

"Ouch!" Donald squawked.

Served him right. "What was an accident?"

"The bridal magazines. They were an accident."

He tugged his arm up and my fingers slipped off the silky fabric.

"What about bridal magazines, you great big idiot?" I slapped his arm.

"I picked up a pile of mags from the salon for Nana and the Cronies to read. I didn't know there were bridal magazines in the mix until she rang me." He paled.

I glared at him.

"She rang you? You knew what would happen and you didn't warn me?"

"How was I to know she'd make something of it?"

Credit where credit's due, he attempted to sound innocent, and it was a good attempt.

"Have you met our Nana? Because it's sounding like you haven't." I smacked his arm a mite harder. "For future reference, she's that little old lady who thinks you're straight and keeps trying to fix you up with nice young women." Granddaughters of her thinning elderly friend circle, and daughters of caregivers at her retirement village. Nana was a woman on a mission and Donald was firmly in her sights, until now, until he did a stupid thing with bridal magazines and the crosshairs landed on me. I was not having it. Nope. I was not.

He cringed. "Stop being so mean, Ronnie."

"I haven't even started!"

"What do you want me to do?"

"Fix it! Explain to Nana there *is* no wedding and there will not *be* any wedding."

Not the easiest task in the world. Which is why it was unwise to give Nana ammunition. She had firm ideas on how people should live their lives and didn't mind a jot letting everyone know what they were. It was worse now that Nana liked my on-again, off-again man-friend, Ben. She repeatedly told me that Ben wouldn't buy the cow if I kept giving the milk away for free. I was pretty sure I was the cow in that scenario, and I didn't like the analogy much.

I puffed air through my closed lips.

Donald's right eyebrow rose, his piercing twinkled in the sun. "Ronnie?"

"Just fix it, Donald. I have to go back to work." I shot out a further comment, "Why is it that you get away with being a charming bachelor, but in Nana's eyes I'm a shrivelling spinster who can't find a man to put a ring on my unworthy finger? And clearly need someone to plan my life for me?"

I'm over this double-standard old-world rubbish. It's not as if I'm five years older than Donald. The family was thoroughly delighted by our arrival within hours of each other. One little seven-pound nine-ounce baby Māori boy and one seven-pound Pākehā baby girl. Yin and yang. We went to the same kindy, primary school, intermediate, and college. We were in the same classes most of the time.

"Life in Nana's day was all about double standards," Donald replied, with his trademark wide grin.

"It sucks." I glared at him. "Fix the Nana problem or there'll be dire consequences for you."

He grumbled under his breath, but I chose not to hear his words of derision. My eyes landed on the greyhound patiently waiting in the back of the car. It was time to go. "Romeo is waiting. I'm off and you … you, Donald. You will fix this situation!"

Truth was, my spidey sense was tingling and it wasn't about Nana's delight in planning a non-existent wedding. It had a lot to do with the phone call from Dave Crocker. I was interested to see what he knew about *Witcher* and was absolutely sure that was what he wanted to talk about.

In case you were wondering, I'm Veronica Tracey and I own an investigation firm with my two best friends. We mostly deal with wayward spouses and theft-as-a-servant jobs. Mostly, but not always. Every now and then an interesting job was flicked my way from former colleagues at NZSIS. Occasionally an old friend reached out with something fun for me to do which enabled me to keep one hand in my former life. This time an old friend from another agency reached out. William MacKinnon. We go back quite a number of years.

My specialty is finding people. I have a knack. Last time a big job came my way I had to find garden gnomes for the Yanks. Turned out to be scarier than it sounded and more world shattering than anyone could've imagined. It also brought an actor into my life, and he had floated in and out on a regular basis ever since. Nana likes him, but that is not the reason he's still in my life.

I drove back to the office, less annoyed with Donald, but still harbouring the feeling that something was about to happen. I unlocked the door and climbed the stairs with Romeo next to me. I liked his presence. He gave off a deceptive softy vibe and that was handy. He was getting on and, for a retired racer, was doing pretty well. Romeo is the best dog in the world and the older he grew the harder I knew his eventual death would hit me. I settled at my desk and flipped through a case report that needed emailing to a client. My cell phone rang. The name on the screen caused a smile. 'Ben the actor'.

"Morning, Ronnie."

"Morning, Ben."

"How goes the Nana situation?" Wherever Ben was, it was noisy. A loudspeaker announced a Hutt Valley train leaving from platform six. Wellington Railway station.

"Told Donald to sort it. Might've involved a threat."

Ben laughed. "I've been called back to set. Won't make it for dinner tonight."

"Damn."

"It happens."

"It's been happening a lot lately, Ben."

"Almost sounds like you miss me."

"Almost." I let a smile fill my voice. "The new job; any idea when more information will come to light?"

"I'm coming out to the Hutt. I have a gift for you from MacKinnon."

"Okay, but you're back on set?"

"I'm on the train now. Meet me, then I'll go back to town."

"Okay, if you insist," I replied, smiling.

"Hey, don't be too hard on Donald. Tell Nana I'll visit later in the week."

"I won't and I won't. I'll be keeping your name out of all conversations until she drops this wedding march." Romeo stood, stretched, and elegantly padded over to the desk. He nudged me. "Bye Ben."

I hung up and walked over to the window. People scurried across the road from the railway station, then disappeared from view. Romeo stretched once more, then lay down on his bed at the back of the office near my desk. He couldn't see outside unless he climbed on the sofa under the window.

I went back to my desk and finished the reports and then emailed them to respective clients. Just as I started to enjoy the peace and quiet, and give some thought to Dave Crockett and our afternoon meeting, Nana rang.

"Veronica dear, the girls and I were wondering ..."

I steeled myself. It's never good when Nana wonders anything.

"Yes, Nana?"

"You see dear, it's like this …" Nana paused. I detected mutterings of discontent in the background. The *Cronies of Doom*. "We think there was a prowler in the garden during the night."

"Was it an inmate?"

"That's not nice, Veronica. We're not prisoners."

"Was it a res-*i*-dent?" I laboured the word with a smile on my face.

"No. It was a youngish woman."

To be fair, I had heard her call seventy-year-olds young. Young was a relative term and included most people under ninety.

"Define youngish."

"A bit older than you I suppose."

I am nowhere near seventy and found that almost reassuring. Almost.

"And define prowling, because walking through instead of going around isn't technically prowling."

Nana huffed. "She prowled. She walked all around and seemed interested in several of the apartments that open onto the back garden. She was almost in the bushes at the far end, and then she left, in a hurry."

"Did you alert security?"

"Yes, but she was gone before they arrived."

"Staff see anything?"

"No. Just us three."

"How late was this occurrence?"

"A little after midnight."

And yet she rang to discuss wedding ideas bright and

early in the morning and never mentioned the prowler. I decided not to mention the earlier conversation. I also didn't want to know why they were gathered at that time of night. Some sort of coven meeting perhaps. Whatever it was, it was best left alone. The prowler notion gave birth to a small mercy; at least Nana had moved on from planning my wedding.

"What would you like me to do, Nana?"

"Come and look for clues ..." The exasperation in Nana's voice warned me not to fob her off. Much better to have her actively pursuing anything that wasn't my love life, or in her opinion, the lack thereof.

"I'll come over soon."

"How long do you think you'll be?"

I looked at my watch. "As long as nothing crops up, I'll be there in an hour, tops."

"We'll be waiting."

"While you're waiting, would you each write a description of the woman? No conferring, please."

"Yes, dear." The tiresome tone to her voice gave me pause. The *Cronies of Doom* were up to something. The creation of mountains out of molehills, and drama from thin air, was their usual modus operandi.

"Nana, try and keep out of trouble. Romeo and I will be there soon."

"Will you stay for a cup of tea?"

"I'm sure that will be fine. Is there cake?" I am, after all, a dutiful granddaughter and tried to spend as much time as sanity would allow with Nana. Time was precious, but so was the thin thread that tethered my sanity to my functioning brain. I did like cake though.

"I think I have some of that light fruitcake you like."

Romeo whined. I said goodbye and hung up the phone. The big dog moved to the door at the top of the stairs, his head cocked to one side.

"I can hear it too, bud," I said, as I listened to slow footsteps climb the stairs.

Eventually there was a knock on the door.

I sent Romeo back to his bed with a quick flick of my wrist and moved towards the door. The solid core door opened to reveal an elderly lady. Not our typical client.

I smiled, welcomingly, or at least that's what I was going for. No telling what my face was really doing.

"Hello. Come in." The lady tentatively walked through the doorway. I closed the door after her. "How can I help?"

The visitor was approximately eighty-five years old, with short straight silver hair and a fringe brushed across her forehead. She wore a light-weight tan coat over a pair of navy slacks and a white blouse. Her aged blue eyes were bright, and I bet they missed nothing despite her unsure countenance. She clutched a navy handbag under one arm.

"Are you Veronica Tracey?" she asked in a quiet voice rimmed with apprehension.

"Yes, I am." I ushered her toward a chair in front of my desk. Romeo snuck up to greet the woman.

"Oh, my goodness," she said, and patted Romeo on the

head. He went back to bed, satisfied with the attention.

I sat behind my desk and pointed to the chair in front. "Have a seat."

The lady hesitated at first, then with gathered momentum and purpose, she perched on the edge of the seat, nestling her handbag on her knee.

Romeo bumped my chair as he settled himself for a spot of grooming.

"How can I help?"

She licked her thin lips and sighed. The dog moved again and then changed position completely.

I waited for the woman to speak.

A train rumbled in the distance, almost lost under the traffic noise that rose from the busy road below. Old lady, dog getting fidgety, neither of those things were ideal. While the lady fished for coherent thoughts, I extracted my phone from my pocket. "Bear with ... looks like I need reinforcements," I said, and flicked off a text to one of my business partners.

Ronnie: *Steph, I need help in the office.*

My phone buzzed with a reply.

Steph: *Be there in ten.*

Pocketing my phone again, I turned my attention to the woman. Romeo paced. The tags on his collar jingling with every movement.

"Settle bud," I murmured when he nudged me. "Cross your legs or something." He huffed and paced some more and then folded himself awkwardly into a corner of the couch.

The lady cleared her throat. "I am Isabella White, and I believe I require your services," she said, "I recently discovered that someone has been following me."

"Has been, or is?" I took a notepad from my desk drawer and wrote the lady's name on the top of a clear page.

"Is. Sorry. I should have been clearer."

"Have you been to police with this?"

"No, no. They wouldn't be able to do anything. It's just an old woman's word." Her voice crumbled at the edges. "Why would they listen to me?"

"Were you followed here?"

She nodded. "I think so. I felt someone behind me, but when I turned, I didn't see anyone."

"Have you ever seen the person you suspect is following you?"

Her head shook ever so slightly. "Not really. I'm not sure."

I stood, and crossed the room to the large windows that overlooked the street below. A woman sat in the small park opposite the fancy new railway station. A man sat facing the road on the seats at the northern corner of the station. A bus pulled in. Neither person moved. Not unusual. People sometimes just sit on sunny days.

Railway bells clanged. Romeo whined, jumped off the couch, and paced some more.

Mrs White twisted in her chair. "Do you think the person is still out there?"

I smiled reassuringly at the woman. "I see no one

suspicious."

The woman startled when Steph barrelled through the door, puffing. "I'm here!"

"You have a choice, take Romeo out to relieve himself, or ..." I waved a hand at the lady waiting at my desk, knowing exactly what Steph would opt for. "Gather relevant details from Mrs ... Mrs White. What I have so far is on the pad on my desk."

"Go," Steph said, and hurried over to the desk. "Not in a dog poop mood."

I grabbed the leather dog lead that hung on the wall by the door, clipped it to Romeo's collar, pocketed doggy bags from a bowl on the coffee table near the couch, and took off out the door muttering, "Sorry, bear with."

Romeo finished a long pee as another train rumbled into the station. He then wandered in the green space sniffing. Made him happy to sniff. A few minutes later I double bagged a steaming pile of poop and dropped it into the nearest council bin. Luckily, the joy of dog companionship outweighed the stench.

Someone waved at me from the platform of the train station. Ben! Romeo and I hurried across the road.

Ben hung back by the last door of the train with a gift-wrapped box in his hands. It was about the size of a ream of printer paper. The wrapping bore birthday greetings and roses. His smile dimpled his cheeks.

"Fancy meeting you here," I said, with a grin. Romeo bounced around Ben's feet until he gave him a pat.

"You're hard to resist." He thrust the brightly wrapped

package at me with a cheeky grin on his face, leaned in and kissed my cheek. "Happy birthday from MacKinnon."

I gave the package a gentle shake. "How kind. We'll do dinner later in the week then?"

"Might be next week, Ronnie," Ben said.

"Pretty sure I can entertain myself until then. What's in the box?" I whispered, stepping into his arms.

"A little more information on *Witcher*," Ben said, his lips close enough to my ear that the words tickled.

"Tell MacKinnon thank you. But I have another new job ... she's sitting in my office," I whispered with a laugh, and took a small step away while I pretended to give the package back.

Ben grinned. "If she's paying a quarter of a mil, then I'll take this back."

"Quarter of a mil?" They really want this woman found.

"You might be on your own with this one. You okay with that?"

"I won't be on my own. Someone reached out from the Aussie's late yesterday afternoon. One of MacKinnon's boys, I think. I'm meeting with him later today."

"Interesting." He attempted to look hurt but failed. "Thought I was letting you down."

"You're not, you have other stuff happening. I can deal with this, whatever it is, with Dave Crocker."

"Did you just say Crocker?"

"Yep."

"Dave Crocker?"

"Yeah, he said Dave Crocker, I said Dave Crocker."

"He's the one everyone used to call Crockett. He's a legend." Ben's enthusiasm bounced through his words. "I heard he was in New Zealand, has been for a few years. Never run into him though."

"Seriously? Fan boy much?"

Ben grinned. "Ronnie, he's the man. He was undercover with Inferno Jesters in Australia and then in Virginia for years. He's *the man*."

"And here he is working in New Zealand with me. Now I feel special," I said, laughing again. "I hope he lives up to your hype."

"Speaking of legends ..." Curiosity sparkled in Ben's blue eyes. He continued, "Nana ... anymore wedding plans?"

"No. But she's up to something."

Surprise replaced the curiosity. "Fill me in." He glanced at his watch. "Make it fast, Ronnie."

"She wants me to drop by and investigate a person acting suspiciously in the gardens."

"At least she's moved on from planning our wedding." Ben said. "Are you going?"

"Yes. I think I should. You know what the *Cronies of Doom* are like."

"Good luck."

A female voice over the public address system announced the Wellington train was about to depart, stopping at all stations until Petone. We said goodbye and Ben vanished into the nearest carriage. The door shut behind him. A hand waved from the gloomy interior. I waved back.

* * *

Back in the office, Steph was knee deep in discussion with the old lady in front of her.

Romeo settled on his bed, yawned, and fell asleep. Awake one minute, sound asleep the next. Tough life he had.

Steph excused herself from the new client.

"Present?" she said, looking at the brightly wrapped box in my hand.

"Would seem so, early birthday by the look of it ..."

"Very early, six months early in fact." Steph narrowed her eyes. "It's something else, right?"

I winked. "I hope it sparkles. I'll put the jug on." I walked back through the door and down the hallway to the break room with the box in my hands. I checked the water level in the jug, switched it on, then sat at the table. I used a knife to slit the paper at the sellotape points. The paper fell away to reveal a lidded box containing a document packet. Grasping the packet firmly by the end, I slid a clipped bunch of papers free. I half expected to hear Jim Phelps' voice stating, "Your mission should you choose to accept it ..." Thankfully the Mission Impossible theme song didn't fill the room. The only noise came from the jug beginning to boil. With a hint of disappointment at the lack of theme music, I placed the papers on the table.

On the top of the stack of pages was a photograph clipped to several sheets of paper. The photograph was a head shot of a thirty-five-year-old woman. Non-smiling, no expression at all, possibly a passport or ID photo. The woman was on the pretty side of plain. Dark wavy, shoulder length hair, pale brown eyes, high cheek bones, straight nose, all set on a heart-shaped face. Light skin tone and minimal lines. The paper it was stapled to recorded her name as Tania Bateman. Unremarkable, but not unattractive. A cryptographer. The brief contained instructions. Locate Tania Bateman. She was last seen leaving work on Friday afternoon.

It was Tuesday morning.

She'd been officially missing since Saturday. According to the paperwork, she had a meeting scheduled for Saturday which she failed to attend. She hadn't answered her cell or home phone since. Nor had she been sighted. The thirty-five-year-old, had never missed a day of work. She was intelligent and had a good private sector job with TechSynth. Tania lived alone and was an avid reader. She had no significant other according to her employment record. Her parents lived in the Marlborough Sounds. Tania lived in Poets block in Upper Hutt. She owned her own home. Mortgage free.

Her vanilla bio held nothing to suggest where she was or what went wrong.

Maybe she'd spiced things up a bit and gone on an impromptu holiday. Financial information was included in the file. Her savings account contained fifty-seven thousand dollars. Her daily account contained twenty-thousand four hundred and fifteen dollars. There was no debt on credit cards. She withdrew five hundred dollars two weeks before her disappearance. Her debit card recorded zero transactions for two weeks, but automatic payments went from her daily account as normal. No larger withdrawals. Nothing in her financials indicated she was planning a holiday or looking to disappear. There were no untoward large deposits. The only credits over the last six months were salary.

The last sheet of paper was a statement from TechSynth saying her employer had nothing to contribute as to the whereabouts of Tania Bateman. I snapped a picture of the ID photo of Tania Bateman with my phone. That way I had something to compare to random people on the street, or to jog my memory.

Upper Hutt might be a quiet town to outsiders, but under the surface lurked danger and mysteries. People did sometimes disappear never to be seen again. The hidden depths, the underbelly of the city, was where the axe wielding maniacs, perverts, and killers lurked. There was a phone number for TechSynth. I picked up my cell phone and called it.

A recorded message said: *Enter the extension you require or press zero to talk to reception.* I pressed zero and waited. A woman answered.

"Tania Bateman, please," I said.

"I'm sorry she's no longer with us."

That was fast.

"Do you have a number where I can reach her?"

"She didn't leave any forwarding information."

"Thank you." I hung up and flipped through the papers again. A cell phone was mentioned but there was no number for it. I did a fast search for Bateman, online in the white pages, using my phone. Nothing. Nothing using one of the many people search engines either.

I tried her home number. It rang off the hook. I hung up and considered the situation. There was something iffy about the job.

Time to get serious. I gathered up the paperwork and went into the third meeting room, closed, and locked the door.

From a tall oak credenza, I took a carved wooden box and placed it on the table in the middle of the room. Back at the credenza, I picked up a map from the shelf below where the box lived. I spread the map on the table, moving the box out of the way as I smoothed the creases and folds. Once I was sure it was wrinkle free, I found two white candles, two silver candle sticks and a zippo in the cupboard on the other side of the room. I climbed on a chair and removed the smoke alarm. If that went off, it'd give the game away. Natural light streamed in the uncovered windows. I opened one wide. Fresh air filled the space. I breathed slowly for a count of ten, clearing my mind and focusing my intentions. With my intent cemented I lit the candles and called to spirit. I opened the box and removed my amethyst pendulum. Holding it in my right hand I felt my intentions flow from me to the stone. The amethyst slid through my fingers until all I was holding was the end of the silver chain. The amethyst dangled above the map. Working in a grid formation, right to left, I concentrated on Tania Bateman. The pendulum swung in wide circles. As I moved my hand slowly left, the circles continued. Over Trentham the pendulum faltered. She lived in Trentham, made sense for it to indicate there, but it wasn't the complete stop I expected. Further left, the circles continued, always wide, always moving. I covered the entire map, but it revealed no definite area we should concentrate on to find the woman. I moved back to Trentham. Smaller circles, but nothing drew the pendulum. No energy pulled it in.

I lay the pendulum down and found another map, a bigger map. One that showed the valley from Lower Hutt up. I started as far south as I could. The energy peaked at TechSynth but faded to almost nothing by the Silverstream area.

It was as if she never travelled into Upper Hutt. Yet I knew she lived in Trentham.

I thanked spirit and packed everything away, closing the window and putting the smoke alarm back last. It made no sense that I couldn't get a clear reading. I could usually get something usable. Hell, I'd even picked up residual energy from garden gnomes back in the day. Yet, Tania Bateman didn't appear to leave an energy trail. Perplexing.

As I walked down the hall to the kitchen, Steph's voice

echoed in the hollow stairwell. "You can come out now! Mrs White has gone."

I ducked into the kitchen before I replied. "I wasn't hiding," I said, lifting my voice to be heard. "Just making the coffee."

I put the papers back on the kitchen table and made coffee, double quick.

"Are you coming out?" Steph called again. This time her words fell away as if sucked into a void.

I gathered the papers and shovelled them back into the envelope, stuck my phone in my pocket, tucked the envelope under my arm, and picked up the two coffees I'd made. "I'm coming."

Sun rays bounced off the edge of a desk and into my eyes. I squinted and carried on, almost walking into the first desk. Coffee sloshed in the cups. Steph relieved me of one.

I moved to my desk, further back in the room. With the coffee cup safely on the desk, I placed the envelope into the top drawer, locked it, and then pocketed the key.

"I think we need some venetian blinds on the front window," Steph commented. "I'm going to ring the curtain place and get a quote." Sun streamed into the room, filling every corner with bright light.

"Good idea. Now, fill me in on Mrs White."

I checked my watch. Plenty of time before my meeting with Dave Crocker, the *legend*.

Romeo left Steph and flopped onto the floor by my desk.

"She thinks she's being followed. I managed to get a description. Male, mid to late thirties, six feet tall, dark wavy hair that sits on his collar, with a large blonde streak in the front." Steph stopped talking. Our eyes met.

"Donald?" The description was uncannily close to cousin Donald. "Was he wearing silver tipped black boots and a diamond watch?"

Steph nodded. "She said he was a very good looking Māori boy and quite flashy."

"Definitely Donald."

My hand reached for the landline on my desk. I rang Donald's hair salon. The phone rang three times before Mags the receptionist answered, "Mirror, Mirror. How can I help?"

"Mags, it's Ronnie, is he in?"

Background kerfuffle segued into Donald's voice through the receiver. "Ronnie ..."

"Donnie ..."

"Don't be horrible." A sigh swung after his words. "How can I help?"

"I just had an elderly woman in here saying she's being followed, and the description sounds awfully like you." I paused to let that sink in. "Something you'd like to share?"

"Why would I follow someone?"

"Answering me with a question is not denial, Donald."

"I can't even begin to understand why you think I'd follow an old duck."

"Again ... that's not denial."

He huffed and puffed down the phone.

"I'm not made of twigs, Donald, you can't blow me away."

"I don't know what you want me to say, Ronnie."

I tapped a finger on the desktop. "Tell me why you are following an old woman."

"As if I've got nothing better to do."

The gumboot dropped and bounced a few times. Nana.

I tested the theory. "Why did Nana want you to follow Mrs White?"

"I have a client. I can't get into Nana discussions right now."

I sensed he was about to hang up. "I'm on my way to Nana's now. You go back to your client. I know where you live."

Hanging up first was more satisfying than listening to his gasping panic.

Steph waited.

"It was him?"

"Oh yeah, and it's got something to do with Nana." I shook my head, then rolled my eyes. "Nana appears to be using cousin Donald as her henchman in some nefarious dealings."

Donald wasn't exactly henchman material. If the word henchman conjured up something shiny and sparkly, or even something akin to a unicorn kitten with dragonfly wings, then it would describe Donald.

Steph passed me Romeo's lead. One glance told me it was already attached to the dog. "You better take him.

You know how the oldies love visits from the furry beast."

Before leaving I double checked my drawer was locked and that the key was safely in my pocket. Steph passed no comment. Every now and then envelopes arrived for me and it was often something we couldn't discuss, so unless I needed their help, no one asked. A glimmer of curiosity sparked behind Steph's eyes, but I knew she wouldn't ask details. That was the end of that.

"See you soon. Hold the fort."

Steph smiled and flipped the television on. Cricket. I knew she loved nothing more than uninterrupted cricket time.

"Blinds," I said.

"I'll ring now and get a quote."

"Thank you." The door closed by itself once Romeo and I started down the stairs.

I walked Romeo south on Fergusson Drive and onto Martin Street. A nice day for a walk.

Chapter 3
[Crockett: Thinly veiled threats.]

The morning was moving along nicely, but I still had plenty of time before the meeting with Veronica Tracey. I hopped on the bike and went for a ride. Decided to swing past the house the tradies were working on. It was a long wide, tree-lined street. All the houses were set well back from the road, and expensive. I parked behind a ute, dropped my helmet over my mirror, and headed up the driveway, unzipping my jacket as I went. I knocked on the front door, then opened it, and called out, "Art?"

A voice came back, "Hang on."

Footsteps moved toward me, and a man came into view.

"How's it going?" I asked, extending my hand.

We shook.

"Yeah, not bad, Crockett." He turned and walked back down the hallway. I followed. "I suggested the homeowners spend the week in a hotel."

"Jesus. How big is that bill going to be?"

"Does it matter?" He stepped into the kitchen.

"Probably not in the big scheme of things, just make sure I get the invoice," I said. There was a man up a ladder in the kitchen, his top half inside the crawl space. I watched for a second. "Art, is there anything you need?"

Art shook his head. "We're good. We'll be finished here on Friday. I'll drop round with the security codes for the system."

"Thanks. Text me first, ay?"

He nodded. "What's the next job?"

"There's a place in Ngaio that needs the same kind of overhaul. Then a residence in Wainuiomata."

"Part of *Trojan Horse*?"

I nodded. "You up for it?"

His head bobbed slowly. "The money's good."

"I'll leave you to get on with it. Give me a bell if you need anything."

Twenty minutes later I was back home, looking over the paperwork for *Witcher*. I read the papers twice. No cell phone. No contact details for family. No email address. Strange. There were two phone numbers. Her home phone, and her place of employment. I rang the second number. A recorded voice answered asking for the extension and saying press zero for the receptionist, I pressed zero.

"Tania Bateman's extension, please."

"I'm sorry Ms Bateman is away."

"Cheers." I hung up.

Away. Suppose she is away.

I rang her home number. It rang and rang. I hung up after twenty rings. If she was home, she wasn't answering the phone.

I logged on to a messaging site and fired off a quick message to MacKinnon: *Cell phone number, email addresses, family contact details would be helpful.*

Leaving the screen open I went to the kitchen and

made a coffee. By the time I sat back down in front of the laptop, there was a reply.

MacKinnon: *The cell phone number attached to her personal file is out of service. No info on her family. Email address was disposable.*

Not good. Not good, at all. I fired off another message and got an immediate answer.

MacKinnon: *There are hidden truths covered in a coating of lies. Find out what's going on and find that woman.*

I drank my coffee and read his reply four times. Something fishy was happening. She had a security clearance. Yet vital information was missing from her employment record. We didn't even have her parents' names. Her parents lived in Marlborough. No previous work history.

She arrived in the world fully fledged at the age of thirty. No previous life. Something no one wants talked about in the open, happened. It looked like someone fucked up five years ago and hired her without the proper checks and balances. A security clearance was stamped on her file. But by whom?

MacKinnon was right about the lies.

My cell phone buzzed. I checked the display. Chandler. Reluctantly I answered the call.

"What can I do for you?"

"Meet with me, in half an hour. My office," he said, his voice grating like a two-pack-a-day smoker.

"Why?"

"Because you need to know who you are working with."

"I know who I am working with, Chandler. If you have more information, you can give it to me now." His reputation wasn't a secret. He was a bad hombre and I doubted he had anything useful to share.

"My office, half an hour. You better hop on that Harley of yours double quick to make it in time."

I hung up.

Fuck me. Guess I was going to meet Chandler.

Waiting outside his office, I questioned my reason for turning up. Didn't seem like he would have anything to tell me that couldn't be said over the phone. His assistant appeared from the office. Skittish, but she still managed a smile in my direction.

"Mr Crocker, go on in." She sat behind her desk as her smile faded.

I knocked once on the door and pushed it wide open. A well-put-together man with short grey hair lifted his head and motioned me over. He looked like the type of bloke who had bottles of moisturiser and went for manicures. He pointed to a chair near the desk. I didn't care for the hardness in his expression or the lack of light behind his dark eyes. I pushed the door to, behind me and sat in the chair.

"Mr Crocker," he crooned. "How can I help?"

"You wanted this meeting, so you tell me."

"I hear you are working with Veronica Tracey." His voice held a sharp edge. He folded his manicured fingers together and rested his hands on the desktop.

"And?" I genuinely did not know what the man's problem was and I didn't want to give it any thought.

"You might regret your decision ..."

Ah, here we go.

"I doubt it. Ms Tracey comes highly recommended."

"I'm sure. No doubt by MacKinnon." Derision ringed his words. "Be careful, Mr Crockett, she's insubordinate and hard to control."

"We're working together, sir. I'm not her superior." Controlling people is not how I work.

"Watch your back. She's had assets killed with her reckless behaviour and inability to follow orders. No one wants to work with her now."

That's not the story I'd heard. I knew whose orders she refused to follow, and I knew why. I'd read the full report, thanks to MacKinnon. I got a copy before her former boss, Reede, had the information redacted. Raymond Chandler was Reede's underling once upon a time. I knew this idiot worked with Ronnie, back in the day. Okay, so he wanted to run her down. That probably makes him feel like a big man. Everything I'd heard about Chandler appeared to be true.

"She worked with the Americans a couple of years ago." People still wanted her on their team.

"Under sufferance on their part, and the mess she left behind with that bloody actor ... I can't believe anyone would hire her again. And as for that pathetic agency she's operating. Really? 'Wherefore art thou?' Could she get any cheesier?"

"I heard a completely different story," I said. Enough, he was not getting away with this bullshit. Not on my watch. Pick your fight carefully, Crockett. He's got enough power to be annoying. I shrugged that thought away.

"I'm available for a drink later tonight, if you'd like to hear more." He batted his eyelashes and licked his lips.

"Sorry, sir. I have a prior engagement." With my self-esteem.

"Your loss," he said, flicking his tongue over his lips and looking me up and down. My manhood went into self-preservation mode and shrivelled.

I shook my head. "Busy." Forever.

"Trust me. You don't want to get mixed up with Tracey. She'll drag you with her into the sewer," he said, trying to keep eye contact.

"Wow, man, you're a piece of shit."

"Watch your beautiful back. Be a shame if something happened to it."

I threw a cold smile. "That sounded like a threat. You want to reel that back in?"

His eyes widened. "Not a threat. A friendly warning. She's dangerous."

"I like to make my own mind up about colleagues. Thanks for the concern." Go fuck yourself. "No one needs someone like you poisoning the well."

He sucked in air with a sharp hiss.

"You do not want to make an enemy of me."

I walked to the door, opened it slowly, turned around and smiled. "I see everything I've heard about you is true. Good luck."

"You have my number," he called after me. "Use it."

It'd be a cold day in hell. My skin crawled. I needed a steaming hot shower and a lot of soap. Time was ticking and I couldn't go home before meeting Ronnie. Instead of a shower I opted for a coffee and five minutes to get my head straight, before heading back to Upper Hutt.

Chapter 4
[Ronnie: The trouble with Nana.]

Twenty minutes later, I stood in the light and airy foyer of the retirement home on Ward Street, with the dog next to me. I was fairly confident that old age was caused by a virus and that the virus lived beyond the big glass doors. Bravely, I swung the left-hand door open and entered with Romeo. I knew by his quick glance at me that he and I were on the same page regarding the old age virus.

Margot smiled brightly. "Morning Ronnie, June said you'd be in." She waved a hand at the sanitiser on the counter, and the warning about norovirus. I duly pumped a big dollop into my hands and rubbed it in thoroughly. Sticky and unpleasant, but better than death.

"Is Nana in her apartment?"

"Yes, I think so."

"Thanks."

I walked slowly to the big glass automatic doors that lead down the south corridor. They whooshed open. Side-stepping Zimmer frames and the walking dead, I kept Romeo on the wall side, so he didn't get his toes trampled. Outside Nana's apartment door, I took a deep breath and knocked twice.

A deceptively feeble voice called out, "Come in."

I opened the door, and then unhooked Romeo's lead so he could say hello and lie down wherever he wanted.

Clucking and fussing noises rose from Nana over the

dog. The *Cronies of Doom* joined in. The sitting room buzzed with affection for Romeo, and he thrived on it. With my best smile plastered on my face, I greeted Nana.

Nana offered her papery old cheek for a kiss. Dutiful granddaughter that I am, I obliged. I resisted the urge to rub sanitiser on my lips to stem the transfer of old.

"Sit, Veronica, we have our descriptions ready," Nana said, then snickered as Romeo sat. "Aren't you a good boy."

Not all greyhounds can sit, mine is an exception.

I unceremoniously plopped into a vacant armchair and waited to see who would go first. No surprise that it was Ester Mulholland. She was a former policewoman who worked with Grandad back in the day. Things were different then; Ester was in charge of cups of tea, and on good days she probably supervised female prisoners. It was a vastly different time. Ester was well-rounded, a little bit matronly. I imagined she was slimmer in her policing days. She wore a khaki skirt and a cream long-sleeved blouse with a necklace of peridot-coloured beads. Her soft grey hair sat just below her collar.

"I've written everything down for you," Ester said, as she leaned over and dropped a white writing pad in my lap. "Hope you don't mind, but I got the girls to use the same template."

I flicked my eyes over the outline of a female drawn on the page and the corresponding notes. I didn't mind at all. Ester had drawn the length of her hair and clothing onto the outline and had then given a detailed description.

"Nice work."

Nana and Frankie handed over their pieces of paper. Same deal, but a little less description. I looked for similarities. They agreed on the style of clothing and hair, but not age. The age range ran from early thirties to late forties. I fitted somewhere in the middle, closer to the dreaded forty than thirty. Thirty-mumble was my current age. Donald agreed with my estimate of our age. When we were out together, he liked to chop a good five years off and go early thirties.

Growing up is optional. Growing old is viral.

"Have any of you seen the mystery woman before?" I queried the trio.

They all shook their heads. Something about the description being so bland made me think of the missing cryptographer. Surely not? I compared the photo on my phone of Tania Bateman, to the descriptions offered. So close, it could be the same person. What were the chances? With my luck, it *was* her and then I'd have the three old biddies smack in the middle of a real investigation. That could only end badly.

I passed the phone to Nana. "Is this her?"

Nana studied the image then passed the phone to Ester on her left. It did a circle back to me. They nodded in unison.

"You're all sure?" I watched the women carefully. They all agreed with a solid nod. Buggery bollocks, that's all I needed.

"Veronica, why on earth would you have a photo of our prowler?" Nana asked, with a smattering of delight.

"I don't know that I do, Nana. This is someone that came to my attention in an unrelated matter earlier this morning." I smiled. "Any idea what she was looking for in the garden?"

The three women shook their heads.

"I'll take Romeo for a walk around outside," I said. "Why don't you three accompany me and point out the places she snooped?"

A murmur of approval flittered around the group. I knew they'd like that. I re-clipped Romeo's lead and stood. Nana sprang to her feet and had the ranch slider to the garden open before Ester or Frankie could blink. Nana was a spry old stick and not about to let a silly number like ninety-four get the better of her. Nana had been ninety-four for a while. No one was quite sure for how long, or how much longer ninety-four could go on. The truth was that Nana had fudged her age in an upward direction for a long time. Even she wasn't sure how old she really was anymore. Didn't seem to slow her down.

The women followed Romeo around the garden. He was happy to be sniffing trees. Nana pointed out the area she first spotted the woman. Ester and Frankie added helpful information. Everyone agreed the woman's behaviour was odd.

Very odd if it's the same woman I'm looking for.

"Who lives in that apartment?" I asked and pointed to where Nana said she first saw the mystery prowler.

"Mrs Wright."

"Did you say Wright with a wr or White with a wh?" I watched Nana closely for a reaction.

"Wright," she replied, deadpan.

"Does she have a daughter by any chance?"

"No dear, she had no children."

Ester chimed in, "Sad story that one. They tried for years and couldn't have a baby. Never adopted either. She was a schoolteacher and poured her life into that instead. Mr Wright was a military man."

Could've been an old pupil coming for a visit, or the daughter of a friend.

We moved to the next place the woman was seen. "And who lives here?"

Nana had nothing to say. Frankie stepped in, "No one. The apartment is empty. The old fellow who lived there is in the hospital wing now." She nodded her head sagely. "He's lost what was left of his marbles. Sad state of affairs."

"Children?"

"None that we've ever met or seen or heard him talk about. He never mentioned visitors."

Maybe he didn't like everyone knowing his business, or maybe he'd forgotten he had children or visitors.

"What was his name?"

"James Reading."

"I'll look into his background, just in case the mystery lady was looking for her long lost father or grandfather."

"You're not taking any notes, dear," Nana said, pulling

a pen from a secret side-pocket in her purple flowery dress, and a notebook from another hidden pocket. She handed me the notebook and pen, and in exchange I handed her Romeo's lead. His impeccable manners and consideration of people meant it was quite safe for Nana to hold onto the lead while I took notes. Anything to keep Nana happy and her brain ticking over with a new mystery. Anything that wasn't talking about weddings, was good for me.

Dutifully making notes, I moved over to where Ester stood. She pointed out trampled flowers in a garden bed by a window. I photographed the trampling and a partial shoe print with my phone. Nana clucked with approval; The *Cronies of Doom* nodded and joined in. My approval rating skyrocketed.

It was all going well.

Nana was happiest when she had a mystery to solve and seemed to have forgotten all about Donald's bridal magazines. Hooray for small mercies. But I had not forgotten about dear Donald and his stupidity, or about henchman Donald and the mysterious happenings with Mrs White.

"Nana, a question about Mrs White."

Nana's old eyes widened. Quick as a flash she replied, "No dear, I said Mrs Wright."

"I know what you said, Nana. But I'd like to talk about a Mrs Isabella White."

"What on earth made you bring *her* name up?"

"She came in to see us at the office, said she's being

followed, she gave Steph a description of the person."

Nana shuffled away, suddenly a lot frailer than two minutes ago. "I need a lie down, dear. It's been a busy day." She scurried away to her apartment with Romeo ambling beside her.

It only took me four strides to catch up. Ester puffed along behind, aided by Frankie.

"That carry on won't wash with me, Nana. You're up to something, and I want to know why you asked Donald to follow that poor old woman?"

Her head spun. Fire sparked within her old blue eyes.

"*Poor old woman?*" Nana spat with pure derision.

"Nana?"

"That *poor old woman* is up to no good."

"By whose determination?" I asked, placing a hand on Nana's forearm to stop her entering her apartment.

"It's none of your business, Veronica. You should leave it alone."

"Oh, but it is my business. She hired my firm to find out who was following her, and why."

Nana's lips stretched over her false teeth in a frightening rendition of a smile. "Isn't that the pip?"

"Nana ... I will find out whether you tell me or not."

"You should leave it alone, Veronica. She's a *mad* old woman fabricating silliness for attention."

"We'll see."

I didn't believe that for one second. Nana walked into her sitting room. I gave the situation some thought, and then rang Jenn.

"Hey, Steph has the details of a new job, a walk in, Mrs White. I'd like you to take it."

"Yep, no problem at all. Just about finished this report. Steph will sign off on the expenses shortly, then I'm all over the White case."

"Thank you. See you later."

I shoved my phone into my back pocket.

Nana eyed me with annoyance. "That wasn't necessary Veronica. You should've sent that woman on her way."

"She's a client." She managed to climb all the stairs to get help. I considered that the least we could do was provide some peace of mind. "And if she's a friend of yours, she'll get the friends and family discount."

Nana's hackles rose. "She is not my friend. Don't you go giving *her* a discount."

Ester and Frankie joined us inside. Frankie was keen to know my thoughts on the mystery woman. I didn't even know my thoughts on the woman yet. And I could hardly tell them what I did know about Tania Bateman.

The Cronies were like an ancient Scooby-doo gang. All they needed was a big dog, the Mystery Machine, and a theme song. I glanced at Romeo. Nope, he was much braver than Scooby.

"I'll talk to Margot on my way out and see what I can turn up regarding your mysterious prowler."

"Don't forget the security people," Ester said.

"I won't," I replied, with a smile. I turned to Nana. "If you think of anything that you need to tell Jenn or me regarding Mrs White, you know how to reach me."

I relieved Nana of Romeo's lead, picked my shoulder bag up off the floor near the chair I'd been sitting in, and shoved all the witness information into it, along with Nana's notebook. I left the pen on the coffee table.

"I'll let myself out," I said to the group, still hovering near the ranch slider. "And I'll be in touch."

Frankie and Ester chorused goodbyes. Nana waved and smiled with more saccharine than usual. Jenn would get to the bottom of Mrs White and Nana. Something told me it was a juicy story.

* * *

"Hang on, Romeo, just a bit longer, and then you can read all the lamp post stories on the way back to work." I gave his ears a rub when he looked up at me and then rang the bell on the counter and waited. Margot appeared from a room down the hall, flustered, but smiling.

"You off then, Ronnie?"

"Yep, just a wee question about the intruder incident during the night ..."

Margot rolled her eyes and tutted. "Incident! Really, they're making a meal of it, those three." She flicked her head toward the hallway that led to Nana's apartment. "What do you want to know?"

"Did anyone else see anything?"

"No. We had a staff meeting this morning and had a chat with the residents at breakfast. No one else reported seeing anyone in the garden."

"How about staff? Security?"

"Nothing. The security company was called in. There was no one here when they arrived. They did say flowers were trampled in one of the garden beds." Margot smiled. "Some of our residents get a bit forgetful and it's not unusual for plants to get stood on."

"Really?"

"One or two in particular do tend to forget where the garden entrance door is."

"So, the trampled flowers could be nothing?"

"Yes. Security couldn't determine who or what caused the trampling. There was nothing out of place outside. No one attempted entry. The door to the main building is alarmed at night and the alarm was armed."

"Any thoughts?" I asked.

"Three old biddies with overactive imaginations."

"Highly likely knowing those three." I showed Margot the photo of the missing woman from my investigation. "Ever seen this lady visiting anyone?"

Margot took a moment to look at the photo then shook her head.

"We get it all here, you know, Ronnie. The overactive imaginations, attention seeking, the arguing, and dramas. It's like kindergarten for oldies some days."

Certainly couldn't rule any of that out. Kindergarten for oldies who have the means to cause real strife for someone if they so desired. Mrs White popped back into my mind.

"You don't know a Mrs Isabella White, do you?"

Margot's brow furrowed. "That name is familiar. Give

me a minute." She typed into the computer on her desk. Her desk was below the counter. Anyone in a wheelchair would be hard pushed to see Margot if she was sitting down. "I knew that name was familiar. I found her records."

"She used to be here, and isn't now?"

"That's right. She moved out of the village three years ago."

"Don't suppose you have anything on that computer that says who she was friendly with?"

A small exclamation escaped Margot's mouth, and she popped up from her chair. "Her apartment was next to June's."

"Oh, that's interesting. And she left three years ago?"

"Yes."

"In June, by any chance?"

"July."

"Grandad died in June."

"Why the interest in Mrs White?"

"She's a client of ours. Just wondered if she had a connection to the village at all. You know, background?"

"Of course, well, good luck."

"You're certain you haven't seen this woman anywhere near the home?" I opened the image of Tania Bateman on my phone again and handed it over to Margot for a last inspection.

Margot took a moment, before passing it back with a shake of her head. "I generally see all visitors unless the person accesses an apartment with an exterior door."

"Thanks for that." Then I thought about cameras. "Are there external security cameras?"

"Yes, covering the doorways into the main building."

"Anything in the garden? Is there a doorway there?"

"I'll check with security and see if there is. Can I ring you later?"

"Of course, you have my number?"

"I do, Ronnie, it's in your Nana's file. Have a nice day."

Romeo and I walked back to the office. He stopped at every other lamp post so he could read the latest blogs by the Martin Street dogs and add his own comments. Some days the blogs were endless. Today wasn't so bad. He'd read most of them on the way to Nana's. There were no children playing in the school yard of Upper Hutt Primary to garner his interest. We crossed the pedestrian crossing to the swimming pool without pausing near the back gate of the school for little grabby hands that normally liked to poke out and reach for Romeo.

Jenn and Steph were both in the office when I arrived. Steph was glued to the cricket and Jenn was leafing through a magazine. They looked up, smiled, and went back to doing their thing.

"You know what we need?" I said, unclipping the dog and watching him drink from his water bowl for a moment.

"What?" Jenn asked, putting the magazine down.

"Clinkers and coffee."

Jenn nodded. "Donuts and coffee would be better."

"Clinkers are scarcer than hen's teeth, donuts are a

more available option," Steph commented, ever practical. She turned the TV up and zoned back into the cricket.

At least no one had an opinion about the coffee.

"Watch Romeo for a minute, I'm going for coffee," I said, taking my wallet out of my bag, and hurrying out the door. Jenn's voice floated down the stairs after me requesting cream donuts, not the chocolate iced kind.

Creamed donuts were probably the least I could do, considering I'd dropped the Mrs White thing on her, especially when I knew Nana was wrapped up in it and had dragged Donald along for the ride. Remorse reared its ugly head for a moment. I quelled it with thoughts of the new mission. That was the priority. Nana and her vendetta, not so much. Thoughts of the mystery woman in the garden surfaced as I paid for the coffee at the Dough Bakery. I stuffed my wallet under my arm, carried the take-out tray in one hand and a bag of cream donuts in the other. A bit of concern wriggled around in my mind regarding the *Cronies of Doom* identifying the prowler as the missing Bateman woman. What on earth would she be doing in a retirement village garden? Also, was it really her? The cronies are sharp as tacks, but it was after midnight, and they were also quite well known for their vivid imaginations. A bit of embellishment never hurt, was their motto for most things.

Upper Hutt seemed like a nowhere place to go missing. It was a small city for starters. Two degrees of separation in New Zealand, and in Upper Hutt that held huge truth. If someone didn't know you, their sister or brother did.

Not the sort of place you get lost by accident. And if she wanted to disappear, why would she lurk in a retirement home garden in the middle of the bloody night days after her supposed disappearance?

I eased the takeout tray onto my desk and then passed round the coffees and the donuts. Jenn scoffed her donut in record time, dripping less cream onto her shirt than usual. Impressive.

"That was good, almost as good as the donuts from Broadway."

Romeo sat as close to her as he could, waiting for a chance to swoop in with his long tongue and scoop a blob of creamy raspberry jam from her tee-shirt. If it wasn't for his close attention, Jenn would need more than two changes of clothing in any given day.

Feeling better after a coffee and the sugar rush, I decided it was time to tackle the mystery of the garden woman and work out if it was the same woman Crocker and I were looking for. It already felt off that it took so long after she disappeared for us to be involved. Those important first forty-eight hours rolled past and now it was harder to pick up a trail. I needed some quiet time with a map and something personal that belonged to Tania Bateman.

The *Cronies of Doom* would drive me crazy if I didn't appear to be doing something about the prowler, but if it *was* the woman I wanted, then I'd need a cover story for the Cronies.

They're old, they're not stupid. Troublemakers, but not

usually malicious.

I noticed Jenn watch me open my laptop and take the notebook from my bag.

"Can I help you?" I asked.

"Mrs White."

"All yours. Have fun."

"Why do I get the feeling you know something?"

I shrugged and typed a name from the notebook into a search program. "No idea."

Telling her anything I knew about Nana could run the risk of influencing the investigation. It was much better if Jenn came at it without preconceived ideas surrounding the conniving nature of Nana. So, I said nothing. Shoot me.

The search on the screen in front of me churned on, spitting up very little in the way of useful information. I half-expected to find one of the former inmates of the empty apartment had a long-lost daughter, but it wasn't looking promising on that front. James Reading was a dark horse, but not a randy dark horse with multitudes of stray children from what I could gather.

The lives of Mr and Mrs Wright were a little more open. They were members of several community groups, and friends of the library. I searched the retirement village website and found newsletters. From those I discovered that Mrs Wright organised the Christmas play every year and Mr Wright ran a military history club. When I looked over the list of upcoming activities on the website, up popped their names again. They ran a book club that met every fortnight in the main lounge. The book chosen for the next meeting was one by an Upper Hutt author. Seemed they liked a bit of murder and mayhem. They were busy, active, and not sitting around causing trouble for their non-existent grandchildren. I found no connection to Tania Bateman.

As the day ticked on, my eyes blurred from staring at the computer.

"Hey Steph?" I waited patiently for her to tear her eyes off the game.

"Yep?" One eye still watched the cricket.

"How'd you get on with the curtains or blinds, or whatever?"

She tore her eyes from the screen and flicked through a diary on her desk. "Someone is coming to discuss blinds on Thursday morning. I'll be here."

"Great, Jenn and I will be in and out for the rest of the week."

"You want me to take Romeo if you two are that busy?" Her focus returned to the game. "Six! About time."

"If you could, that'd be great. He's not going to enjoy it much."

I glanced at my watch when I heard heavy footsteps on the stairs. My two-o'clock meeting had arrived.

Chapter 5
[Crockett: Getting on with the job.]

I knocked once, then swung the door open. The interior office was warm, sunny, and filled with noise from the cricket on the television. I was not averse to cricket and I knew Australia was playing New Zealand in a series of one-dayers. A large white and black greyhound with friendly eyes stood and shook but didn't venture closer.

A tidy looking woman with long dark hair greeted me with a smile. "Dave Crocker?"

I nodded. "Veronica Tracey?"

"In the flesh," she said, stepping forward and shaking my hand. She turned to the other two women in the office and said, "Can I have the room please?"

They stood, gathered whatever they needed, and the tall skinny dog.

"We'll be in the break room," one woman replied as she flicked the remote at the TV sending the screen into darkness. "Watching the cricket."

"Who's bowling?" I asked.

"You lot," she said. "You're an Aussie, right?"

I nodded. "I'm Crockett," I said, putting my hand out.

She shook it. "I'm Steph, this is Jenn." Handshakes all round, then I reached behind me and opened the door for them.

"Have a seat," Ronnie said, waving a hand toward the couch under the window.

"Thanks." I unzipped my leather jacket, pulled a document packet out from inside, laid it on the coffee table in front of the couch, then sat on the large dark brown chesterfield. Nice.

Ronnie sat opposite in a matching armchair.

"Can I get you anything?" Ronnie asked.

"No, I'm good. Let's get down to it, shall we?"

"Okay. I know you picked up the packet from the bookshop downstairs and that you're working on a job codenamed *Witcher*," she said.

"The powers that be, have decided we should work together." That was the truth. MacKinnon wanted me working with her. I watched for a reaction.

"So, I heard and I have no problem working with the Australians."

"Good. We're not all bad." I stretched one leg out. "Heard you sometimes do some work for the Americans."

"Is that a problem?"

"Not at all. They pay well, good for you, and welcome aboard the Aussie team." I smiled. "The way I see it, someone isn't telling the whole truth. Be it the missing Bateman woman or her employers." Probably both. "Our job, as well as locating Ms Bateman, is to *lure the lie*."

Ronnie nodded and smiled. "Glad you said that, because I was wondering how she got a security clearance like she has without the information that goes with it? It isn't a high-level clearance, but they should've looked a smidge closer."

"I had the same thoughts," I said. Already I liked

Ronnie. She didn't beat about the bush.

"And I have something," Ronnie said.

"Great start then. I have the feeling we're going to be wading thigh deep in shit to bring this job to fruition."

Ronnie laughed. "Possibly. Get this, our woman may have been seen at a retirement home in the middle of the night."

"When?" I asked.

"Last night. Well, midnight or just after."

"She supposedly went missing on Saturday or maybe even Friday after work."

"Yeah, something doesn't add up," Ronnie said.

She was right about that. Nothing added up. If she went missing on Friday night or Saturday, then vital days were wasted.

"Why would a woman in her thirties be at a retirement home?" Wouldn't be my first choice.

"No idea. Cannot confirm one-hundred percent that it was her, but she was identified by three elderly women," Ronnie said, her voice light and rimmed with humour.

"How?"

"I showed them a photo ..."

Ronnie's cell phone rang. She pried it from her pocket and looked at the screen.

"Speak of the devil," she said with a smile. "I need to take this." Ronnie answered and put the call on speaker. "Nana, everything all right?"

"Have you made any progress?"

"Not yet, Nana. I'm searching databases to see if there

is a link between your prowler and the retirement home *inmates*."

"Residents, Veronica. How many times must I say that we are residents?" said the disembodied voice from the phone. "Now, I'm ringing because the girls and I were wondering if you needed help?"

Ronnie sucked in air. "That won't be necessary, Nana. I can handle this." She paused then offered something else, "Are you certain the woman you saw is the woman in the photo I showed you?"

"Yes, dear. We've told you already."

"Just checking, Nana." Ronnie smiled at me, then said, "Why don't you talk to Jenn about Mrs White?"

The woman huffed and puffed from the phone. "There's nothing to say about that silly old woman."

"Jenn has the case, no doubt you'll hear from her in due course, and you can tell her that yourself," Ronnie said. "Perhaps you could also mention why Donald is involved in your scheme ..."

"I hear the tea trolley. Sorry Veronica, must dash."

Ronnie hung up and placed her phone on the coffee table.

I watched on with amusement. "What was that about?"

"The home where our woman was spotted happens to be the same one that houses my Nana and the *Cronies of Doom*."

"The Cronies of what?"

"Doom. The *Cronies of Doom*. Nana's little circle of friends. Think Nancy Drew and her friends, but older than dirt."

I wasn't sure whether to smile or cringe. MacKinnon did say Ronnie was a colourful character. "Is that going to be a problem?"

Ronnie nodded while saying, "No, not at all. How could a ninety-four-year-old woman be any trouble?"

"The only lead so far is the one involving your Nana?"

"Correct."

"Have you had a look at Bateman's house yet?"

"No."

"I think we'd better. Let's do it."

"Do you want the dog?"

I turned my head slowly and made direct eye-contact with Ronnie. "The dog, the one that was in here?"

"Yes. Romeo." She nodded. "He's a search and rescue dog. He's an awesome tracker."

"Hold on, you're ex-SIS, now a private investigator, and you have a search and rescue greyhound?" More colour. "Don't imagine there are many of them."

"Steph and Jenn are volunteer fire fighters who occasionally help out with search and rescue. Romeo liked to go with them, so they trained him. He's a unique animal."

"Firies?"

"If you must. What is it with you Aussies having to shorten everything and make it sound cute?"

I clicked my tongue and winked at her. "Have you met me?"

"You're about as cute as a pit bull."

"You're dreaming. I'm freaking adorable," I grumbled, then shot her a smile.

"For future reference if you ever call me *Darl* or refer to me as a *Sheila*, we'll have a major problem," Ronnie said. "We going or what?" A smile graced her features. "Dog, yes or no?"

"Yes, and yes." I shrugged. Couldn't hurt to have the dog along.

* * *

Tania Bateman kept a tidy house. The lawns were cut short, and the flower beds weed free. Straight, clean, and professional looking edges.

"You think she uses a gardener?" Ronnie asked, as we walked up the driveway.

"Looks like it. The lawns are freshly mown ..." I pointed to a few stray blades of grass on the path. "Unless she came home this morning and did them herself?"

"Maybe she did."

I knocked on the front door and waited. Ronnie peered in the windows. Romeo sniffed the doormat, then joined Ronnie.

No one answered the knock. "Let's try the back of the house," I said.

We walked down the few steps and around the side of the house, past the garage, and into the backyard. Tidy vegetable beds lined the back fence. A rotary clothesline sat in the middle of the yard with a concrete path leading to it from the back door. I inspected the area. Empty flowerpots of all shapes and sizes gathered near the door. On a hunch, I started looking underneath them. I found a key under one and showed Ronnie. "Didn't think people actually did that," I said. They didn't in my world, and I doubted they did in Ronnie's.

"Makes it easier for us and saves picking locks," she replied. "I didn't think people really did that either."

I stuck the key in the lock. It turned, and the door opened. I pushed it wide and called into the house, "Ms Bateman? Tania? Are you here?"

No answer.

We donned latex gloves and entered the house. A quick walk through determined no one was home. Ronnie let the dog investigate by himself. The fridge contained perishable food. The milk had a week to go before its best before date. The fruit bowl on the bench contained fresh fruit. Ronnie pointed out a few unopened bills on the end of the kitchen bench, neatly placed on top of each other. All bore recent post marks.

"You know anyone who goes on holiday without opening bills or cleaning out the fridge?" I asked.

Ronnie shook her head. "Although, if she was intending to go for the weekend, then there's no harm, is there?"

"Yeah. Fair point."

I stood in the living room. It was a tidy airy space. A bookmark stuck out of a closed book on the coffee table next to a brown fabric upholstered armchair. I picked the book up for closer inspection. The brief said she was an avid reader. I scanned the room. An avid reader without any bookcases. "Hey, Ronnie, do you know this author?" I showed her the book cover. She might know. She has a bookshop.

"Yes." She nodded. "And she's a Kiwi author. That's from the bookshop downstairs."

"You're sure?"

"No one else stocks that author in New Zealand. Pass it here."

I handed the book over and watched as she flicked to the very last page. She showed me the back page. "See how it's blank?"

"Yeah."

"It wasn't purchased online from overseas. This book is also distributed by Amazon and the back of all books printed by Amazon have the place and date of the printing. The copies we have of that book in the bookshop, are printed in New Zealand and don't have printing info on the back page."

"And?"

"I'm one-hundred percent sure it's from our shop."

"Can we find out when she bought it?"

"Yes. There is a day-book in which all sales are recorded by book title. Emily will know how many copies of this have sold and probably who bought them."

"Emily ..." I said. I liked the idea of seeing her again.

Ronnie put the book back on the table. "She's a tidy person," she said, then walked down the hallway that opened off the lounge.

I followed. I was happy to let Ronnie take the lead. Poking around in a woman's home didn't feel right. I knew I was just doing my job, but it still made me feel like a creep. If Bateman was a bloke, it'd be a different story.

Her bed was made, and the general order of the house did indicate a tidy person. In the wardrobe of her bedroom, Ronnie found Tania's handbag. She took the bag to the bed and tipped it out. We found her wallet and car keys. Ronnie looked closer at the keys. As she went through them, I could see the house keys were on the chain as well. Yet the doors were locked. She held them out to me. "People usually take their keys."

"They do," I replied, looking through the other bits and pieces from her handbag. It amounted to pocket litter, but not the useful kind. No receipts or ticket stubs. Hers was confined to half a packet of throat lozenges, a couple of ripped wrappers from muesli bars, and the corner of a chocolate bar wrapper.

"I don't think she planned on leaving," Ronnie said. "She left her wallet. She could've locked the door behind her with the hidden key, so that might explain why the door was locked, but the keys are in here."

"I'd say so."

"The handbag tells me she *uses* a handbag, so she would've taken that with her if she left for a weekend away or went shopping."

Ronnie opened the single drawer in the bedside table

and surveyed the contents. "Chapstick, packets of tissues, four blue pens, a single folded sheet of paper."

She removed the paper, unfolded it, and showed it to me. A roughly sketched diagram. A rectangle with another rectangle drawn on one side, quarter of the way down. On the long side were the numbers three, five, and twelve. "What do you think?"

"What are the numbers?"

Ronnie looked at the picture again. "Don't know ... measurements? Perhaps she wants to rearrange a room?"

"And that's all you found in the drawer?"

"All I found that was interesting."

"That's the thing with this house, there really is nothing interesting." My eyes roamed the walls. I pointed to a picture hung above the bed. "A picture of a field and flowers. But no photos anywhere."

"Yeah. There isn't even anything stuck to the fridge."

"Even *my* fridge has magnets holding receipts," I said, "Bet yours does as well."

"More scrawled notes and photos on mine," Ronnie replied with a smile. "But if people like us have stuff on our fridges that tells others something about us ... mostly that we're human. What does that say about Tania Bateman?"

"She's either an exceptionally vanilla person, or Tania Bateman's life is a load of fabricated bullshit" I said, knowing deep down that I was probably right. I pushed my thought home with another comment, "She's an avid reader with one book. That's what I read on the file, avid reader. There's not even an eReader in the house."

We stared at each other for a beat.

"There's no tech, Crockett. This house is a shell devoid of personality and tech."

"Whoever she is, it's looking like she left in a hurry and there aren't signs of struggle either," I said, from the doorway. "I'm going to look in the garage. The notes said she has a Toyota Camry."

"We'll join you outside in a moment. I want to find something Romeo can use for scent."

"Do whatever it is you do, I'll be in the garage," I said, over my shoulder as I walked away.

This job didn't feel right. What was really going on here? I swung the garage door open and let my eyes became accustomed to the dim interior. The car was there.

Chapter 6
[Ronnie: Fish & Chips and a phone box]

Romeo and I went into Bateman's bedroom. I checked the washing basket and pulled out a tee-shirt, underneath which I saw shorts and sports socks. "This is promising," I said to Romeo.

With the tee-shirt in my hand, I took the dog outside and over to the side door of the garage.

The door was open. I peered into the semi-dark interior. I could see a car. "Hey, Crockett?"

"Yeah," came a voice from the depths, followed by an echo. Footsteps rang on the concrete floor as he walked around the car. I heard him try the doors. "Car's locked."

"Keys are in her handbag inside. Do you want them?"

"No. Maybe later. Got a feeling the car is as personal as the house."

"Guess when you're running from something, taking your car isn't smart." Which reminded me, I needed to switch cars if we planned on returning here. Didn't know how many neighbours had spotted the Mustang.

"Nope. She'd be better off taking an Uber than driving her own car." His footsteps grew louder until he joined me outside the garage and closed the door. "Interesting you said running from something and not on the run."

"Don't know why I said that." I really didn't know why. "Let's see what Romeo can find," I said, holding the tee-shirt in my hand near the dog's nose. "Find her, Romeo."

Romeo buried his nose in the fabric. When he was done, he looked up at me once then hunted the ground for a trail. I bundled the shirt up and clutched it in my left hand. In my right was the dog's long lead. I wound my hand through the loop and held the lead in a firm grip just in case he got excited and pulled. The big dog sniffed, picking up the pace as he followed a scent down the driveway, with us in hot pursuit.

We followed him along the street, across two roads, and into the front gate of Upper Hutt College, between the buildings, and out onto the large sports fields. The dog determinedly dragged on my arm, and I was pleased I'd hooked my hand through the loop. Crockett jogged along beside me as the dog led us through the bushes that formed a boundary between the college and neighbouring intermediate school. Romeo stopped for a moment on the intermediate side, sniffing in a few directions before charging off again, hot on the scent. Nothing he loved more than to follow a trail. He moved swiftly around the buildings, through the courtyard, between more buildings, and across the netball courts. Romeo headed straight for the back gate.

"Having fun, bud?" I said to him. He glanced up once, then went straight back to work. Crockett ran ahead and swung the gate open. The dog slowed his pace and gave me some breathing room. Beyond the gate Merton Street stretched all the way to Fergusson Drive. With purpose, Romeo resumed the hunt. He crossed Rimutaka Street to the Merton Street dairy.

"Have you got a photo?" I asked Crockett. It was easier for him to show it to shop keepers than for me. Most shops didn't appreciate dogs entering.

"Yes." He took his phone from his pocket and tapped for a moment. He showed me. A photo of Tania Bateman was visible on the screen. "I'll be right back," Crockett said, and vanished through the doorway into the dim shop interior.

Romeo circled, but appeared to have lost the scent at the phone box on the corner. He planted his bum and waited. "Good boy." I ruffled the thin fur on his head while I scanned the area. There were houses across the intersection, directly in front of me and flats across Merton Street on my right. Someone might have seen something.

Crockett stepped out of the dairy's shadowy doorway into the bright sun. He glanced at me and shook his head, and then walked to the café next to the dairy.

I took a closer look at the public phone booth, then snapped a photo of the phone, making sure I clearly got the number. I sent the image to Steph and asked her to access the phone records for the last three weeks, in particular looking for incoming calls. Steph replied quickly saying she'd do her best.

Every old thriller movie I'd ever watched jumbled in my mind. It wasn't unusual to have bad guys send the victim to a phone box and then ring them. Maybe Tania got a call. Maybe she ran to the phone box for a reason, and then ran home again. Or she ran over, got a phone call, and followed directions to some other location. My mind spun on and on with possible events. Or, perhaps, Tania made a call. Or she didn't touch the phone at all, and someone picked her up. Maybe it was a meeting point.

But who goes anywhere without a wallet or phone, these days?

Someone who is told not to bring a phone.

Why would anyone be told not to bring a phone?

Because phones track movement. Even turned off, they retain a certain amount of information about where a person went. There was no cell phone in the house. Did she take her phone?

I rang Steph. "Hey, another phone-based request."

"Shoot," she said.

"In my desk drawer is a folder. Find the private phone number attached and get everything you can from it." There wasn't a cell phone number. Didn't mean she didn't have one. For all we knew she might've made a call from her landline that would shed some light on her whereabouts. She could've rung her own cell phone. I've done it when I can't locate mine. Pretty sure a lot of people have rung their cells from a landline to try and locate them in their home, or to hear their voice mail messages. There were reasons, no need to be negative and think she didn't do something like that.

"Locked drawer?"

"Yes."

Steph paused; I heard her breathing. "You have the key."

I did. "There's a spare in the safe. Also, run her name through all our databases. Find out if she has a cell phone no one knows about." A light bulb flashed in my mind. She could use an unregistered phone. Pre-pay. You can buy those at supermarkets. It'd be hard to find a purchase on her financials when it could be hidden within a grocery spend.

"You're sure you want me looking at the file?"

"Yes. Just lock it back up when you're done." I saw Crockett emerge from the café. "Gotta go." I hit end call and shoved my phone in my jeans pocket.

Crockett came out of the cafe and went into the fish and chip shop. I waited. Romeo waited. He was enjoying the smells that floated past him on the breeze.

Crockett walked toward us.

"She buys fish and chips from the chip shop every fortnight on a Friday. They don't know if she came in last Friday or the Friday before. No cameras."

"Helpful," I said. "She either, got in a vehicle at the intersection near the phone booth," I pointed. "Or went back the way she came. There's no trail from this point, except back." Why go back? Why not run on and go around the block home?

"Let's start knocking on doors."

I grinned. "Maybe I should knock on doors and you stay on the street with the big guy."

"What are you saying?"

"I'm saying you're a touch scarier than adorable ... I'll yell if I need you." He looked like a biker. A big guy wearing black. Imposing.

I could see consideration in his eyes for a second. I knew he understood my point of view. With a little reluctance he agreed and took the lead from my hand. "Looks like we're waiting over here, Romeo," Crockett said. I could feel his eyes on me as I crossed the road and found the gate for the house on the corner.

I had my phone in my hand and a photo of Bateman on the screen by the time the lady of the house opened the door.

"Hello, I'm trying to find my friend, Tania."

"There's no one here by that name," the woman said, and started to close the door.

"This is her," I showed her the photo. "You might have seen her around?"

She shook her head and shut the door.

At least it didn't slam. I waved to Crockett and moved to the next house. Same deal. Except a man opened the door.

I crossed back over the road and headed to the flats, giving Romeo a quick head rub on my way past. He managed to get a sneaky lick of my hand.

Crockett and Romeo waited. The man shifted his weight from foot to foot. The dog just sat and watched. I could feel his eyes following me. There were a few flats that faced the shops. I went flat to flat, knocking on doors, asking questions, showing the photo. At the third flat I saw an ashtray in the corner of the small porch. Someone liked to spend time outside on the steps. I knocked just as the door opened. A large woman in her fifties stood there with cigarettes in one hand and a mug of coffee in the other.

I ran through my spiel and showed her the photo.

"She's that runner girl. I see her sometimes. She could do with a meal and less running," she said, wrinkling her pudgy nose.

"Do you know when you saw her last?"

She nodded. I moved down the steps to the path to allow her room to exit and sit on the step.

"Not since Friday evening."

That was hopeful. "Friday? What'd she do?"

"She hung around the phone box, which wasn't unusual, sometimes she made calls there. I think that's what she did anyway. After the phone thing, she goes to the chip shop before she runs back the way she came."

"Did she make a call on Friday?"

The woman nodded, causing her neck to wobble like jelly.

"When she makes calls, how long are they?"

"Not long, two or three minutes. Not long enough for me to finish a smoke." The lady lit a cigarette and blew smoke over her shoulder. "She didn't go to the chip shop on Friday. Broke her routine."

"That's probably why you remembered it so clearly," I said. "Thank you. Hopefully, I can find her."

The woman smiled and took another drag on her

cigarette. "Good luck." Smoke puffed from her mouth as she spoke.

Time to leave.

I returned with a grin.

"See the lady on the steps behind me."

Crockett nodded. "I do."

"She saw her. Get this, she says Bateman makes calls from the phone box when she goes for fish and chips." I took the dog's lead from Crockett. "Let's head back."

"The phone?" Crockett looked at the phone booth.

"I asked Steph to find all incoming and outgoing calls for the last three weeks. With luck, we'll get something." That wouldn't be far enough back. "Hang on." I rang Steph back. "The phone box number ... go back twelve months. Look for calls placed to or from the number on Fridays."

"Got it," Steph said. "You're going to owe me a bottle of wine or two."

"Reasonable," I said with a laugh, and hung up.

"That should be interesting," Crockett said, watching a car turn the corner.

We walked, letting Romeo lead the way. He opted for the exact same route, retracing his steps with dogged determination. I wondered if the missing woman did the same. Did she go home, shower, change, and then disappear? If it was her in the retirement village garden, she wasn't wearing running clothes. More interesting was the phone calls. We really needed to know who she rang, or who rang the phone box. They might know what happened to her and have a lead we could follow.

Crockett waited by the passenger door of my car outside Bateman's. I unlocked the doors and encouraged Romeo into the back, then clipped him to his seatbelt. Crockett climbed into the passenger seat.

I slid behind the wheel and smiled at Crockett. "Office?"

"Yes, let's start running a board."

I knew what he meant. Easier to see what was going on with a running timeline. I had a whiteboard wall in one of the meeting rooms that was perfect for that. Also, it was a lockable room.

Chapter 7
[Tania: Missing.]

Tania Bateman lay curled in the foetal position on a wooden floor. Her feet were shackled, her right wrist handcuffed to a steel pipe. Tania's eyes opened to a blurry, grey world. She lay still and took stock of the situation. Her last memory was walking in a courtyard garden hoping to find a place to leave the package, but not where she was supposed to leave it. All she could do was pray that the old lady she saw in the window of an apartment saw her, too, and got curious or reported a prowler. She'd spent a couple of days sleeping rough under bridges, hoping to evade capture until she could find her way out. It was going well. She'd ditched the package, and she was hours away from extraction.

And now she had no idea where she was or how she got there. Her eyes adjusted slowly to the fading light. She was thirsty but not hungry. There was a dull ache in her temple. She touched her head with her left hand and felt a lump the size of an egg. Tania tried to sit up. Her restrained wrist made that almost impossible. It took a few attempts before she realised she could thread the handcuff up the pipe until she could sit. She checked her pockets, by patting them. Nothing. Tania's eyes roamed the room.

Radiators and windows lined one wall. Dull golden rays of sun slipped through the grime-coated windows and streaked across the dirty floor. The opposite wall had two doors with glass windows. The doors were three metres apart and closed. A full-length blackboard presided over the front of the room. The back wall was blank except for yellowed pieces of sticky tape and the occasional drawing pin. Tania's prison was an old school room.

She cleared her throat and tested her voice. It croaked a few times before releasing a single word, "Hello."

No one answered. Tania inspected the shackles around her ankles. She rubbed her handcuffed wrist. She was uncomfortable. Life was uncomfortable.

She remembered the things she'd learnt from the bi-annual hostage training her work ran. When you reach the place you're being held, be hyper alert. Where are the potential exits? Are there any obstacles? How many abductors do you have? What is their routine? Are they armed? Do they seem fit? What is their mental state? The more intel you have, the higher your chances of a successful outcome.

Maintain dignity, be vigilant, take mental note of the kidnappers' routine, and remain disciplined. Now is not the time for hysterical outbursts or tears. Be human, be polite, and be nice. Be true to your values and integrity, no matter what you are enduring or what threats are made. When you get an opportunity, exploit it. Assume the worst. Fortune favours the brave.

Tania didn't know if her captor or captors knew who she was. If they did, it would get messy, and fast. If they didn't then she had more time to find an exit route.

Tania was alone.

She still had her watch on her left wrist. It was an analogue watch, not a smartwatch. The time was eight-forty-six. The fading light from the windows changed to pinks and purples. She knew it was sunset because the sun rose well before seven in the morning. She leant on the radiator. Cold from the metal seeped into her back. Tania closed her eyes to relieve the ache in her head. It didn't work.

Long shadows crept across the floor from the windows, slowly at first, then faster as the night grew deeper.

Alone in the dark with creaks and groans, she listened, trying to hear over her pounding heartbeat. Was it a floorboard that creaked?

She held her breath, concentrating on the room beyond.

She tried to determine if it was someone moving around or the wood settling as it cooled. The noises stopped.

She cast her mind back to the events prior to waking up in the school room. Was this connected to TechSynth? Blurry memories refused to sharpen. What happened?

Where was the thumb drive? She touched the front pockets in her jeans with her free hand. Nothing. Did they get it? Did whoever grabbed her have it? Did she pass it to her contact?

What could she remember?

The bookshop. She liked the bookshop. Her mind

drifted to thoughts of books until she remembered the note. There was a note in a book. Did she leave it or take it? It wasn't in her pockets. If she left it someone could find it. That felt bad, even though she couldn't remember why. She thought about Emily at the bookshop. There was something wrong with Emily. Tania visited the bookshop regularly, but Emily had never remembered her. They spoke often, and yet Emily showed no recognition. Tania remembered that Emily was always writing in a notebook. She wondered what she wrote. Then another thought emerged, and it occurred to her that the people who wanted the thumb drive wouldn't know that Emily couldn't identify anyone. Whoever left the note, the coordinates, they also wouldn't know Emily didn't seem to recognise anyone. Sucked to be Emily.

What else could she remember? Nothing. Not grey fuzz, but deep dark nothing.

Tania rubbed her head with her free hand. It didn't matter how many ways she approached her recent memories, they refused to be anything more than a blank screen.

Her eyes skimmed the walls of her prison. Footsteps resounded outside the room. Her heart leapt into her mouth.

Chapter 8
[Crockett: An incomplete timeline.]

Ronnie clasped a blue whiteboard pen in her hand and added information to the large board. I had a black pen and started drawing a timeline. Being tall had advantages. I could draw over her head without any problem.

"When did you hear about this job?" I asked, moving from behind her to stand next to her and continue my line.

"Monday, but it was more a heads up than actual information."

"I got a whiff of something Sunday night," I replied. Something was up. There was too big a delay in anyone being asked to look for the woman. Friday night to Sunday night, and even then, like Ronnie, I didn't have much to work with at all.

"More information arrived after your phone call to me," Ronnie said.

I added that to the timeline. "MacKinnon reached out to me and you, separately. Then I was asked to contact you and bring you in," I said, watching her from my periphery to gauge her reaction: there wasn't one. Her expression remained impassive.

"So, bring me in because I'm working privately and therefore harder to control, or for another reason?"

"Two reasons." I smiled at her comment. "Yes, because

you're working privately, but also because you have a rep for getting things done."

"If this woman really works in private industry, like we've been told, why are government agencies so keen on finding her?"

I shot Ronnie a fast smile, that went all the way to my eyes. "Agencies plural?"

"I didn't come down in the last shower."

"No one has mentioned multiple agency interest," I said.

"They don't exactly advertise, do they? But if she is missing and important enough for us to be called in, then, it's agencies."

"Fair point," I said. I felt my smile falter, then came back strong. "Remember when I said something about luring the lie?"

Ronnie smiled. "I do. And I think you're right about people not telling the truth about Tania Bateman." She wrote a big question mark on the board next to Bateman's name. She turned toward me. "I know you would've heard from an old colleague about me. If you hadn't reached out to him for more information, you'd be an idiot, and you don't strike me as stupid." She paused, then continued, "And that nasty piece of goods probably already knew about the missing woman."

"Why do you think that?"

"Because we are looking for a cryptographer." She shrugged. "I just have a feeling there might be security implications beyond the company Bateman works for."

"You're right about Chandler, by the way. He said a few things." I turned back to the board and added more dates. She was on the money with her ex-colleague being nasty. He was a horrible bloke. I still felt dirty. "He doesn't like you much, does he?"

"That, Crockett, goes both ways. I'm sure he warned you about my insubordination and how I'll drag you into the mud with me."

Sounded like it wasn't the first time Chandler had done a number on her. "He's a bad hombre, all right. Men like him ruin reputations for shits and giggles."

"I'm sure he makes his partner wish he was dead every single day." Ronnie laughed. "Did you meet him?" She shook her head slowly. "I'm sorry if you did. Hope you had time to shower after that."

"Not just me that feels filthy after being near him, then?"

After listening to Chandler run Ronnie down, I knew why Ronnie reacted the way she did to him, and I knew where the blame lay ... it was not with Ronnie. Although, she could've stepped back at any point and stopped inflaming the situation. I had a feeling that wasn't in her nature.

"Not just you, Crockett. It's anyone who still has a soul and a heart." Her laugher rang out. "You still came to meet me. I'm guessing it wasn't all bad or you're a good judge of men."

"It was bad enough. Your rep for getting the job done is well-known. And I knew his reputation before I met the

93

prick." He's known for throwing up brick walls, and not valuing his officers' input. "I also know he likes to throw his officers under the nearest train rather than support them." Not the first wanker I've come across in an ivory tower. "He slept and blackmailed his way to the top?"

Ronnie shuddered. "That's the truly gross part. His predecessor, Reede, groomed him well, and I sort of helped end her career. Chandler got his knickers in a knot over that. He idolised the bitch."

We completed the timeline as much as we could. Then we sat down in chairs facing the board and gave it consideration.

"I have some questions," Ronnie said, pointing at the noticeably short timeline. "If this woman went missing on Saturday, what was she doing in a garden on Monday night?"

"That's a very good question."

"Okay. If she's so important, why did I get partial information on Monday and more on Tuesday. She went missing Saturday and they let those first forty-eight hours run out."

"I knew about the case on Sunday night, but I certainly didn't have enough information to start anything beyond a fast and dirty internet search. That's a very good point, and it feels like something was going on."

"Did they put their own people on it, and they came up empty?" Ronnie mused aloud. "If it was her in the garden last night, early hours of this morning ..."

"... then she didn't go missing on Saturday," I finished.

"And who was it she talked to on the pay phone? That's information we need."

"I'll be right back," Ronnie said, and stood up. "I'll go see Steph about the phone box."

"Okay."

She left and I sat looking at the timeline, feeling more and more that everything hinged on those phone calls. I zoned out staring at the writing on the wall. Who was she contacting?

My phone rang. I jumped and was glad Ronnie wasn't around to see that. I swiped my finger across the screen to answer the call.

"Crockett."

"Is there progress?" Mackinnon asked.

"Yes," I replied. "We'll find her."

"How are you enjoying Ronnie's company?"

"She's nice. I think we'll get on fine."

"Not prickly or standoffish?"

"No, why would she be?"

"She's worked with the same partner for a few years, thought she might not take kindly to a new partner. Usually, her and Ben Reynolds handle jobs together."

I knew that name. Reynolds had a bit of status in the spy world.

"He's the actor slash spy?"

"Yes."

"Good to know. She's fine. We're working." I hung up. I started hearing stories about Reynolds when I was desk bound in Wellington. Until then I was deep undercover and heard very little about anyone else in the industry. Not gossip wise; I heard things I needed to know. For instance, who was undercover in my vicinity. He never was.

The door opened. Ronnie stepped in with a big whack of papers held against her body.

"We're going to need highlighters," she said, and placed the stack of papers on the table. "Steph got a printout of all the activity from that phone box for the last year."

"That's almost a full ream." I didn't even know people still used pay phones that often. "This is going to take a while," I said.

"Yes, it is. She couldn't get a break down by day, so, we got the lot."

Ronnie dug around in the top drawer of a credenza that sat in the corner of the room, then produced a packet of highlighters.

I split the pile of papers roughly in half and took the top section for myself. She handed me an orange highlighter and she took pink. We settled in to search for phone calls made on Fridays.

"Got a calendar?" I asked. It'd make it easier to find the Fridays if we knew the dates we were looking for.

"Yep." Ronnie went back to the credenza and produced a rolled piece of A3 paper. She flattened it out and used magnets to fasten the calendar to the whiteboard. It was a year at a glance. Now that was helpful. Ronnie chose a green highlighter and drew lines down the Fridays. She was definitely a thinker.

An hour and a half disappeared as we hunched over printed pages with our highlighters and marked all Friday activity. We wrote down every phone number that called in or out on a Friday in our respective notebooks.

Eventually, Ronnie stood and stretched. "Who knew phone boxes were still used so much?"

"Not me," I replied. "Need a break?"

She nodded.

"It'd be helpful if we could work out where she was over the weekend and when she really went missing. She could still be wherever she was prior to the garden appearance," she said.

"What was she wearing?"

Ronnie picked up the sketches from the *Cronies of Doom*. "Dark pants, maybe jeans and a dark-coloured jacket, zippered with a hood."

"Footwear?"

"Sneakers."

"Most people don't run in long pants and a jacket, do they?" I said, fishing my phone from my inside jacket pocket as it buzzed. I read the screen, then said, "I've got a meeting."

Art needed to touch base about *Trojan Horse*. I hoped it wasn't trouble.

"Correct, most people don't wear jeans and a jacket while running. I'll see if I can get somewhere with this for the next hour or so," Ronnie said. "There were shorts, socks, and a tee-shirt in her bedroom hamper. I'd say she changed after the run. We don't know if she packed clothes to take with her. Or if she's been back since."

"What if she had clothes somewhere else?" The generic state of her house bugged me. People have stuff. Stuff that tells a story. Receipts stuck to fridges. Takeaway menus. Photographs. Books. Personal possessions. She had nothing that really indicated someone lived at the house, apart from minimal food in the fridge and unopened mail. There were a few addresses around the world that had received mail for me over the years. Looked like I was "living" at those addresses, but I never was.

"Anything is possible," Ronnie said. "So, far I'm not seeing a pattern. As in the same number called over and over."

"Nor am I, but if she was using the phone box to call someone, we'll find it." I hoped I sounded sure. "I'll check in tomorrow. Back here bright and early?" I stood and gathered the paper stack I was working on and my notebook. "I'll finish this off tonight."

"I'll be in at eight tomorrow," Ronnie said, looking at the whiteboard.

There was a look in her eye that made me think she was up to something. "I wouldn't snoop into TechSynth. It could be dangerous on your own, something we should do together. But if you do dig around, don't advertise your interest and keep it to internet snooping."

"I wouldn't be open about my snooping. This is not my first job." Ronnie grinned and waved as I left.

It was getting dark by the time I got home. I garaged the bike and let myself in the back door. Knowing Art would arrive in ten minutes, I took my paperwork to my office and locked the office door. Separate jobs. He didn't need to know anything about *Witcher*. And Ronnie didn't need to know anything about *Trojan Horse*.

Chapter 9
[Ronnie: Impromptu field trip.]

I opened my laptop, connected to a VPN, then opened a secure anonymous browser. I dug around the internet looking for anything I could find about Tania Bateman and TechSynth. Browsing through tabs on the site I looked for any mention of our target. The last tab was employees at various events. Team building and functions. Photos with captions. Not a thing. Five years with the company and zero photographs of her doing anything and no mentions. No employee of the month awards or commendations for anything. But then if she was what I suspected she was, then she wouldn't agree to photos or references that included her name anywhere online.

Bored with the lack of information on the website, I packed up, locked the door, and then checked the main office. The room was dark. I flicked the lights on. It was late. Steph would've taken Romeo home to Donald hours ago. I dropped the meeting room keys into my desk drawer and grabbed my handbag. With one last look around the office, I locked the door and left. I intended to work on the printouts from home, like Crockett. But I couldn't get the lack of information about Bateman out of my mind.

I sat in my car for a minute thinking. Where would Tania Bateman go? I fired up the engine and pulled into the deserted street. Twenty-minutes later I cruised past TechSynth. He didn't say specifically not to go to the TechSynth building; I guess that's what he meant, but he didn't say those exact words. I smiled as I found a car park about fifty metres from the front entrance of the building in a dark area on the street.

Time to get into character. One non-threatening mum with a broken-down car, coming right up. I turned my cell phone off and carried it in my hand.

I adopted a harried look and walked up to the front door of the building that housed TechSynth. Light spilled over the walkway from the lobby. Someone sat behind a desk to the right of the door, about five metres away. A man in a uniform. Security guard, maybe.

I pushed the door. Nothing happened. The man didn't move.

Kick it up a notch, Ronnie. I knocked, adjusting my expression to something I hoped was akin to distress, and knocked again. Louder more panicky.

The guard approached the door. He called out, "We're closed."

"I just need to use a phone, mine died and my car broke down," I said, "Please. I don't know this area." I showed him the black screen on my phone before putting it in my pocket.

He shook his head. "Go back to your car."

"Please, my kids are waiting for me, I need to get a tow truck, and to tell the babysitter." I injected panic into my voice to garner a reaction from the guard. His expression softened. I was winning. "Please!"

He pressed a button beside the door. "Make it quick, lady. Over there, on my desk. You can use my phone."

"Thank you, so much, I really appreciate it." I hurried to the desk he pointed at. He followed but not too close. Behind the desk on the wall was a building directory. I glanced up at it, scanning fast looking for the name Bateman. It was a long shot and there were no Bateman's on the board. I picked up the phone then looked at the guard. "Sorry, I don't know your name. I'm Ronnie."

The guard hovered by the edge of the desk. "Angus. I'm Angus. Hurry up."

"Sorry, Angus, do I have to dial anything to get an outside line?" On the desk was a list. One page, small print, single spaced. Surname, first name, office number, extension.

"Dial 4 and then the number," Angus said.

"Thank you." I dialled Crockett's number, and while the phone rang, I noted a black line through the list, across the words: Bateman, Tania extension 3512. That's interesting. We've seen that number before but spaced apart. Clearly, they're not expecting her back if her name is crossed out. I committed a couple of other names with the same office number to memory.

"Crockett," said a gruff voice in my ear.

"I need a tow truck to ..." I threw a helpless look at Angus. "... um."

"TechSynth on High Street. 430 High Street."

I mouthed, thank you, then spoke into the receiver.

"TechSynth, 430 High Street. My car is up the road a little way from the building."

"Ronnie, is that you?"

"Yes, that's correct," I replied, nodding at Angus.

"I'll be there in ten, do you really need a tow?" He didn't sound thrilled.

"No, that should be fine."

"Exfil, now, Ronnie."

"I'll be with the car."

I hung up before he could say anything else. He said enough with his exfil comment. I could pretend I don't know that means exfiltrate. But I doubt he'd buy it. His tone suggested it was more order than comment. Must have pushed his buttons. Oops a daisy.

"Okay if I quickly ring my babysitter?" If I had kids and someone was waiting for me, I'd want to call and tell the person I was running late.

Angus nodded. "Make it fast, I've got rounds."

I smiled and dialled my office number. As soon as the answer machine kicked in, I said, "Hope everything is okay. I'm so sorry. I'll be home in ..." I checked my watch. "Forty minutes. Sorry, car trouble." I hung up.

"Okay?" Angus asked, ushering me to the door.

"Yes ... and thank you. You're very kind." My eyes flicked around the walls looking for cameras. I spotted four. "Hope you don't get in trouble for letting me use the phone."

"Nah, it'll be fine."

"They are cameras up there, right?"

"Yes. There won't be any trouble." His voice was gruff but with a smooth edge. "Nothing happened and no one checks the footage unless there's a problem."

"What a relief," I said smiling. "I'd hate to think you'd be in trouble for doing a nice thing."

He unlocked the door. "Be careful ma'am."

"I'll lock myself in the car," I said.

I knew Angus would watch me walk back to the street. "Stay safe," he called after me.

With a half turn toward the building, I gave him a wave before the darkness swallowed me.

I unlocked the car and climbed into the driver's seat. I checked the mirrors to make sure no one was around and locked the doors. Then I turned on my cell phone. The screen lit up with text messages from Crockett. I wrote the extension number for Tania Bateman in a text and sent it to him.

He didn't reply. Seven minutes later I recognised the roar of a Harley and looked up in time to see it cruise past my car. That's got to be him. I started the engine and followed the motorbike another hundred and fifty metres or so from where I'd parked. I pulled in behind the Harley. Crockett swung off the bike and stalked toward me; he didn't stop to take his helmet off.

I unlocked my door, and he jerked it open. "What the hell were you doing?"

"Finding out that Tania Bateman doesn't work there anymore," I said with a grin. "They've crossed her name and extension out."

"Really?" He rested an arm on the roof of the car and leaned down. "And that information helps us find her, how?"

"It doesn't yet, but it's interesting. If she was missing, but they expected her back ... why would they wipe her out like that?" And it tied to the phone call I made when I heard about the job.

"Good question. You should've come to me first. What did I say about snooping?"

Probably would've been smarter to at least let him know what I was doing. But then I didn't know myself until I'd done it.

"It was light snooping at best," I replied. "Easier for me to play the damsel in distress card than you."

"Tell me next time. We don't know what we are up against."

"Fair enough." He had a point. "As you said, we need to lure the lie, but I'll try and give you a heads-up next time."

Crockett sighed. "There will be no next time. I'm going home and so should you."

He ran back to his bike, jumped on, fired the engine up, and roared away. I followed, sticking to the speed limit until he was gone from sight. Time to ditch my car. Switch my car. I headed for Hutt Road and the garage I kept there. Once safely inside the garage, I thoroughly cleaned the Mustang ready for its next outing and drove off in a silver Toyota Corolla. The Corolla was one of the most common cars on the road and few people remembered silver sedans. I was sure every other car was silver. As I drove home, I wondered if Crockett knew something I didn't. Couldn't quite put my finger on why I thought that, or what it was he knew.

Chapter 10
[Ronnie: Nana's mysterious man.]

I watched my phone screen come to life. Nana's image sat quietly under the ring tone. The only time she's ever quiet, I thought, then took a breath and answered with as much perk as I could muster, "Morning, Nana."

"Veronica dear, something peculiar has happened."

"Again, Nana, or is this the mystery garden intruder, extended version?"

"Something completely different, Veronica." Nana paused. In the background I could hear garbled chatter. Ah, wonderful the *Cronies of Doom* had gathered for the new mystery.

"I wouldn't worry about the woman in the garden. The girls and I think she was just lost, perhaps tipsy, and wandered in by accident."

That was a relief.

"You are probably right. Now, how can I help you with this new mystery?"

I doodled on my desk jotter. Three little stick figures running amok. The likeness to the *Cronies of Doom* was uncanny.

"A courier arrived this morning with the photographs from our trip south, dear. I was just showing them to the girls. They delightedly admired my very beautiful grandchildren."

"I bet there's more to this than our beauty, Nana?"

"Oh, yes, dear. Ester noticed a strange man in the background on the Ferry."

Of course, she did.

"Nana, I'm sure I can speak for Donald here when I say we are delighted you think we are beautiful." Because that's clearly what matters in life. "And as for a strange man in the background ... the boat was full of strangers."

My pen added moustaches to my stick figure faces then topped them off with hats. Now they were dastardly moustache-twirling villains.

"Ronnie, the man is in the photos from the Ferry, from the café in Picton, the restaurant that night, Pelorus bridge, and all the photographs taken on the trip, apart from the ones at your father and uncle's home in Christchurch."

I stopped drawing and started paying attention. "You're absolutely certain it's the same person, no doubt at all?" Someone inserting themselves in our photos did not bode well.

"Yes, dear."

"Well, Nana, it seems you have a real mystery on your hands."

"Do you have the original photos dear?"

"I have some, and Donald has the rest. I'll see if I can enhance the image and find out who your mystery man is."

Glee resounded in Nana's voice. "We shall see if we've seen him in any other photographs. Such fun."

"I'll visit tomorrow Nana. I have a full day here today. Don't cause too much trouble."

"Isn't it exciting having another mystery, Veronica? The girls and I will keep you posted."

"Talk to you tomorrow, Nana."

I hung up, relieved she'd dropped the Bateman mystery and the wedding march, but someone appearing in so many of our photos smacked of trouble. Trouble with a capital T. A nana-sized dilemma. I scrolled through the photos on my phone. Sure enough, it did look like the same person lurking in the background of several of the images. I zoomed in as much as possible on the first photo Nana mentioned. Then I abandoned the phone in favour of my computer. Bigger screens are handy for such things.

Steph swung the hall door open. Romeo padded over. I stared transfixed at the screen in front of me. I could hear Steph talking to the dog and moving around the office.

"All right, what's so exciting that you didn't even say good morning?" Steph asked, while switching her computer on at her desk.

"Nana found something in the photos we took during our Christchurch trip." I looked up at Steph. "Nana. Actually. Found. Something. Steph."

"Well done that woman." Steph gave me a long look. "You're not swearing under your breath, this is new."

"Come and look at these images," I said, beckoning her over. "This is troubling."

I showed Steph the first eight photos and enlarged the background of every picture, then pointed the man out. It was hard to determine his height as he wasn't near enough to the camera lens, or anything that gave an indication. He wore sunglasses in all the photographs I'd seen of him, even inside. Who does that?

"How many photos include the mystery man?" Steph asked, leaning in for a closer look. "Is that a motorbike jacket he's wearing?"

"Forty photos so far and it does look like the sort of leather jacket a bike rider would wear."

Steph stepped back and frowned. "How many?"

"Forty!"

"Let's find out who he is then. Forty photos is a bit stalky."

I took a screen shot of the man's head and shoulders, then added it to our database. "Somehow I doubt he'll appear in this search. Can you add the image to an internet search and see what you dig up? I'm going to see Donald. He took photos too and printed some for Nana. He might have an idea, or at least different shots of mystery man, maybe one without sunglasses on."

"Done. Off you go."

I stood up, pocketed my phone, and grabbed my sunnies. "Romeo is with you," I said, patting the dog. "Sorry boy, but you don't like the smells in the salon. See you soon."

I headed out the door.

As soon as I rounded the edge of the building, sun bounced into my eyes. I slipped my sunglasses on and hurried around the next corner and into Donald's hair salon. I pushed my sunglasses up on top of my head. The smell of hair dye with an undertone of developer, wafted in the air-conditioned room, and irritated my nose.

His receptionist greeted me with a cheery smile and a bright good morning.

"Is he in?"

"Out the back. Go on through, Ronnie."

I wound my way around chairs and customers, saying hello to a couple I recognised as I went. I knocked once on the door at the back of the salon and opened it. Donald was sitting on a bright red leather sofa drinking a coffee.

"Don't tell me you finally want me to fix that?" Donald said, waving a finger at my hair.

"How very rude. Nothing needs fixing." I smiled and wrinkled my nose. There is nothing wrong with brown hair. "Have you got your phone with you?"

"Yes."

"Good, can I see your photos, please?"

Donald frowned and started to shake his head.

"Donald, please, the photos from our trip with Nana." His frown deepened. "Trust me, Donald, I don't want to see your messages or sexts or whatever you get up too." A sudden thought popped into my mind. "I also don't want to know about any dick pics, or whatever it is you share."

"I'll find the photos for you," he said, unlocking his phone and scrolling quickly through some screens.

"Could you send them to me?"

Donald looked up. "That might be safer." He winked.

"Eww. Just make sure nothing icky gets through."

"Airdrop, okay?"

"Perfect."

Donald selected the photos and airdropped them. "And this is all because?"

"Nana found something odd in some of the photos and I wanted to check yours."

"Is this about her intruder?"

"No. This is something else."

"And it's in our photos?"

Oh, yeah.

"There's a man, the same man, in forty of the photos so far."

"Did we take someone with us by accident?" He arched an eyebrow. "I think I'd know if we had a man along."

No doubt.

"Looks like this person was on the Ferry with us and at every bloody place we went from then on."

"And you, the spy, didn't notice?"

"That's correct."

"You're slipping, Ronnie."

"Why would someone purposefully get themselves in so many of our photos?" I said and slid onto the sofa next to Donald. "If it's something akin to my old job, they'd be making sure they didn't get into any photos, but this person seems to have inserted themselves." I scrolled through the images from Donald. "Look …"

"Oh, my, he's delicious." He fanned himself with his phone. "Big and strong looking," Donald crooned, licking his lips. "What do you think, six-three or four?"

"Keep it in your pants," I replied. "What vibe is he giving off?" I regretted my words as soon as they left my lips.

"Delicious, we've established that." Donald scrolled through a few more of the photos on his phone.

"What else?"

"Probably rides a Harley. Look at him. He's all rugged and tough. That jacket is well worn. He's wearing a black shirt and black pants. Don't think they're leather, more's the pity." Donald enlarged the small area of the man's shirt that was visible. "Can't make out the image. What's that look like to you?"

"Wings?"

"Harley tee-shirt, perhaps." Donald licked his lips again. "And this hunk of manhood came along on our trip and we had no idea? What a waste."

"How many motorbikes do you remember hearing or seeing on the way to Nelson?"

Donald pursed his lips as he thought. "Several Harleys, and some other less gorgeous affairs."

"You drove on the way down. I was in the backseat writing case files and client letters. I didn't take a lot of notice."

"Clearly, Sweetie, we had a tag-a-long and you didn't spot him." Donald gave me a look.

I didn't need reminding. "This photo ..." I stopped scrolling and held my phone closer to Donald. "You, your dad, and Nana ... and our biker friend propping up the bar behind you all. You took this with your long monkey arms. Where were you, and what night was that?"

"That was at The Brickworks on Centaurus Road, our last night."

I thought aloud, "Dad and I were across town visiting the *God Mother*." We'd left it to the last minute and made sure we had to hurry off after dinner. It was a duty visit.

"Ronnie, he must be enchanted by me!" Donald's joy filled the room. "My big, rugged prince charming."

"Settle, petal. Now we know biker dude has taken an interest in *you*, we'd best be on high alert while I dig around and find out why," I said, hoisting myself from the low sofa. "See you tonight. You're cooking."

"I don't think we need look too far for the reason, Ronnie, I'm fabulous ..." Donald's voice drifted wistfully. He flapped a hand at me in a simulated wave as I left. He was already engrossed in the images of the mystery man.

I slid my sunglasses over my eyes and checked more images on the short walk back to the office. Toward the end of the trip south with Nana, I found one with the mystery man's face unencumbered by sunglasses or hidden in shadow. Gotcha. I hurried up the stairs to the office. I knew I should've been devoting my time to finding Bateman, but this guy in the photos was creeping me out and I wanted to know who he was, and why he attached himself to our holiday.

* * *

Steph greeted me as soon as I stepped through the main door into the sunny office space. "Nothing so far."

"I've got a better picture. Sans glasses," I said, striding across the room to my desk. Romeo waited on his bed close by. I bent down and rubbed the top of his head. "Good boy," I said. "You're a very good boy." He wrinkled his nose. Salon smells stick. "Sorry Romeo. I stink."

Steph continued working for a few minutes while I uploaded the new image and add it to our database search, then dragged her chair over to my desk. The pair of us sat in silence and waited.

The phone rang. I jumped. Steph laughed and picked up the receiver. "Good morning, Wherefore Art Thou." A moment later she handed the phone to me. "Dave Crocker for you."

I gave her a weak half smile and took the phone.

"What can I do for you?"

"Find Tania Bateman," he said quietly.

"Working on it."

"Good to know."

"I need to show you something," I said, then added, "Did you come up with anything?"

"Not yet. I'll be at your office in ten minutes - you can show me whatever it is then. By the way, we're visiting your Nana."

A sigh landed on the desk in front of me. "Great." What else could I say? I hung up and gave Steph a sidelong look. "I'll be out for the rest of the day. Can you drop Romeo around to Donald again before you lock up?"

"Of course."

The program on the screen pinged. I stared at the information and photograph on the screen. A known associate of the Inferno Jesters, Brisbane chapter.

"How did he get into New Zealand?" I asked the dog in a whisper.

"Did you say something?" Steph said, frowning in my direction.

"I did. The man in the photos is a biker."

"He does look the part."

"I don't like this at all." I saved everything, shoved my cell phone in my pocket, picked up my laptop, the pile of papers from yesterday, and the keys. "Crockett is coming in. I'll be in the room we're using. Meeting room one."

"You all right?"

"Yes, just wondering why a biker would be so interested in Donald. Time to do some digging."

With the laptop under my arm, I unlocked the meeting room door. Once inside I closed the door and flipped the light switch. The room had no natural light source. I liked it for exactly that reason. No one could see into it from anywhere. I placed my laptop on the table and stared at the whiteboard for a minute.

Nothing at all about Tania Bateman's vanishing act felt right. I was more than a hundred percent sure there was information missing - information that would help us. And now, the biker thing. I recalled a conversation with Ben. Didn't he say Crockett was undercover with a biker gang?

I rang Ben. He answered fast.

"Crockett was undercover with bikers, you told me that, right?"

"Yes. Inferno Jesters in Virginia," He paused. "He was undercover for a long time. Why?"

"Just wondered." I hung up.

I pulled myself away from the whiteboard and sat at the table. With the laptop opened, I logged into a website I hadn't used in a long time. My login still worked, which I took as a sign that I should run the biker's image through all security camera footage at points of entry. Border surveillance cameras. I used a separate search for his name. Enzo Giuliano. I heard footsteps outside the door just as the search returned an image match from Auckland International Airport, and the name search returned the same match.

A single knock vibrated the door before it opened.

"Ronnie," Crockett said, with a half a smile. "Wasn't sure you were here. Didn't see the Mustang."

"Morning," I replied with a smile. "I switched cars last night."

He entered the room and closed the door. "What do you need to show me?"

"This," I said and carefully spun the laptop to face him. "Apparently this guy is an associate of the Inferno Jesters ... he also got himself in almost every single photo from a trip I took last week with my cousin and Nana."

I watched Crockett. His eyebrows almost met as he frowned at the screen. "Enzo Giuliano," he said softly. "He's aged a bit."

I didn't feel like letting on I knew he was undercover with the Inferno Jesters himself.

"You know him?"

"Yeah. It's taken them four years, but it looks like they know where I am and who I associate with."

I leaned on my elbows. "This was before you reached out to me."

"Then they have good intel. Someone knew I was going to reach out."

"How could anyone know that?"

We stared at each other. My mind raced. "This is bad." If they knew he was going to reach out, then they knew there was a job coming that would involve both of us.

I blinked. The mesmerising eye-contact with Crockett broke. "What the hell, Crockett?"

He shrugged. "No idea."

"Great."

"Did you get anything helpful off the printout?" Crockett asked, changing the subject.

I opened my notebook and showed him my list of Friday times and numbers. He opened his and showed me his list. Cross reference time.

It didn't take long for us to find a pattern. "How many Fridays are there?"

A laugh fell from his lips. "Fifty-two weeks in a year so around fifty-two."

I shook my head, a smile on my lips. "Yeah, okay, smarty pants. How many correspond with Friday calls that could be her, is what I meant?"

"That's trickier. None of the calls were made at the same time, but more were made in the afternoon than the morning, look ..." He ran his finger down the list on the first page of his notebook. "We need to run the phone numbers and see how many are registered."

I nodded. "Pass your notebook over, I'll combine them and look for any that were called more than once." I opened the program I like to use to check the validity of phone numbers and look for any registered to people.

"Want a hand?"

"Yeah, here," I shoved my laptop closer to him. "You can use mine, and I'll go get another one."

"You just have laptops sitting around on the off-chance?"

"I have a spare or two," I said on my way out the door. I opened the storeroom across the hall and looked at the row of laptops charging on the shelf. The closest one had a green light, so I knew it was fully charged. I unplugged it and rejoined Crockett.

"Two numbers are registered so far, and both were government agencies," he said, looking up as I sat down.

We spent half an hour typing in phone numbers and writing down the information that came from the searches.

"There's the pattern," I said, linking a bunch of numbers with a red pen. "Over thirty-seven weeks, there were eighteen calls that lasted two to three minutes. The number changed every four calls."

None of the phone numbers were registered.

"We need to trace those phone calls," Crockett said. He started typing in another screen. I hadn't noticed him pull up a new screen. "If they're doing what I think they're doing then the phone calls are forwarded to another number."

"And those two phone numbers change every few weeks ... a version of a break phone," I said. Except she was using a pay phone instead of a pre-pay cell phone. "How was she getting the new number?"

"Could be given to her on the last call before the number changed."

Or a dead drop.

I leaned on my elbows and looked at the list and the phone numbers we now knew came from unregistered pre-pay SIMS across three different providers.

Crockett turned his attention to the board on the wall and the timeline.

"Has anyone else gone missing in Upper Hutt?" He stood and leaned against the table near me. "Is Upper

Hutt the type of city that has a long history of random disappearances?"

I'd wondered if she chose Upper Hutt on purpose but couldn't work out why anyone would. "Not recently, that I know of. I mean people sometimes go missing but it's not the Bermuda Triangle of New Zealand or anything. The last one I can recall was about eighteen months ago a woman disappeared ..."

"And?"

"They found her in Tahiti with her boyfriend and a missing two-hundred grand that she embezzled from the bank she worked at."

"Impressive that they got so far."

"Yeah, did the new identity thing and sailed out of New Zealand to Tahiti, as crew on a yacht."

"Thought it out then. Gave their new lives a good shot."

"They found them when someone at a resort they decided to use as their temp home, saw them on the news."

"Anyone else?"

"Not that I'm aware of, teenagers and an older lady, once upon a time. Nothing that rings any bells with this disappearance."

He nodded. "If this is a kidnapping, why?" Crockett leaned against the wall and fixed his gaze on the board. "Other than to bring me out into the world again?"

I watched him, wondering when he was going to address the biker situation, but also happy to concentrate on the Bateman problem, and not let myself think about Nana and Donald and the danger potential.

"No demands," I said. "There should be demands by now." We looked at each other. I spoke first. "Unless there were?"

"She could be dead already," Crockett said.

"Where are her family? Where are her friends, in all this?"

"Why aren't they carrying on all over the media about wanting her to come home?" Crockett added.

"They don't know?" I wondered aloud. They don't know or they were given a cover story.

"That won't work forever, surely, unless she regularly breaks contact and vanishes for undetermined periods of time," Crockett said, and stood up straighter. "Or the family down south is fictitious. Who don't people look for?"

"People like us. Spies. But even we have family and friends and eventually someone would notice."

"Could be weeks though, depending on the job."

"Someone snatched a spy ..." I said, because her behaviour fitted, her bland life, her bland home. It fitted. "That changes everything. It's not about money. It's about intelligence. Who the hell does she report to and what does she have?"

Crockett was already on his phone. I could hear his side of the conversation. It was clipped and gruff. Not a happy call. I stopped trying to work out the other side of the call.

Was Bateman a spy and was she grabbed? Was that her in the garden? Was she there to meet someone? Where was she between Saturday and the wee small hours of Tuesday morning? Did she leave everything behind to start a new life? Or was that what someone wanted us to believe?

I looked at the board. No mortgage. Who has no mortgage at her age? I pushed myself up from the chair. I had no mortgage. A couple of big jobs saw to that. How much is the intel inside Tania Bateman's head worth? Was it more than that? Was she holding something? The payday on the job was hefty. She was worth a lot. I got a feeling I could ask for more and they'd pay it without question. I wouldn't. I didn't need it. Crockett broke off his phone conversation and joined me. Standing side by side we read the board again.

"I think you're right," Crockett said slowly after a few minutes. "She's an asset. She's not one of ours. But she became a person of interest two years ago. That's all I got from the call."

"Maybe we should've had that bit of information at the beginning," I said, tapping my fingers on the table. "The only thing we found in her house was that piece of paper. No photos, no letters, no diary, no laptop, no phone, no tablet, no music. Nothing personal at all, except one book and a piece of paper. It's a generic house with a generic interior. A curated shell." Pretty sure she was someone's spy. Person of interest. In what context?

"Now we know for sure that the piece of paper means something," Crockett said, he picked up a whiteboard marker and circled the reproduced sketch from the piece of paper, on the whiteboard.

"Why didn't whoever took Tania Bateman, take it?"

"Didn't see it?" Crockett stepped back. "If the house was tossed it was done so with care. Nothing looked to be out of place."

"More than likely not a robbery or a home invasion ending in a kidnapping," I said.

"We don't even know where she was taken from, or if she was taken. She could've walked away of her own volition."

"I guess she could've. Did you look at the text I sent you last night?" I paced up and down the room.

"The extension?"

"That's the one."

"Yes," Crockett said.

I paced some more. "Okay, then, isn't it curious that the extension is those numbers on the piece of paper?"

"Very. But what does the paper mean?"

"Probably not her extension, but I guess if someone saw it, that's what they'd think ..."

"You should know that we've been reminded that our job is to find her and find out who is muddying the waters surrounding this case." Crockett slouched a little.

"Reminded or warned?"

"That's open to interpretation," Crockett muttered.

"It's my experience that the past has a relationship with the present," I said.

"Take me to visit your Nana," Crockett said, pushing off from his lean against the table. "If that was Bateman in the garden then we are missing something. Something big."

Agreed.

The laptop he was using pinged. Crockett spun it to face him rather than moving around the table.

"The calls were forwarded to other burner phones. A different one every three calls," he closed the laptop.

There was no doubt in my mind that she was spy.

Chapter 11
[Crockett: Old boilers]

Ronnie pulled into a park outside the rest home. She climbed out of the car and waited for me to do the same before locking the doors. She didn't seem to be in much of a hurry as she led the way down the drive and into the main building. Ronnie paused briefly, squirted hand sanitiser onto her hands, then signed in using her own pen. A middle-aged, cheerful woman poked her head around a doorway from the back office.

"Afternoon, Ronnie. Didn't know you were coming in." She fully emerged from the doorway. Her gaze moved from Ronnie's face to my chest, lingered, then meandered upwards to find my eyes. "Hello. Please sanitise and sign in. Who are you visiting?" she asked, with a slow bat of her eyelashes.

If this is what it's like for the ladies normally, then I need to be more aware and reign this shit right in. Eye contact. No roaming.

"He's with me," Ronnie said. "Crockett meet Margot, she keeps the riff-raff out and the *inmates* in."

I smiled. *Inmates.* "Pleased to meet you." I squirted hand sanitiser into my palm and rubbed it thoroughly into my hands.

"Likewise," Margot replied. "June is in her apartment."

"Okay, thank you." Ronnie swung the interior glass door open.

The air smelled of lavender and something else. Age? Do old people smell?

I fell into step beside Ronnie. We dodged relics and walking frames as we made our way through the wide corridors to the apartments.

"This is it," Ronnie said. She knocked three times on a solid wooden door before twisting the handle and swinging the door open. "Nana?"

"Come in, Veronica," an elderly voice replied.

She whispered to me, "Remember this was your idea." And walked into the apartment.

I closed the door behind me then strode after Ronnie.

She walked towards someone sitting in an armchair, looking out at the garden. Alone. "I have someone with me, Nana."

"I'll put the kettle on then, dear," The old woman replied. She stood and turned to face us. Aged canny eyes looked me up and down, but it wasn't creepy, it was knowing. Then she smiled. "You must be a friend of Veronica's." She stretched out her hand. "I'm June." I obliged and gently shook the thin-skinned proffered appendage.

"Pleased to meet you. I'm Dave Crocker, a colleague of Ronnie's. I'd like to talk to you about the lady in the garden."

"You are very straightforward, young man," June said, and continued into the open plan kitchenette. "We'll have a cup of tea."

I got the feeling she wasn't easily dissuaded from her

path. I learnt a long time ago, that going with the flow tends to have the best outcome in these situations. Old hands rattled teacups while setting them on saucers. She busied herself.

"Where are the *Cronies of Doom*?" Ronnie asked above the boiling kettle, as she motioned for me to sit down. I watched the kitchenette manoeuvring from a chair in the living room a good six feet away. It was a well-practiced dance between grandmother and granddaughter. The scene brought up memories of being in my grandmother's kitchen as a kid.

"Veronica, it's unkind to call the girls, *Cronies of Doom*. They are my very good friends." She glanced at a clock on the wall. "And they're due in shortly for tea."

June reached for a large tin on a shelf above the sink. "I'll get it, Nana." Ronnie's hand took the tin from the shelf and passed it to her grandmother. Ronnie took a tray from under the sink and placed it on the bench, then pulled a tea towel from a drawer and spread it on the tray. Ronnie loaded the tray with the cups and saucers and a plate of biscuits. "I'll take this through, Nan."

June followed her, carrying the teapot stuffed inside an orange and yellow cozy. She placed the teapot onto a cork mat next to the tray on the coffee table in the middle of the room.

"Now, young man, what would you like to know about the mysterious garden lady? I'm sure Veronica told you we think she was tipsy and lost. No mystery at all really," June said, sitting down.

Seems sure of herself. I smiled. "That probably is the case, but I was hoping you wouldn't mind telling me what you saw?"

"I don't mind at all," June said, scooting forward in her seat to pour the tea. "Tea?"

"Yes, please."

"Milk, sugar?"

"No, thank you," I replied, taking the offered saucer and cup. It was going to be a challenge holding the cup with the tiny handle. I opted to grasp the cup with my whole hand. It was safer that way. My hands aren't made for delicate china.

June looked at Ronnie. "An Australian with manners?"

"Nana, be nice."

"Now, Mr Crocker, what can I tell you?" June sat with her cup balanced by the tiny handle between her thumb and age-gnarled fingers and took a small sip.

"Where were you when you first noticed the lady?"

June sipped her tea and appeared thoughtful for a moment. "I was sitting where you are now. My girlfriends were with me." She paused. "I was facing the ranch slider. Frankie was sitting where I am now, and Ester was where Veronica is. So, only Frankie and I could see the movement outside."

"And the curtains were open at midnight?"

"Yes, I put small solar fairy lights in my rose bushes. We often sit with the drapes open at night."

"Did the woman look in as she passed?"

"Yes, I believe so. Just a glance. The light from the

apartment no doubt drew her attention."

Light pouring from a retirement village apartment at midnight would draw anyone's attention.

"Did she see you?"

"I don't know. Perhaps, but it wouldn't have been much of a look. I only noticed her because I happened to look out as she passed."

"Then what did you do?"

"Frankie, Ester, and I thought it was a bit strange having someone wander into the garden, so we all went to the window and watched what she did."

"And what was it you saw her do?"

"She walked across the grass and stopped at three apartments."

"Three?" Ronnie said.

"Yes, dear."

Ronnie said nothing else.

"Did she pick anything up?" I asked.

"I don't think so."

"Think carefully."

There was a light tap at the door a split second before it opened with a *whoosh*. I turned my head. Two more old boilers entered the apartment. Must be the *Cronies of Doom*. They looked the part.

Ronnie stood up to greet them. "Hello, ladies."

"Oh, hello, Veronica," a shorter, chubbier one said with a smile. "Nice to see you again."

"Come on in, I'll get some more cups. I have my colleague with me, Dave Crocker. He has a few questions about the garden intruder."

A tallish slim woman stepped forward. "Hello, young man. I am Frankie Mount."

I set my cup down and stood. I towered over Frankie as I held out my hand, but she was still taller than the other two. She came midway between my elbow and shoulder.

"It's a pleasure." We shook then Frankie took a seat.

The smaller chubbier woman moved in. "I'm Ester Mulholland, former police officer with New Zealand police" she said, grasping my hand.

"Pleased to meet you, Officer," I said, extracting my hand from her surprisingly strong grip.

Ronnie smiled. Nana snickered. Mum instilled manners in us boys and I was glad she did. I waited until the newcomers were seated before I sat, and judging by the smiles, I earned some points.

"I would appreciate if you all could think back to the night the intruder in the garden appeared." I paused to gauge the energy in the room, then continued, "What was the weather like that evening?"

Ronnie listened as I wound back time and restarted the interview. No doubt she'd used the same technique a few times.

Ester spoke, "It was a lovely calm evening."

Then Frankie continued, "Yes, it was. Quite warm. We sat in here with the drapes pulled back so we could enjoy the garden lights."

"What did you do earlier in the evening?"

June poured more tea, and then looked at me. "We played cards, drank a lot of tea, and talked."

I nodded. "Who won the cards?"

June's thin lips stretched across her teeth. "I did," she said.

"What were you playing?"

I expected it was canasta or cribbage and when June replied with poker, a surprised laugh from Ronnie made me smile. Guess she didn't expect poker any more than I did.

"Veronica, really," Nana scolded. "We play poker every Monday, Wednesday and Friday night."

"Good for you Nana," Ronnie said. "How much did you win?"

"We don't play for money dear; we play for chocolates."

I grinned at Ronnie and mouthed the words: *I like her.* Ronnie looked away.

"When you went outside to look at where the lady had been ...," I said, "... what did you see?"

Ester shifted in her seat. "How did you know we went outside?"

"That's what a police officer would do," I replied, then added, "even though she shouldn't because it could've been dangerous. And there was no way of knowing what you'd be walking into."

Ester appeared to give my comment consideration. "I suppose it wasn't wise, but we did go and look. Just in case she was lost and needed help."

"And?"

"She was gone so quickly we thought we'd imagined seeing her."

"But you did see her?"

"Oh, yes."

"And you were shown a photograph?"

"Yes. It was definitely the garden lady. We didn't see her face long, you understand, but there is nothing wrong with our eyesight or brains."

"Do you mind if I take a look, with Ronnie, out in the garden?"

"Go on," June said. "The girls and I will finish our tea."

* * *

Ronnie and I entered the garden leaving the old boilers drinking their tea. I steered her in the direction the woman must've come from rather than where she'd gone. We emerged through a tree lined path and found a gate to the street. I opened it and stepped out. I looked up and down the road then turned to Ronnie, still inside the gate. That was when I saw it, a small mark on the gate. It was about the size of a fifty-cent piece. I'd seen marks like that before. I pulled my phone out and turned on the built-in torch. I directed the beam at the mark and sure enough it reflected right back.

"What is it? And are you done shining lights?" Ronnie said, looking away blinking.

"There's a reflective mark on the gate. Let's walk back

through the garden and see if we find any more." Reasons for a mark on the gate trailed through my mind. Could be a target for thieves. Could just be a kid playing. Could be a sign for a drug deal. Could be a mark for a dead drop.

I latched the gate behind me, and we walked back the way we'd come, mindful that we were looking for a small reflective mark. At the end of the path, Ronnie pointed out a small mark. It was on the left side on a tree branch.

"Left," she said.

We walked on. Another mark a few feet past Nana's door. Then two more, and one on the far side of the lawn, in what would've been a dark area. That mark was a two-centimetre line.

"Here," I said, crouching. I observed leaf matter on the ground under the mark looking for signs of disruption. None. My eyes moved left; scanning under a bush several feet away, I saw a discarded wrapper. I shuffled, still crouched, to the bush. From my jacket pocket I took a pen, which I used to lift the wrapper for closer inspection. "Piece of plastic wrap," I said. "Out of place. This garden is well maintained, and there's no rubbish strewn around." I shoved it in my pocket rather than dropping it again.

"Might've blown in," Ronnie said. "It's gets windy, rubbish appears in even the tidiest of gardens."

"Possible." I stood and turned, looking at various bushes around the marked plant. Ronnie joined me. "We found the mark and there's nothing near it. Did she pick something up?"

"Perhaps she did."

"Doesn't look like anything was disturbed. And it was dark. The oldies didn't mention her using a torch."

I bent down and peered into the shadows.

Ronnie dropped to one knee with her back to me. "Crockett?" she said, pointing to something small and quite a way under a drooping fern. "Could be something?"

I've got long arms, but even at full stretch I had to use the pen to flick the object closer. "A small cardboard box." I flicked it again. "An old matchbox."

Ronnie handed me a latex glove from her pocket. I used it to wrap around the box and pick it up. I gave it a shake. Something shifted and rattled. Ronnie's eyes brightened in the dim light of the surrounding camellias. "I heard that," she said.

Using the glove, I slid the purple drawer in the box out far enough that I could see the contents.

"Not matches. The question is ... did she leave this or was she supposed to pick it up?" I said, holding the matchbox so she could see the contents. "Look."

Ronnie peered at the box. "A small USB."

"Can we go back to your office and see what this drive is all about."

"Of course."

Chapter 12
[Ronnie: Secrets and lies.]

Steph and Romeo were gone by the time we returned to the office. Late afternoon clouds rolled in, making the stairwell lights seem brighter than usual.

"Main office," I said, from the top of the stairs. "There's a desktop computer on the back desk. Not sure if you saw it. It's up against the back wall. It's not internet capable. We'll use that for the USB." I had the computer purpose built without any kind of internet connectivity. Paranoia is part of the job. Sometimes devices have built in 'call home' features and I didn't want to find out the hard way if this one did.

Crockett nodded his agreement and waited while I unlocked the door.

I walked ahead of him and pressed the power button on the tower. Crockett grabbed a chair and dragged it over. I sat in the chair already at the desk.

"What do you use this computer for?" he asked.

"Things like what's in that matchbox, writing client letters, storing some files that we want to keep away from potential hackers. Jenn likes to play SIMS on our down days, and this is the computer she uses."

"You get many random thumb drives?"

"A few. Who doesn't in a job like this, over the years?" I moved the mouse and entered a password on the login screen. "Pays to be ready."

I opened Launchpad then clicked on an app icon. I motioned to Crockett to put the drive in one of the USB ports. The app I'd opened brought up a new screen with a lock symbol at the top.

I dragged the USB icon inside the new screen.

"We'll give it a moment to run some checks. I don't particularly want a virus on this machine."

"Good idea."

We waited in silence until a green tick popped up on the screen.

"Ready?" I asked. My hand guided the mouse pointer to the icon for the thumb drive.

"Yes."

I clicked the icon and opened the drive. "Here we go."

Four folders sat on the screen. "Guess we start opening folders," Crockett said, "In order?"

I nodded. It'd be silly to be haphazard about it. I clicked the first folder. It housed files. I clicked on a file to find it was encrypted. No problem.

"What is that?" Crockett asked, pointing at the odd file extensions.

"Encryption."

"Any way for us to see the contents?"

I smiled. "Perhaps." I ran the mouse pointer over a few of the file extensions. "That'll be high level encryption. I have a little something."

With a few keystrokes an icon spun into view. I tapped it. It opened. I dragged all the folders into the program. One by one the program unpacked the folders contents.

"How do you have something that cracks top level government encryption?"

I shot him a fast look. "How'd you know that was top-level government encryption?" Officially Bateman was supposed to be private sector.

"Good guess." His eyes remained fixed on the screen. "How'd you get something that can unpack files like this?"

"A friend designed it and then installed it here. Just in case."

"Fuck me," Crockett whispered.

"Looks like this is one of those 'just in case' moments." I clicked on a file and watched as a screed of information appeared.

"What the hell ..." Crockett leaned forward to get a closer look. "Names and locations."

"Names, codenames, and locations," I corrected. Shit. No one should have this information. "This is an atlas."

"Could be a list of employees ..." Crockett said with a hint of hope, even though I could tell by his expression that he knew that wasn't the case.

"I doubt they're employees of the company she works at, unless TechSynth isn't what it's reported to be." I scrolled down the list. "I know some of these people."

"What do you mean you know some of them?"

I pointed to five names. "They were colleagues of mine back in the day." I swallowed hard. I was looking at a list of current spies and officers working for a number of different intelligence services around the world. "Most of these people are still in play." I slowly moved down the list and saw my name. Except me. I'm not in play. I scrolled further and spotted a few more people in the intelligence community that were technically retired. "I'm on it."

"Not just current spies," Crockett mumbled. "Unless you forgot to mention you're an active officer?"

I saw the handle next to my name. My last official job. Codenamed: *Eternal Sunshine*. They should've called it: *Misery*.

"I'm not active," I said, chewing my lip. Well, not like he meant. "The questions now are … did she drop this drive or was she supposed to pick it up?" I said, looking at more names. A feeling of dread grew. We should not be looking at this. "Who is she? And who is she working for?"

"Does it matter? Someone is trying to share sensitive information that will get people killed," Crockett replied.

"Of course, it matters. Is she a traitor or is someone else the traitor? Was she blackmailed, was she coerced, or is this of her own volition?" I scrolled through more documents. It was too late to unsee it. "Is she selling this?" No one was going to give it away. "Why am I on the list? Why is it multi-national? Who made the list?" I saw Ben's name. Both of us on the list, but not Crockett. Why was my last job on there?

"Will asking those questions help us find her?"

"It might. We're hunting a foreign spy, Aren't we?"

"Starting to look like that."

"If the person who was supposed to pick up this little box couldn't find it and took her ..." I looked at Crockett. "I think she left, I think she's running, and I think she hid it away from where it should've been left."

"Why leave it in the garden? If she wasn't going to hand it over, why leave it at all?" he said.

"So, she wasn't caught with it? Maybe we're not the only ones after her. She could've left it for someone to find it." That's when I knew I was onto something. Maybe, the marks were so she could find her way back to it, later. Once whoever wanted it was gone. "A spy with cold feet or a better offer?"

"But why that garden? Why not somewhere else with less risk of being seen?" He moved his leg. It brushed mine. "Did she want someone to see her?"

"There are easier ways to be seen, than skulking in a retirement home garden at midnight," I said, with a smile.

He gave me a long look. "You aren't exactly invisible. Could she have done it on purpose?"

"Clearly it was purposeful. The question is why there?" I grinned and nudged him. "I'm not invisible, but my life before becoming this delightful PI you see before you, was."

"No one knows what you were?"

Not no one. "Steph and Jenn know."

"Nana?"

"No, not exactly, she thinks I was in law enforcement."

"You live with your cousin ..."

"Donald knows, and despite how annoying he is, I trust him."

"But you're saying the placement of the device isn't about your former life?"

"Yep. Those closest to me knew what I was, but it wasn't public knowledge. It's not like they published articles in the paper naming names after ops," I said. We don't even get a truthful death notice. The placement of the USB drive bugged me, but I might know why someone would leave something so valuable in that garden. "Nana and the *Cronies of Doom* solve little mysteries around the retirement village."

"I gathered ..."

"A month ago, the local paper did a story on them. Nana mentioned my agency," I said.

"Could that be the connection?" Crockett mused. "Bateman escaped and made sure your Nana saw her and left the thumb drive knowing your Nana would investigate and find it."

"I doubt it happened like that. I don't think she escaped from anywhere, I think she's been hiding." But where?

"You don't like my narrative?" Crockett asked.

"It isn't very likely," I replied. "How would Bateman know Nana was up at midnight playing cards? How would she know Nana liked the drapes open on nice nights to see the garden lights? And finally, how would she know Nana had a garden apartment?"

"If you're going to shit all over my theory of this being

connected to you, then I'm expecting you to have a better one."

"Then you'll be disappointed," I said, and paused for thought. "If I was Bateman, I'd have couriered the drive to someone. If she knew about me and wanted help, why not send it to the bookshop? She was a customer. No one would've blinked if she'd sent herself a parcel to the bookshop and just didn't pick it up. We'd hang onto it."

Crockett nodded slowly. "Emily did say that customers sometimes had parcels dropped at the bookshop for people to collect on their way home."

I sighed. "This not getting us any closer to finding her."

"No," Crockett said. "It's not. Where was she, from Friday night to Monday night?"

"Still at home? Hunkered down." I knew she wasn't, I just knew. Nothing pointed to her being home.

"I'd be surprised if TechSynth didn't send their own people after her." Crockett stood and stretched. "She went to ground, had a change of heart, stashed the drive, and was snatched after that?"

"By whom? TechSynth? And then what? They made up the rest?" I picked up my phone and made a call. I walked to the window and looked out at the railway station across the road. "Shit," I whispered.

"What?" Crockett joined me.

"That?" I pointed at a man on a seat by the railway station. "Looks like your mate, Enzo."

The phone in my hand stopped ringing and a voice answered. More convinced than ever that I wanted Ben on the job with me, I said, "I need you out here. All hands, on deck."

"All right. I can pull that off." He coughed a few times. "Looks like I'm coming down with something." Post-COVID no one wants anyone working if they have even a hint at illness.

"Soon as you can, Ben." I hung up.

Crockett watched the man across the road. "Can he see in here?"

"Not very well," I replied. "The angle isn't great."

"Who did you call?"

"A friend. We often work cases together." Didn't refer to him as my boyfriend generally because it sounded weird. I smiled. "His name is Ben." I walked down the back of the office and placed the phone on my desk, then moved to the computer we were using before. "He'll be here as soon as he can get out."

"Ben?"

"Reynolds."

"Never met him, but I've heard about him. Why do we need him?"

"Because we need back up," I said. "We have the Enzo situation. We have god only knows what going on with TechSynth, and Nana is somehow caught up in it." That was the switch for me. Ben would make sure Nana was safe, no matter what. "And we still need to find Bateman, the job we were hired to do."

Crockett sat in his chair.

"All right, then we'll bring Ben Reynolds in."

Yes, we will.

"Our brief was to find Bateman, regardless of anything else, it doesn't matter what we think she did or didn't do, I guess. But it might impact on our ability to find her if we don't know what was happening in her world." I looked at Crockett. "I'm assuming here, that your brief is the same as mine, to locate Bateman."

"What does that mean?"

"Are you here to find her and bring her in, or find and eliminate?"

Crockett ignored the question and asked me to open the next folder. It felt like the answer was elimination. I opened another folder on the screen in front of me, then the next, and finally the last folder.

All three contained complete personnel files on the officers named in the list. I saw my file. Curiosity got the better of me and I opened it. I moved through the file looking at reports, a lot of which were redacted. As I read, I slipped into my former world and recalled the missing details from the reports. Things I never wanted to revisit bubbled to the surface. I shut the file. Then re-opened it. And looked at the bottom right-hand corner again. What looked like a page number was in fact the numbers three, five, and twelve. I opened a few more files and scrolled to the end. Found another with the same "page number".

I closed the files and opened the atlas itself. It was a spreadsheet. I didn't fully open it the first time, I just looked at the names and visible information. This time I scrolled right and up popped more columns.

"This is definitely something," I said, pointing to several columns of numbers. "Three, five, twelve. Appears next to a lot of these. Including mine and Ben's."

"Shit," he said, on an outward breath.

"The questions, Crockett, are, how did Bateman get this information and what she was planning on doing with it? Did she download this from TechSynth, and if so, why was this information on their servers? What is it they actually do? And what on earth does three, five, twelve mean?"

"They are not our questions, Ronnie. Our question is, *where is Tania Bateman?*"

Ben and I might disagree with his assessment considering our personnel files are included in the data. The names on the list didn't have anything that tied them together. Or nothing obvious anyway. We weren't all working the same theatre or even at the same time. The numbers tied them together, but how?

"Do police know she's a missing person?" I asked. "Because I didn't see a police report in my dossier on her."

"This isn't a police matter," he said, with care.

"Are we one hundred percent sure that no one will report her missing? Because if someone does, it'll become a police matter." And if that happened and Crockett's mission was elimination, then he'd better be damn good or he'd be up on murder charges.

"You went to her place of work. She doesn't exist now, right?" he asked.

"Pretty much. But she worked with people; people who must've known her at least a little bit."

"What are you saying?"

"I'm saying, we should talk to her co-workers, just like I would if this was a regular missing person case."

"You want to know if they've been told something different ..."

I nodded. "I do."

"You didn't happen to get a look at any other names and extensions while you were annoying that security guard, did you?"

A smile tweaked the edges of my mouth. Of course, I did. What would the point be if I didn't?

"I did."

"Let's find out."

I didn't expect Crockett to be so accommodating. But that's exactly what I would do if I wanted someone to think I was on their side but really I was gathering intel. Polite, friendly, accommodating. My mind wandered briefly as I considered whether there were sides in this situation, or just a job to be completed. It's a job. Let's get on with it.

I tapped two icons, closed the files, ejected the USB, and shut the computer down. I had the tiny USB in my hand and Crockett was watching me.

"You couldn't get a glass of water from the kitchen, could you?"

His brow creased. "Okay."

I waited until he left the room, took a small key from

my drawer, turned the computer screen a bit and quickly unlocked the secret compartment in the back of the computer screen. I stuck the USB in it and closed the hatch. It locked.

By the time Crockett came back with a glass of water, I'd moved to another computer. This time, it was a laptop at my own desk.

"Thanks," I said, and took the glass while I lifted the lid and waited a moment before opening a browser and typing in a name from memory: Marion Sylvester. It took a matter of seconds to find all her social media accounts. She had Instagram, LinkedIn, Twitter, Facebook, and Pinterest. Yay for people who give no thought to privacy and security. I sipped the water under Crockett's watchful eye.

LinkedIn told me she worked for the same company as Tania Bateman and confirmed I had the right person. I found a cell phone number. After a quick search I paired the phone number with an address.

"Right, let's go," I said to Crockett, and scribbled the address on a post-it note. "It's a twenty-five-minute drive." Give or take. I looked at the time. We'd be turning up around about five-thirty. Probably not the best time to surprise someone.

* * *

I suggested Crockett stay in the car when we arrived. It didn't pay to have a big biker-looking man front up to someone's door. No one needed beating or knee capping. It was a conversation, that's all. I strolled up the path to a latched gate, checked for 'beware of the dog' signs, saw none, and let myself in the gate. I closed it behind me, in case there was a dog somewhere. Nothing came rushing barking around the side of the house. I knocked on a green painted, solid wood, front door. Inside the house I heard children playing. I knocked again. Footsteps, and a woman's voice overrode the sound of kids. The door opened. A thirty-something woman with short dark hair, a friendly smile, and a barbie doll in her hand, greeted me, "Hello. You're not selling anything are you?"

"No," I replied, with a light laugh. "I was hoping you could help me. I'm looking for an old friend and I'm sure she mentioned your name. I think you work together."

"Oh, okay." She passed a small child the toy she held in her hand. The child ran away down the hall behind her.

"Her name is Tania Bateman and she worked for TechSynth until recently."

"Yes, I do know Tania. We shared an office. Quite a sad story. Her Dad had a stroke and she left rather suddenly to take care of him."

"That's awful, was it recent?"

"Friday evening."

"Oh, poor Tania. Did you hear from her?"

"No, she asked our boss to let us know." Concern creased her brow. "It must've been quite a shock for her."

"It'd be awful." I started to move away from the door. "Her dad was in Marlborough?"

"Yes, Blenheim."

"I'll try her dad's place. Thanks, Marion."

"Give her my best." Marion smiled, and closed the door.

I hurried back to the car to find Crockett in the driver's seat. I rolled my eyes at him and climbed in the passenger side. "Jump in my grave as quick?"

"Probably not, that'd be weird." He started the car. "And?"

"Her boss told her co-workers that her dad had a stroke on Friday, and she left to take care of him."

"Now you know no one will be reporting her missing."

I sank into the seat and thought about everything. It didn't bode well for Tania Bateman. "What if someone is hunting Bateman and she's gone off the res to protect herself ..."

"Not our problem," he replied, navigating traffic.

"You're one hundred percent sure about that?"

"Yeah, we find her, Ronnie. That's our brief."

A Harley roared past. We watched it disappear from view.

"Let's find out what old Enzo rides and get a rego," Crockett said. "Might help."

I twisted in my seat to look at Crockett. "Has this situation got something to do with our holiday hopping biker?"

"How could it? That was before this."

"Thought you were some hotshot tough guy with smarts," I said, disappointment ringing in my words.

"What does that mean?"

"You know this guy." I paused. "Did he turn up to flush you?"

"How would he know I'd contact you?"

"Because Bateman is the sort of person I'd be asked to look for. Discount nothing, Crockett."

"Okay, sure, I can see that. But how would he know anyone would want me looking for her?" Crockett asked. "Feels like fishing, Ronnie."

"Not at all." I smiled and zapped the window down a few centimetres. "I did my homework." The early evening breeze felt refreshing on my face. "You wanted out from behind a desk and there wasn't much happening. The world's been fairly quiet since COVID-19. Then all of a sudden, here you are."

"Or," Crockett muttered, "he really does like your cousin Donald and it's all a coincidence." His voice trailed off.

I glanced at his face. "What's that look then?"

"Just a memory. I knew someone once who didn't believe in coincidence." He gave a small smile, which I saw in my periphery. "Enzo could be a coincidence."

"Could be. But when he isn't, I told you so."

Chapter 13
[Crockett: The bookshop.]

"Ronnie, is the bookshop still open?" I asked, as I pulled into a park behind the building.

"Yes. Emily will be there," she replied. "We're open until six, two days a week over the summer."

"Long days for her."

"It was her idea, and she does it so the people who catch the train out from the city can get their reading fix," Ronnie said.

"I'll meet you back in the office," I said, and climbed out of the car.

Ronnie closed the car door. I tossed her the keys and she walked away.

I meandered in the large front door of the bookshop and smiled at the pretty woman behind the counter.

"Hey, Milo, how's it going?"

She blinked a few times and took a breath before she formed a response.

"People call me Emily, but you call me Milo," she said with precision. "Hi, Crockett,"

"Didn't think you'd remembered me," I said, the smile in my voice genuine, and I hope, reflected on my face. She was easy on the eye and there was something about her that drew me in.

She smiled back. I pulled my notebook from my back pocket and flicked through it to find the name of the book that Ronnie said came from the bookshop.

"Can you look at this for me?" I showed Emily the title written on the page. "Do you know who bought this book and when?"

"Not immediately." Emily reached into a cupboard, then placed a big blue ledger on the counter. "This is the daybook. Every sale is recorded. What I need to do is find the sale and the date then check my diary, okay?" Her smile faded. "I forget things. I write everything down."

I nodded. "Sure."

"We can also look for the sale on the computer. That will tell you how the person paid."

"Okay." I didn't remember seeing any credit card purchases from the bookshop in her financials, but maybe I didn't look back far enough. An idea surfaced. "Do you have a customer reward card?"

"Yes."

"Does it tell you what they purchased?"

"Yes, and how many purchases."

I stepped back to give Emily space to do what she needed to do. I had a feeling crowding her wouldn't help her memory. While I waited, I wandered further into the shop and browsed the bookshelves.

"There is information here for you," Emily said.

"What've you got?" I asked with a smile. I walked over to the front counter.

"That book was purchased a few weeks ago." She pulled her diary from her backpack and checked the date of the sale. "It was a lady. She is a regular customer."

"How regular?"

She read her notes on the day and shrugged. "I do not know. That information is not in my book."

Part of me wanted to look at her diary for the first time I came in, just to see what she wrote.

I showed her a picture of Bateman on my phone. "Is this her?"

Emily studied the photo. "The lady is familiar. It is possible."

I put my phone away. "Can we find out when she came in from the store card?"

Emily nodded, and opened the program attached to the cards. She stopped at the first screen. "What do you call her?"

"Tania Bateman."

She typed and hit enter. Emily shook her head. "Our system does not know that name." She blinked a few times. A lost look settled on her face. "I do not know what to do now."

I changed tack. "It's okay. Don't worry." No sense stressing Emily out over the name. "When she came in, Milo, do you remember where she spent the most time?"

Emily came out from behind the counter and walked clockwise, slowly around the shop. She stopped when she reached the counter and walked back the other way. At the crime section she stopped again and pointed. "Here."

"Thank you, Milo." I stepped up beside her. "I guess she likes thrillers."

"Yes. These are the shelves for people who like those

types of books. Some of the books on that wall are true crime." Emily went to move away, then looked back at me. "She used a credit card once, I think."

"You're awesome," I said, with a smile.

I stayed looking at the books while Milo went back to her computer. Whatever happened to her really did a number on her brain, but there was something about her that stirred me up. I heard pages turn but not typing. When I looked over, she was looking through her diary. I carried on looking at the books. Patience is a virtue and I'm a patient man.

I thought about the sketched rectangle we'd found at Bateman's house. It was the one thing that was out of place and didn't fit with her generic no personality house. I spun around and looked at the layout of the bookshop, then walked the length and looked at it again from the door.

Shit.

The sketch could be the bookshop floor plan. Roughly drawn, but that's what it looked like. The numbers had stuck with me. Ronnie said it was Bateman's phone extension at work. It could easily be something else as well. The way the numbers were spaced meant something more than a phone extension. I started counting the books and writing the titles in my notebook. The third, fifth, and twelfth book on each shelf. One set stood out. *Nothing Bad Happens Here, Eraserbyte, Carlswick Conspiracy*.

"Hey, Milo, did she ever buy one of these?" I strode

across the floor, slid the notebook next to her hand on the counter, and tapped the page with the last three titles on it.

"I will look."

I watched with interest as she opened the daybook again and worked backwards searching through the days until her finger rested on the words '*Carlswick Conspiracy*'. She found the day in her diary and told me it was a regular customer. "The lady with dark hair. That is what is written down."

"Is it the same lady that bought the book we talked about before?" I flipped the pages to show her the title of the book found at Bateman's house again. "This one, Milo?"

Emily's eyes widened. "I am not sure."

"It's okay. We know the day. Can we look at shop banking records and see if she used a credit card?"

Emily nodded. She opened the app they used to keep track of sales and to scan receipts. She found the right day and showed me the day's receipts.

"There it is," she said, pointing to the name of the book on an image. "Sharon Kleine."

So, she had another credit card, if indeed Kleine is Bateman, and not another woman who came in around the same time.

I wrote the name and number of the credit card, in my notebook. "Sharon Kleine." I touched Milo's hand with mine, briefly. "You're doing great, Milo. Now we have a name can you see if that person has a store card?"

Emily did as I asked and found the store card records for the woman. And there was the book we found at Bateman's. Half a chance Kleine was Bateman. For the first time, I felt like I was making progress.

"That's great, Milo. Really great. Can you print the information for me, please?"

She nodded and did as I asked. She really was nice. The printer at back of the shop whirred. I walked back there in time to catch the paper before it landed on the floor. Something on the crime thriller shelves gave me reason to pause. A niggle made me look at the shelf where I'd thought there was some kind of message in book titles. It was not unusual in my world to find hidden messages. "Hey, are all these books in the right places?"

"Is something wrong?" She made her way to me.

"She liked these books, yes?"

"Yes, she did."

"Are all of them, on this shelf, in the right place?"

Emily looked at the books. She walked the length of the shelf, touching each one. When she walked back the other way, she stopped with her finger on the spine of a book. "This one should be another book over." She nodded her head and ran her fingertip along the spines of all the books that ended in *byte*. There were twelve such books. "These are true crime. She was real."

"Who was real, Emily?"

"The lady the stories are about. I don't remember her name." Her fingers tipped *Eraserbyte* forward. "It needs to be where it belongs."

I smiled. "Thank you." As I watched, she removed the book from the shelf. "Can I see it?"

"Yes." She handed me the book.

I read the blurb on the back. The minute I saw the name of the main character I knew it was indeed true. Someone had written about Ellie Iverson. Fuck me. I ran my eyes along the shelf. No way were all these written since her death. I flicked through a few pages. There was a term for this particular type of book and it wasn't true crime. Creative non-fiction. The author wrote these from Ellie's point of view, like a novel but this was no made up story. The whole thing was nuts. How could anyone get this information? I handed the book back to Emily. Now's not the time to worry about stories concerning a dead woman.

"Do you know when it was moved?"

She shook her head. "Sorry." Emily created a gap and tried to slide the book in where it belonged, but it stuck out a little. She pulled it out again and checked the cover hadn't bent. She slid it back and the same thing happened. Emily took the book out and peered into the gap. Her fingers fished out a crumpled piece of paper. She opened it up.

"What is that?" I asked. Emily handed me the small piece of white paper. It was a piece from a memo pad with three typed words separated by full stops, and then it said, 'glow dots'. We found glow-in-the-dark paint in the retirement village garden. What were the odds of this being about that? But the three words made no immediate sense. "Funny thing to be in the bookshelf."

"Yes, unusual," she said, and finished straightening the books on the shelf.

It wasn't just the titles that held a message; one of the books did too. I wondered if Bateman saw it, read it, and left it behind knowing no one else could understand the message, or if she didn't find it at all. There was something about the way the three words were written. Not those actual words, but a sequence like that. I'd seen it before. But where?

"You're the most helpful retail assistant I've ever met," I said, "Thank you." I pocketed the note. "Ronnie will want to see this."

"Sometimes I do not feel helpful. Thank you for saying that I am."

"You are. You really are. I'll buy you that hot chocolate, I promise."

Milo smiled. I gave her a wave as I left the shop. I hurried past the big display window, along the wide footpath, and took the stairs two at a time to Ronnie's office.

"Ronnie!" I called from the stairwell. "Where are you?"

Her voice floated in the air as my feet hit the landing at the top of the stairs. "Where you left me."

"I left you near the car."

"Main office," she called back. Laughter followed.

I opened the door and walked in. "We've got something." I waved my notebook at her.

"Lay it on me," she said smiling.

I dropped my open notebook on her keyboard. "Sharon Kleine. Tania Bateman used a credit card in the name Sharon Kleine." Our first real break with this case.

A commotion outside the door interrupted our conversation.

One of Ronnie's business partners, Jenn, burst through the door with a male in tow.

"You, sit," she growled at the disheveled man, and pushed him toward the couch under the window. As soon as she turned her back, he bolted for the door. Jenn tripped him. The man hit the ground in an ungainly sprawl. "What'd I say?" He rolled over, she reached down and grabbed him by the arm. "Get up and go sit down. Idiot."

I moved away from Ronnie's desk, and closer to Jenn. "Problem?"

"Little one. This moron thinks he's clever. He tried to take my phone and iPad."

"Police?"

Jenn looked up at me with a half-smile on her lips. There was something different about her - her hair. I dragged my eyes away from the super bright colours. It takes a brave woman to wear a hairdo like that.

"Eventually. But first, I need to find out why. Clearly, he's not good at thievery so there must be a reason." Jenn looked over at Ronnie. "I was working the job you gave me ..."

Ronnie stifled a laugh, but I heard the little pieces clinging to her words. "Had your hair done then?"

Jenn glared across the room. I kept quiet. It seemed safest. I got the impression by Jenn's glare and body language, that the hair colour job wasn't what she expected.

"This ...," Jenn said with a scowl while waving her hand in the vicinity of her head. "Is something Donald called *Sunset Fiesta*."

When she said it, I could see the sunset. The very top of her normally blond hair was a deep inky blue which faded into purple then pink and orange.

"It's beautiful," Ronnie said, throwing her a cap from her desk drawer.

"Thank you," Jenn muttered, jamming the cap on her head. Pinks and oranges peeked out the gap between the cap and her shirt collar. "I'll just give you some highlights while we talk, he said."

I remained silent.

"I take it he did that out the back, no mirror?"

"He's a little sneaky bastard," Jenn said, turning her attention to the man who was chuckling. "Shut it!"

Raucous laughter erupted from the man. He could do with some lessons in manners. "They told me to look for the lady with clown hair," he crowed. "They weren't wrong."

"Dick," Jenn said, and whacked him on the arm.

Good job.

"Let me get this straight," I said. "Donald did this to make you easy to spot?" It wasn't a silly idea on his part, but I wasn't sure I understood what was happening.

"Yes," Jenn replied, tears glistening in her blue eyes.

I nodded slowly. "I think it's cool," I said. "Definitely Sunset Fiesta and not clown."

Jenn frowned under the rim on the cap, then a small smile grew. "Thank you. Donald's a tool."

"No question about Donald's tool status," Ronnie replied, and stood up. "See what you can find out from your light-fingered mate. I'll be back in a few."

She left, right in the middle of our discovery, and Jenn's obvious distress?

I glanced at Jenn. "Want an extra pair of hands?"

She gave me a small smile. "Absolutely."

Chapter 14
[Ronnie: Finding Kleine.]

It's rather bad form to disappear in the middle of something. I didn't want to listen to the guy Jenn caught trying to pinch her tech explain his light fingers, and I had something I wanted to try. It was pretty clear that Nana had branched out from using Donald as a henchman. Donald as a henchman still stuck in my throat as impossible. He was a hair stylist for goodness sake. Oh. God. Jenn's hair! How could he?

I walked down the hallway to the third meeting room, let myself in, locked the door, and set the room up ready to dowse. I called spirit and opened the window. Then lit the candles.

No breeze this evening, just calm warm air.

Leaving Jenn and Crockett wasn't a great move, but I didn't want to explain my workings. Not everyone gets it. And I don't know on which side of the spiritual being/paranormal fence Crockett sits. We had a new name, and that could help me do what I do best.

"Spirit, show me what you can. I have limited time and we need to find this woman."

One candle flickered once, then straightened.

I focused on Sharon Kleine. The pendulum swung in wide even circles as I moved carefully across the map, drawing the flame with it in a slow dance. This time I started on the left and moved right. Sometimes it helps to change perspective.

Kleine led me to the bookshop downstairs, Countdown Supermarket near the bookshop, then Quinn's Post. Lastly, Kleine's energy centred on the same street as Bateman lived. That was important. It meant she didn't have another home.

There was a small energy field near the river end of Moonshine Road. Interesting. I thought about what was there. A petrol station. A playground. The stopbank and the Hutt River Trail. Definitely places to investigate. But I couldn't exactly tell Crockett why I was interested in them. I needed to find another way of explaining my interest.

Sometimes working with someone isn't as easy as working alone. This was one of those times.

I packed up, closed the window, and shut the door behind me. I hit the kitchen on the way back and took a bottle of water from the fridge. I opened it and drank a few mouthfuls as I let myself back into the office, wondering if Sharon Kleine was her real name.

"You're back," Crockett said from my desk.

I looked around. Jenn sat at her desk, still wearing the cap, but looking happier. "What happened to the guy?"

"He gave me what I needed, and Crockett gave him a stern warning," Jenn said, with a smile. She flicked her thumb toward Crockett. "We could keep him around."

Nice to know he's useful.

"And what did your wee thief have to say?"

"He was paid by someone we know to find out how the

investigation I'm working on is going ...," Jenn said, shaking her head and biting back a smile. "I can't believe bloody Donald is in cahoots with ..."

"Nana?"

"Oh, hell yes. She's really got it in for Mrs White."

"So, I gathered. Where did she find that slimy low-life?" I leaned on Jenn's desk. "He doesn't look like one of Donald's mates."

"She advertised in the bloody paper," Jenn said. "She put the bloody thing in the classifieds and said she was looking for someone to do odd jobs."

That woman!

"Can you deal with her, Jenn?"

"Yes. I'm off down to visit her shortly. I'll write this up then leave you two to get on with whatever it is you're doing. It's time I had a wee chat with her anyway," Jenn said. "I swear she's getting worse. Now she's getting Donald to dye people's hair!"

"She definitely is getting worse," I said. "Good luck."

Chapter 15
[Crockett: Brambles and trolls.]

Jenn left on her mission to tackle Ronnie's Nana over the hiring of a thief. I was beginning to see what Ronnie meant when I asked her if her elderly Nana would be a problem. The woman was resourceful and relentless. I wondered why Donald played along with her madness. It didn't make sense.

"I have a question about Donald and your Nana."

"Just the one?" Ronnie replied with a grin.

"For now. How did she rope Donald into her, whatever it is she has going on?"

"Ah, you see, Donald is a dutiful grandson, and he has a secret. He's terrified Nana will find out his secret, and he isn't brave enough to tell her himself. He thinks it'll kill her, or the disappointment will."

"How bad is it?"

Ronnie tipped her head back and laughed. "It's not. But Donald can be a bit over dramatic at times. He's convinced that it'll kill Nana to find out he's gay."

"Would she care?"

"Hell no, she's known for years. She told me once she knew before he did."

"I don't understand ..."

"Donald doesn't think Nana knows. And Nana thinks it's great fun to set him up with granddaughters of her friends, and daughters of the staff at the home. He squirms and wriggles, but then goes out with these poor women to keep Nana happy."

"Wow, she's a piece of work."

"She is. But I'm as bad. I could've given him a heads-up, but I didn't because it's fun for me to threaten him with Nana."

"You both get on really well, don't you?"

"We do. We're almost siblings."

I could see that.

"Before the interruption," I said, running my fingers through my hair. "I was going to tell you there was a note behind a book on the shelf, one of the books that interested Bateman."

"What does it say?"

I pulled it from my pocket and handed it to her. Ronnie read it then looked up at me and handed it back. "Do you know what it means?"

"No, but I think I've seen something similar before, in the past. Give me a minute."

My mind kept flipping over random images from long ago and a black op. There was only one person I could ask, and I wasn't sure he'd know. I walked to the other side of the room and made the call anyway.

Mitch answered on the fifth ring. I could hear the girls in the background before he spoke. Every time I heard them laugh, small spikes of what we'd done, and what they'd lost, drove deeper into my heart. Sometimes this job blew chunks.

"Iverson household."

"Hello, mate. All good down in the Sounds?"

"Crockett, good to hear from you. You up for a fishing weekend?"

"Next month, if you're okay with that."

"Absolutely." The girls' laughter rang over the airways.

"I have a question about something I remember Ellie using, or rather I remember her saying."

A door closed. All background noise ceased.

"Okay, lay it on me."

"I remember her saying three words once and everyone knew what it meant. What was that? Some kind of code?"

"Ah, I know what you mean. It's a way of giving coordinates."

"Fuck me."

"Not my type," Mitch said, with a chuckle. "Thanks though."

"Funny man. Was it an app?"

"Yeah, hang on, I've got her phone."

"Didn't that ..."

"Her work phone was with her that day. I have her personal phone. She had the same apps on both."

Was it strange that after four years he still had her phone and kept it charged? Not to me. Not when I knew how much they loved each other, and how much they loved those little girls. Guess her phone was like a time capsule. Memories of happy days.

"I found it," Mitch said. "It's called *What3Words*."

"Thanks matey, I'll ring ya before I head down next

month." The stories about Ellie wouldn't go away. "Hey, did you know someone wrote a set or series of books about Ellie?"

The slow response told me he did. "Long story, long time ago there was an author who caused utter chaos in D.C. She'd apparently been gathering info on cases and writing about Ellie for years. Why?"

"What happened to her?"

"She was killed. Why?"

"How long ago?"

"A few years before we were married. Again, Mitch, why?"

"Because I came across some books today. Mitch there are twelve."

"That's not possible, she was killed and I only know of four books."

"Then someone else carried on where whoever it was left off. Maybe, look into it."

"I will."

"Looking forward to seeing those rowdy little sprogs of yours."

"They love their Uncle Dave. See ya, pal."

I hung up and rejoined Ronnie with a grin on my face. "There's an app. I'll download it, and we should be able to work out what those words mean."

"Cool, get on it then," she said. "I'll start running that credit card and see if there's been any activity this weekend." Ronnie interlaced her fingers and stretched her arms out above the laptop. Her joints cracked.

Without any further comment, she opened the program needed, and typed.

I found the app Mitch told me about in the app store and downloaded it. It didn't take long to work out how to use it. It was designed for people who got lost. The idea was that you sent the coordinates to emergency services and they could find you. It's accurate to a square metre or something. At the top of the screen were three words, and the map pinpointed my location. I added the three words from the note.

Wow. The map moved and the location was the garden in the retirement home.

"Ronnie, the note, it's a location. It is the retirement home garden, specifically an apartment on the left side of the garden. Looks like three away from your Nana's, outside not inside. So, a part of the garden."

"That's not where the matchbox was," Ronnie replied.

"No, it was the other side, it was at least five metres away and then hidden."

"What does it mean?" Ronnie asked, staring at the screen in front of her. "We've got something from the credit card."

"I don't know what it means, except maybe she didn't leave it where whoever left the note wanted her to leave it. For whatever reason." I pulled a chair up and sat next to her. We still know fuck all, that's what it means. "Show me the something."

She pointed to a short list of transactions. One was on Saturday afternoon, at a petrol station on Moonshine

Road. Same place again on Sunday morning. The third transaction was at a cinema on Miro Street Monday afternoon.

"She may not have gone home, but it looks like she wasn't far away," Ronnie said. "Let's go visit the petrol station. They've got forecourt cameras."

"What about that last transaction? Where is that?"

"Down the road and round the corner from Nana's."

"She was checking it out." Recon.

"It appears that way," Ronnie replied, shutting down the laptop and hooking a blazer from the back of her chair. On our way out, she picked up her keys and locked up.

Ronnie pulled into the petrol station and parked out of the way of the pumps. We sat in the car on the forecourt for a moment, both of us surveying the area before alighting from the vehicle. I spoke over the roof to her. "There's a park or playground or something, nearby?"

"Yes, there is. Moonshine Park. You can also access the Hutt River Trail and walk either to Silverstream, or north up toward Akatarawa."

Finally, some places to check.

We walked into the petrol station. A lone figure stood behind the counter.

"Can I help?" he said, as we approached.

"I hope so," Ronnie replied. She had her phone ready in her hand with Tania Bateman's photo on the screen. "Have you seen this woman in the last week?" She showed him the photo.

"Maybe. Who wants to know?"

Ronnie tugged a business card from her jeans pocket with her free hand and gave it to him. "Ronnie Tracey, Private Investigator. She's missing. Her family hired me to find her."

I watched her work and enjoyed it.

She eyed the man's name tag. "It's important, Patel. She might be in trouble."

"She looks like a woman who came in a few times over the weekend."

"Prior to that, have you seen her?"

He shook his head. "No. I haven't, but one of the others might have."

Ronnie smiled. "Do you have CCTV's operating?"

I knew they would because I couldn't think of a petrol station that did not operate CCTV. Armed robberies and drive-offs saw petrol stations installing CCTV before it was super common in other areas of retail.

"Yes."

"Does it record and store footage?"

"Four weeks, off site," he replied.

"Any chance we could take a look at particular times from over the weekend?" I thought it was time I said something. I tried for friendly, but probably came across a bit scary.

"I guess," the man replied with a shrug. He typed on a computer keyboard then said, "Date and time?"

I read the first time and date out. "Try a few minutes before that time, if you can."

Patel typed again. When he finished, he motioned for us to come closer and angled the screen so we could see it better. We watched. Tania Bateman walked in the door and over to the cabinets of food on the far wall. She chose a few things and moved to the counter.

"Great," I said, "Can you check the next time for me?" I wanted to make sure it really was Tania Bateman using a credit card in the name of Sharon Kleine.

Sure enough, the times matched the bank statements.

"Thanks," Ronnie said. "If you see her again, give me a ring."

Patel smiled. "Sure."

I knew he wouldn't. Something about his manner told me that was too much effort. He wasn't paid enough to get involved in any extracurricular activities surrounding a customer.

* * *

Back in the car, Ronnie looked at me while I wrote notes.

"Park?" she said.

"Yeah," I replied, and finished writing in my special Crockett shorthand, before closing the notebook.

Ronnie started the engine.

She drove up the road and down the track that led to Moonshine Park, then pulled into a car park near a kids' play area. There were no other cars in sight.

"Where would she go?" I said, looking around. There was a stopbank, a lot of grass, a play area, and beyond that, the river. I could see a green structure on our left about two hundred metres down the road. "What's that?" I said, pointing into the distance.

"Toilets," Ronnie said. "If she was sleeping rough, then under the bridge would make sense. Fairly sheltered and unlikely to be disturbed. Close enough to the toilets."

"Let's go look under the bridge then." Although why she'd sleep rough, I did not know. She had a house not far away. She clearly had another identity that we weren't told about. She could've checked into a motel. It looked like she had options and that puzzled me.

Ronnie angled out of the car just as her phone rang. She answered it and put the call on speaker.

"Donald?"

"Ronnie, that biker, he's parked across the road from the salon."

"Do not interact, Donald. Just stay inside."

I moved closer to better hear the conversation.

"He's lovely."

"No, Donald, he's dangerous and not in a good way."

I pointed to the license plate of Ronnie's car and mouthed the words "Ask him". I hadn't met the famed Donald Henere-Tracey, so didn't want to jump into the conversation.

"Can you see his license plate?" Ronnie asked.

"Yes." He paused, then read out the number. "Five-five TLX"

"Five, five, Tango, Lima, X-ray," Ronnie repeated.

"You and your fancy speak," Donald said, with a

mocking laugh. "If you must sound like a wanker, I suppose you must."

I grinned.

"Stay inside, do not interact. Call me if he moves. I'll send Ben to you as soon as he gets out to Upper Hutt." She hung up and looked at her watch. Then she made another call. This time not on speaker. But I was close enough to hear without much effort.

"Can you go to the salon when you arrive. Donald will fill you in. Also, keep an eye out for a Harley with the plates: Five, Five, Tango, Lima, X-ray."

"Of course. I'll be there in fifteen." His voice crackled a bit. "You all right?"

"Yeah, things are getting more interesting than I'd hoped they'd be."

If I had to guess I'd say the guy on the phone was Ben Reynolds.

She hung up, shoved her phone into the inside pocket of her jacket, and motioned to me. We walked across the grass toward the river and followed a self-propagating, rambling blackberry hedge under the bridge. Didn't take long to conduct a search of the area. There were signs of recent occupation.

"Look, someone's been here," I said, finding a pie wrapper on the ground near a bush.

"Kids hang out under the bridge like trolls," Ronnie said, with a smile. She moved branches and searched under low hanging scrubby bushes. "There's something under here. I can see some sort of fabric." She reached right under the bushes. "This isn't kids leaving rubbish about the place." She dragged a small backpack out. "Someone stashed this."

We inspected the exterior of the bag before opening. It wasn't a cheap Warehouse bag. It was a branded daypack. Ronnie unzipped the top and opened it up on the ground.

She removed items, one by one. Wet wipes. Tissues. First aid kit. Protein bars. Torch. Spare batteries. Space blankets. Fleece blanket. Change of clothes. Multi-tool. Matches. Lighter. Waterproof storage bag. Small zip lock bag. Notebook and pen. Portable power bank but no phone. Parachute cord. Duct tape. Safety pins. Identity documents. She picked up a red passport and showed me. "Red not black. Russian. We thought we were looking for a kiwi." She opened it, read it, and passed it to me.

"Lissette Markova. Looks a lot like Tania Bateman and Sharon Kleine," I said.

"No wonder I can't get a clear bead on this woman," Ronnie muttered.

That was a strange thing to say.

"What? You can't what?"

She looked up at me for a split second, then went back to what she was doing without answering my question. "This is a go-bag," Ronnie said, as she rifled through the smaller pockets and held up cash in three denominations for me to see.

Russian, New Zealand, and American. "If we needed proof we were looking for a foreign spy, I think we found it," Ronnie said, and put the money back.

"Why didn't she come back for her bag?" I mused. "She stashed it, but why leave it?"

"Because something happened to her before she could. But was TechSynth that something?" Ronnie didn't look up when she spoke.

"If they'd grabbed her, we wouldn't have the case, or if they were working the case and stumbled upon her, we would've been called off," I said. I was pretty sure they wouldn't be paying us for a job they'd already done. It'd come down to money. Everything does.

Ronnie re-packed the bag, stood up, and slung it over her shoulder. "Not leaving this here."

I tore a page out of my notebook, wrote my phone number on it, and placed it carefully where the bag was hidden. "Let's leave her with something."

"She must have a wallet with her, or maybe just a credit card, and there was no phone, but the power pack suggests she had one," Ronnie said, as we walked back to the car. "She stashed her pack. Walked to Nana's street, did a reccy of the retirement home, and went for a coffee and maybe something to eat at the cinema coffee shop, and then what?"

She unlocked the car and dumped the pack in the backseat. We sat in silence for a few minutes. I presumed Ronnie was thinking because I was.

Eventually I said, "Where was she until the middle of the night?" The last place she used her credit card was the cinema café. She wouldn't want to be out in the open.

Not if she thought someone was coming for her, and not while she had the device on her. And she probably had it with her until midnight. Movies? "Did she go to the movies?"

Ronnie played with her phone. Not using it, fidgeting.

"Is there something we need to talk about?" I asked, watching her run her fingers around the edge of the phone case and back, and then do it all over again. "Ronnie, is this about the comment you made about not getting a bead on the woman?"

Her eyes flashed with gold lights as she flicked her head to face me. "Yes."

"All right, lay it on me."

"What'd MacKinnon tell you about me?"

"That you were good at finding people. You had knack for locating the missing. And that you were good to work with," I said, forming each word from the sentences MacKinnon fired at me when he suggested I work with Ronnie. Actually, it wasn't a suggestion.

"That's pretty well true," she said, her smile fading fast. "I have a special skill. I like to employ it, but I don't share my technique with anyone."

"Okay ..." I had no idea where this was going.

"I couldn't get any reading to speak of for Tania Bateman except around the vicinity of TechSynth and little low residue energy emanating from her house." She took a breath and continued. "When I tried to get a reading using Sharon Kleine, I found her at home, at the bookshop, the petrol station, down here, and the last read was near the Quinn's Post pub."

"You're going to need to explain the reading thing. Why didn't you tell me you already knew about some of the places we just visited?"

"Because you'd ask how, and I had no way of backing my wild claims."

"But now you do?"

"Well, sort of, I guess. I always knew I was right, but now I am one hundred percent certain I am right about where she was, but I don't know where she is now."

"Why don't you know?"

"I think maybe if I use the name on the Russian passport, we'll get closer."

I was pretty pleased with how non-judgmental I'd been so far. "How *do* you know?"

She took a big breath in, then released it slowly. "Do you know what dowsing is?"

A couple of old blokes wandering around dry paddocks with forked willow branches looking for water didn't feel like the correct answer, but maybe it was.

"A way of finding water?"

She nodded. "Yes. But you can dowse for energy too. People's energy. Sometimes objects as well if someone handled them and a bit of their energy hung around."

"This a bit woo woo ..."

"Bro, it's totally woo woo. Believe it or not, it works."

"And you want to try this magic dowsing with the Russian name, before we go looking any further?"

"I do."

"Where does this take place and can I watch, or is that not how it works?"

"You can watch, you can even have a go if you want. Just keep an open mind."

"I can do that." There is more to heaven and earth than the fraction of things we know about. I can do open minded, woo woo shit. There's half a chance she even gets results from her woo woo. MacKinnon said she had special skills, and not the Liam Neeson kind. I suppose this is what he meant.

"Let's go find out," Ronnie said. "I have a room in the office suite that no one uses but me."

"Let's do this. Back to the office then. After that we'll resume our tracking."

Ronnie smiled. "We might have a better idea what she was doing after this."

Chapter 16
[Tania: Death is coming.]

He smashed his knuckles into her face, splitting her lip. Blood splattered onto her clothes. She snapped her head upright, and aimed a defiant glare at him.

"Who are you?" she asked, wiping blood from her face with her free hand.

"I ask the questions," he growled, slapping her with an open hand. "You must be worth something to someone. Husband, father, someone will pay to get you back."

"I doubt it," she said, touching her face gingerly.

"What's your name?"

She swallowed blood. "Tania. Tania Bateman."

He used his phone for a few minutes then showed her a screen. "This you?"

It wasn't, but she nodded. She had no internet presence. If he thought she did, it might buy her time. Time for what, she wasn't sure. Just time.

He scrolled through the person's social media. "See, husband," he said and smiled. "Tomorrow."

She said nothing.

He smirked. "You're not bad looking." He grabbed her face. "We should have some fun."

She jerked her face from his hand.

He grabbed her again. Fingers digging into her flesh. "I'd be nicer if I were you."

"People will be looking for me and they're not going to

be nice," she said, her voice rasping over her dry throat.

"No one will be looking yet."

"They will be." Tania closed her eyes. They will be and you will die, she thought, and so will I, once they have what they need.

He let her go.

"I'm thirsty, can I have water, please?"

He left the room and returned with a bottle of water. She gratefully accepted the bottle and drank over half. Her captor watched.

"What's your name?" She put the bottle down on the floor.

"Paul," he replied.

She got the impression that was his real name. He didn't seem bright enough to use a fake one.

"Thank you for the drink, Paul."

He didn't reply. He knelt on one knee and removed the shackles from her ankles, then the handcuffs from her wrist. He straightened up and dragged her to her feet. She looked around for an escape route. "Come on." Paul took her arm and encouraged her to walk. Something clattered to the floor. He stooped and picked it up.

"You lied," he growled, holding the smartphone so she could see it. "Thought you said you didn't have one."

Tania stared blankly at the phone in his hand. Damn. She didn't realise she still had it. Not that she could've reached in the back of her waistband. The screen glowed. It was on. There was a chance they could still track her. She didn't know if there was a way to track the phone he'd given her, but suspected there would be. That's the sort of thing they'd do. She'd intended to ditch it before getting on the train and leaving town.

"Don't know where it came from," she said, trying her best to sound innocent.

He opened-handed her across the face. "Liar."

She wiped blood from her lip.

"Unlock it," he growled, and handed the phone to her.

She did and gave it back. There was nothing to find apart from a few coded text messages. They wouldn't mean anything to him, and they looked like regular texts.

"Who is this?" he asked, showing her the last text conversation. "Who were you talking to?"

"A friend."

"Why doesn't the friend have a name?"

"New phone, I didn't get a chance to add my contacts."

"I bet this friend will pay something," he said with glee. "Probably not a friend, probably your husband."

Definitely not a friend, she thought. The only thing *that* contact will bring is death.

He put the phone in his pocket. "Let's go."

He marched her out of the room and into a corridor. Lights flickered as they passed them. She counted doorways. He stopped at the fourth and swung it open. He shoved her through the doorway. A dim light bulb in the middle of the room gave enough light for her to see a bed, an old school desk, and a broken chair. Tania took another few steps. The room swayed.

"What did you do?" Her vision blurred along with her

thoughts as she staggered.

Chapter 17
[Ronnie: Asking spirit.]

Crockett trailed behind me as I climbed the stairs and turned down the corridor. He followed me to the meeting room. I swung the door open and ushered him in.

"What is that smell?" he asked, as I closed the door behind us.

"Candles," I replied. I pointed to a chair by the credenza. "Have a seat while I set up. Just remember, open minds solve crimes." I remembered when I first heard that phrase and how apt it was; still is.

He froze, turned slowly to face me, his eyes seeking mine. "Who said that?"

"I did," I replied with a laugh. "No one else here, yet."

"No, Ronnie, someone else said that. Where did you hear it?"

"I heard it years ago. I was working with a couple of Americans and a Russian down south," I said. Crockett paled. "You all right?"

"Course." He sat heavily in the chair. "Who did you work with back then, when you heard that phrase?"

I shrugged. "Doesn't matter."

"Ronnie, it matters. Who were they?"

"Mac Connelly and Sean O'Hare. They're both deceased now."

"And the Russian?"

"Misha Praskovya. He was drop dead gorgeous. His

accent slayed me. Heard he was killed in an explosion in Europe somewhere, a number of years ago now."

"Fuck me," Crockett said, shaking his head. "Fuck me."

I grinned. "No thanks." His reaction spoke volumes. "You knew them?"

His head shook and nodded in quick succession. He looked confused, then sad. I watched him as his expression snapped to surprise. Our world isn't as big as people think, especially down here at the bottom of the world.

"It's a small world. We worked joint ops, and I did a joint op with those three," I said. "You did know them, didn't you?"

"I knew Connelly's wife, a little. I knew O'Hare, a bit. Never met the Russian, but I worked with people who knew him."

"Feels like there's a big story there just simmering under the surface." I smiled as I carried on setting the room up. "Hey, be useful, take down the smoke alarm for me?"

Crockett did as I asked. Having a tall guy around was handy for some things. He placed it inside the credenza. Crockett began to relax and sat back down.

"How does this work?" he asked. "Do I need to do anything?"

"Just make yourself comfortable and you'll see how it works in a minute."

I opened the window, lit the candles, and picked up my pendulum. With it held over the map, I said, "Spirit, I ask you to guide this pendulum and show me the truth. Locate Lissette Markova."

As if to answer, the right candle flickered, then straightened. The pendulum swung in broad slow circles. I focused on Lissette. And moved my hand slowly around the map. This time right to left, starting with Silverstream. The swings changed as I got nearer to her street. Over the part of her street that was where her house would be, the pendulum stopped and hung.

"What does that mean?" Crockett asked, he was standing across from me. I hadn't noticed him move.

"Her energy was there," I said. I moved my hand, and the circles grew. As I approached the retirement village the circles became smaller and tighter, then stopped. "Retirement village," I said. I moved again, this time east toward the hills in small progressions. Big circles, small circles, and at the pub, then the vicinity of the movie theatre. I couldn't get anything definite, but she was there at some stage.

I increased the distance, carrying on toward the hills and over into the rural land beyond. Moving south the pendulum spun in large circles. As I reached Whitemans Valley, the swinging slowed and came to an abrupt stop in the middle of what looked like farmland.

Trying again, moving my hand north, the swinging began. I continued north over the farms and open spaces then moved back. As soon as I reached the earlier spot, the pendulum stopped dead. It looked like a fairly big area to search. I couldn't see anything on the map where someone could hide. No obvious buildings. I knew the map was two years old. No reason to assume there wasn't a building, back then, or now. It was a map, not a satellite image. The area the pendulum pointed to was at least a kilometre from the nearest road.

I thanked spirit and place the pendulum on the map. It rolled and stopped.

"What does it mean?" Crockett asked, his gaze fixed on the motionless pendulum.

"Spirit thinks she is over the hill in Whitemans Valley. Here-ish," I said, placing my finger next to the point of the purple pendulum.

"And what's there?"

"I have no idea. I hope it's a structure of some sort."

"If it isn't?"

"Most likely a grave in that instance."

"We should go to the picture theatre and see if anyone recognises her," he said.

"Yes, we should, and see if we can work out how she got from Ward Street to Whitemans Valley, and why. Also, it would be handy to know what's in there, and what we might possibly be walking into."

"Yeah."

I couldn't tell if he was freaked out by my skill set, or if he took it in his stride and filed it under 'weird shit that happens in New Zealand', and I didn't want to ask. As long as he appeared okay with it, I could ignore the niggling in my stomach that started as soon as I decided to share my skill.

* * *

There was a perfect park across the road from the movie theatre on Miro Street. We piled out of the car and entered the café which was the foyer of the cinema. In my peripheral, I caught Crockett scanning the interior for cameras. There weren't any, so I knew he wouldn't find one, but didn't mention it. I was pleased my dowsing had paid off, and now Crockett might be receptive to my ways of working.

The barista smiled and greeted us.

"Could we grab a cappuccino and a ..." I nudged Crockett who was next to me.

"Flat white, thanks," he added.

"No problem." She set about making the coffee.

I took the opportunity to look around. A couple of people sat at a small table near the door, but no one else was obvious. Past the counter were more tables and a wide doorway that led to another seating area. A woman entered while we waited. She looked at me and smiled, then greeted the barista by name.

Okay, so she's a regular.

The lady moved down the café to a table at the side. As I watched her move, I felt there was something familiar about her. The barista handed us our coffees, took the payment, and moved on to making another order without a second glance. Clearly, she was busy. I took my drink and decided to join the lady at the table. Time to see if I

188

had met her before. Being a regular could be helpful to us.

"Hello, I'm Ronnie Tracey. Have we met?" No sense in beating about the bush.

The lady smiled. "Not directly, Ronnie. It's nice to put a face to the name I hear a lot."

"Really?" Colour me surprised.

"I know your Nana. I'm Pat."

That explained it then. But how did she look familiar to me? I rummaged about memories of Nana. Ah, I had it.

"You were on the Wairarapa wine tasting trip with Nana, I saw the photos."

"Yes, what a marvellous time we had."

"Certainly looked like a great day out. Nana showed me the photos." I smiled. "Do you live nearby, Pat? Seems like you're a regular here. You don't strike me as the retirement home type."

"Across the road," Pat said. "What are you doing down this way? Thought you usually got your coffee at the Mayfair in town."

She knew Nana all right.

"I'm looking for someone."

"Both of you?" Pat said, with a nod in Crockett's direction. "Perhaps your friend would like to join us."

I smiled, "He does look a bit out place, and lonely standing over there." I beckoned to Crockett. "Dave this is Pat, a friend of my Nana's."

"Pleased to meet you, Pat," Crockett said, placing our

cups on the table then sitting next to me, taking up nearly all the space on my side of the small table. Men. Crockett spoke, "Hope you don't mind us joining you for a minute."

"Not at all," Pat said. "Ronnie said you are looking for someone?"

Crockett showed Pat the photo of Tania Bateman.

Pat took careful stock of the woman in the photo. "Monday afternoon. She was in here ordering a coffee and a slice of cake."

"Did she go to a movie?"

"I'm not sure." Pat looked past Crockett as the barista walked toward her carrying her coffee. "Thank you, Sarah." She took the coffee from the barista. "You might know. The new woman on Monday afternoon ... did she stay for a movie?"

"Which woman?" Sarah asked.

"Dark hair, squirrelly, fidgety almost."

"Ah, yes, coffee and carrot cake. She was here for about half an hour, then went somewhere else. She did come back for the evening session."

"I knew you'd know," Pat said, with a smile at Sarah.

"Was she with anyone?" Crockett asked.

"Not when she came for coffee, but someone came in after her and went to the movie. I don't know if they were together and couldn't tell you where they sat in the theatre."

"Can you describe the person?"

Sarah glanced at the queue forming by the counter.

The other barista signalled for help.

"Tall, male, with short brown hair, mid-thirties perhaps, tidy clothes. Nothing out of the ordinary." She smiled apologetically. "Sorry. Not much help."

Sarah hurried back to her workstation. Pat, Crockett, and I sipped our coffees.

"Sounds like you have a mystery on your hands," Pat said. "Your Nana mentioned a garden intruder. Is this related?"

"Might be," I said. "It just might be." I sipped my coffee and thought for a moment.

Where did Bateman go? I hadn't picked up anything apart from the movie theatre, retirement home, and the pub. It wouldn't take very long to check out the retirement village, a quick walk around the outside was less than ten minutes. She wasn't seen until midnight. Movies run two hours, maybe two hours thirty at the outside. She could've used the time between coffee and the movie to do a reccy, she certainly didn't enter the buildings. Margot would've seen her and challenged her reason for being there, and by the time the movie finished the main doors to the village reception would've been locked. Where was she between the movie and the midnight sighting? I thought about how long it would take her to walk back to her makeshift camp. There wouldn't be much time left from three-quarters of an hour.

"Enjoy your coffee, Pat, we've got to get going," Crockett said, as he nudged me to stand.

"Very nice to meet you," Pat said. "No doubt I'll catch up with your Nana soon, Ronnie. Take care."

Back in the car, I was still thinking about where Bateman was before being seen at the village. I drove back toward Ward Street. On the right-hand side at the corner was a playground. A path cut through the green space to Ward Street, from Miro Street. There was a building set back from the playground, and large trees on the corner. She could've hung out near the building or under the trees. It was close enough to the movie theatre that spirit might not narrow right in. I kept that in mind. Or she could've gone left and found somewhere to wait at Heretaunga College. That would make more sense because it was closer to the retirement village. She wouldn't be out on the street for long if she was keeping a low profile. Which she seemed to be.

Was the college close enough to the pub to confuse spirit? Yes, it was.

But why stay outside lurking in college grounds with a perfectly good pub right there? Quinn's Post was right next to the retirement village. I'd go to the pub. I believed the pendulum said she went to the pub.

"She went to the pub?" I said, turning left and driving up Ward Street.

"I'd go to the pub," said Crockett. "That thing you do, showed us the pub."

That thing I do, did indeed show us the pub. I smiled.

"I don't doubt you'd go to the pub," I replied, and turned into the Quinn's Post car park. Wonder how busy the pub is on a Monday night? I couldn't imagine it being a full house. "It's handy, it'd be open then, and it'd be more comfortable than lurking in a park or school."

"She didn't use her credit card," he said. "But when you did your thing, it definitely looked like she came to the pub."

"Dowsing, Crockett, my thing is called dowsing." I still had a smile on my lips. At least he wasn't being a closed-minded dick about it.

"When you used your *dowsing* talent it really looked like she was at the pub." He looked at me for a beat. "How big a margin of error is there?"

"That depends on the energy field. She might not have gone into the pub. She could've lurked near the pub and the retirement village. She could've holed up in the garden, because physically the pub and the village are close to each other."

"If she went to the pub, she didn't use a credit card," Crockett said, as if to jog my memory to his earlier comment.

"She didn't use the two we know about. And she had cash in her bag. Maybe she took some of that with her," I said. "And yeah, I think she was here."

"Good point. If she had cash, why did she use that credit card at all?"

I didn't have a decent answer for that question or maybe I did. Words formed. "Because she didn't think anyone would trace it to her." And no one would've if she hadn't used the bookshop as a dead drop. "Or, because her ability to get more cash is limited." I leaned my head back on the headrest. "Whoever she was passing information to, used the bookshop as a dead drop. That means if they didn't get the information, and we have it, they do not ..."

"Not necessarily. Playing devil's advocate here. What if it was left for her? The thumb drive I mean. What if she was told to go to the bookshop after the last phone call she made," Crockett said. "That piece of paper I found there was another part of the dead drop puzzle. Now we know what the words on it mean, it could've been left for her as instructions on where to leave the device. She left it, but not where the coordinates said."

I guess she could've been given the USB by someone and not taken the information from TechSynth, but why would TechSynth be looking for her if she hadn't stolen intelligence from them? And why did TechSynth have that intel, or did they?

"Good points," I said, keeping the rest of my thoughts to myself.

"Emily saw the person who left that note in the bookshop. She saw them, even if she doesn't remember seeing them, or doesn't know what they did," Crockett sat up straight. "She writes notes about everyone who comes through those doors in her diary."

Then her diary contains valuable intelligence and if anyone else knew that, she could be in danger. Whoever was supposed to pick up the device that we now have, is probably not a friendly, and could look to retrace

Bateman's steps.

"We need to protect that intel and Emily," I said.

"Then we need to get tooled up."

I nodded toward the pub. "Let's go in there and see if anyone remembers Bateman first." May as well, we were already here. And I really wanted someone to prove me right so Crockett would be receptive to acting on my information alone should it come to that. I grabbed my bag, removed my wallet, and looked through a selection of business cards. Who am I going to be tonight? No one. I chose a card that simply had my company name and the words 'Private Investigator' followed by the phone number we reserve for this particular card. We have a few cards. This one is the preference if we don't really want to give our names and numbers.

We walked through the doors into a more spacious area than I remembered. It'd been a long time since I'd visited Quinn's Post. It wasn't just a bar. It was a restaurant. I went to the nearest till with a photo of Tania Bateman on my phone screen.

"Hi, have you seen this woman?" I held the phone up to the girl behind the till.

"No," she shook her head. "Charlie might have." She turned and called out over her shoulder for Charlie.

"She was in on Monday night," I said.

"I don't work Monday nights. I knocked off about six, but Charlie was here with a couple of casuals."

A brawny looking bloke with tattoos of frogs up his right forearm, sauntered through a door behind the girl.

He looked like a Charlie or maybe a Wally. He did not look like the description from the barista at the café. "How can I help?"

I showed him the photo on my phone. "I'm looking for this lady."

"Don't remember her," he said.

"Are you sure? Would've been Monday night that she was here, probably between nine and midnight."

"Yeah." He paused. "Don't know her."

"Are Mondays busy?"

"Depends, lady."

"Was Monday this week busy?"

"Not really."

"And you didn't see her?"

"That's what I said."

I guess he might not see many people who come in if he's out the back cooking.

"Who else was working here that night?"

He shrugged. "I can't remember."

"Is there a roster?"

Usually there is.

"I dunno. Boss sent a couple of ..." He paused. "He sent a couple of people to work the shift."

"Thanks." I passed him my curated card. "If you think of something, give me a ring, or text. You can just text that number if you like. It's important."

"She in trouble?" he asked.

"She's missing," Crockett replied. "She's my sister."

The man looked at the card, and then at me and

Crockett. "If I think of something."

I was pretty sure he'd already thought of something and wasn't intending to ring us ever. There was a glimmer in his eye when he saw the photo, fleeting, but definitely a glimmer of recognition.

We left. My phone buzzed. Ben texted to say he didn't have eyes on Enzo.

"Enzo is in the wind," I said to Crockett when we reached the car.

"Eyes open then."

"Your place?" I said, throwing my car keys to Crockett. "You drive."

Crockett caught the keys and grinned. "Okay."

Enzo roared into the pub carpark just before Crockett and I pulled out. He saluted as we drove away.

"He seems nice. Let's invite him to dinner," I said, checking the wing mirror to make sure he wasn't following us.

I texted Ben: Eyes on Enzo at Quinn's Post tavern. Stick with Donald.

Ben: Roger that.

"Sure, tomorrow night work for dinner with Enzo?" Crockett said, with a chuckle.

"Absolutely. I'll cook."

Crockett checked the rearview mirror several times as he drove. I kept an eye on the wing mirror. There was no sign of Enzo. Crockett lived on a back section about halfway down Merton Street, only a few streets away from where Donald and I lived. He pulled the car into the driveway and parked behind his Harley, which was in his carport.

"Trusting," I said. "I don't know if I'd leave a Harley in a carport in this area when I wasn't around."

"Trust me, no one's dumb enough to touch it," he said.

"I can see that would be a thing."

"Come on in," Crocket said holding the side gate open for me. I followed him along a path to a door. He climbed the steps ahead of me, unlocked the door, stepped inside, and disabled the alarm before motioning me to enter. "Welcome to my humble abode. Have a seat wherever you like." He waved a hand to a big couch and several armchairs. "I'll just be a minute."

I looked around the room. Framed pictures of motorbikes and a few family portraits hung on the walls. There was a framed photo of Crockett with two little girls on top of a five-shelf bookcase, that stretched across the wall between the lounge and what I guessed was the kitchen. They were cute kids with blonde curls and wide smiles. They didn't look like him. I sat down and waited.

I checked my watch twice and my phone once. Heavy scrapping sounds came from down the hallway.

"You need a hand?" I called out.

"Nah, I got it," he said, with a grunt as punctuation.

A minute or so later, Crockett came back into the room with a slight flush on his cheeks and carrying a black duffle bag. "Sorry, had to get some gear out of the floor safe." He put the bag on the floor and unzipped it. "The spare bed covers the hidden trapdoor to the safe."

That explained the noises.

He removed two pistol cases, two holsters, belts, magazines, and boxes of ammunition from the bag. Then he delved in again and brought out magazine pouches. With everything carefully laid out on the floor, he looked at me "You good with a Glock?"

"Yes," I replied. I sure am. I reached for the weapon case he held out to me and took it from his hand. I opened the case. Inside was a Glock 17, 4th generation. Nice.

I picked up the magazine from the Glock case and pulled a box of ammunition closer. The next few minutes were spent loading ammo. I slid a magazine into the butt of the Glock 17, racked the slide, and then did a press check. I released the magazine and added one last round to it. Now there were seventeen rounds in the mag and one up.

"Try this holster," Crockett said, and handed me a paddle holster and a belt. "This is the shortest belt I have."

I threaded the belt through the loops of my jeans, slipped the paddle holster inside the back of the jeans so the clip was over the belt. Then I put two spare magazines into a leather pouch and snapped over the belt so they sat just behind my hip and didn't obstruct the gun in my lower back.

"Comfortable?" Crockett asked.

"Yeah, not bad."

"Takes a little getting used to."

I moved the holster a couple of centimetres to the right. "Yes, it will. Been a long time since I've worn a sidearm. I'm not carrying the right paperwork for this."

"I am, we're working together."

"The Aussies are going to provide my get out of jail free card?" I laughed. "I'll look forward to that."

"Maybe we shouldn't put it to the test," Crockett said, with a wry smile. "Don't kill anyone."

"Smart."

He tapped his head. "Smart like tractor, strong like ox."

Laughter bubbled up. "You're not bad for a roo rooter."

Crockett laughed, a deep belly laugh. "At least I'm not a Tui poker."

"Well played," I said, through laughter.

"You ready to head out into the world?" Crockett asked, settling himself.

"What vibe did you get off that big guy at the pub ... Charlie?" I asked, adjusting the belt to a tighter setting.

"Nothing good," he said. "Nothing good at all. I'm a pretty good judge of blokes, and something about him plucked a few warning strings."

"I'm not his biggest fan. Let's get back to the pub - we need to follow him or get a tracker on him. If one of us can get close enough, let's try cloning his phone."

"I see he pinged something in you as well. Good to know. You clone and track people's phones much?"

"I track all my friends and clone their phones. For shits and giggles," I said with a wicked grin.

"Yeah, me too." He shrugged. "You're right though, something felt off about ol' Charlie and I think we need to find out what."

"Another thing before we do that. Emily," I said. "We should go by her place and convince her to spend the night at mine. I know she'll be safe there with Ben."

"That's actually a really good idea."

"Stick around, they come in swarms," I said, making for the door.

He followed. I heard the door close, and the lock click.

Chapter 18
[Crockett: Keeping Emily safe.]

Ronnie and I stood side-by-side at Emily's front door. Anxiety brewed in my gut. Been a while since anyone had an effect on me like that. I rubbed my palms on the sides of my thighs. Get a grip, Crockett. She's not the first pretty girl you've met.

Emily answered the door without asking who it was. Dangerous.

"Ronnie?" she questioned, as if she didn't trust her own eyes. After a short pause she said my name. "Crockett?"

"Yes," Ronnie replied, with a smile. "I know this is a surprise visit, but can we come in?"

Emily nodded and opened the door fully. I followed Ronnie inside and closed the door. Emily led the way to her living room. "Why are you here?"

She folded her good leg under herself as she sat on the couch.

I glanced around the room and saw a laminated list near the light switch. It was a check list and hanging from it was a red whiteboard marker. The last thing on the list said, 'wipe list clean'. I knew she had memory issues, but the list made me think they were worse than I realised.

Ronnie spoke, "Something has happened, and we are worried about you."

"Did I do the wrong thing?" she asked, looking from

Ronnie to me.

I shook my head. "Not at all. It's nothing you did or didn't do. We need to keep you safe."

"What from?"

Ronnie looked at me. My eyebrows rose at her and I sat down next to Emily. "Someone came into the shop and left a note in a bookshelf."

She nodded. "I found it ... with you."

"Yes. The person who did that might think you know who they are."

She frowned. "I *do not* know who did that."

"I know." I waved my index finger between me and Ronnie. "We know."

"Then why does it matter?"

"The person who left the note doesn't know about your memory. They might think you can identify them. If they find out that you can't, or if they suspect that you keep a detailed diary, they might still come after you to get your diary."

Her frown deepened. "But I do not know who it is. If someone took away my diary, I would not be able to check things." Her voice wobbled at the edges.

"That's right."

"Why would they do that. And what would they do to me?"

"I don't know, Milo. I don't know. I don't want anything to happen to you," I said, trying not to panic her, but really wanting to get the message through that she could be in danger.

"What do you want me to do?" she asked, unfolding her leg, and placing her feet on the floor.

"We'd like you to stay at Ronnie's house tonight," I said.

"I like to be home in my house," she said, with quiet authority. "Everything I need is here."

"Where is your diary?" Ronnie asked.

"In my bag. I have not taken it out yet." Emily looked up at Ronnie. "Here is home."

"You can come home again as soon as we make sure you are safe," Ronnie said. "I can help you pack. It's just for the night. You can do one night, Emily," she said.

She had me convinced, but Emily appeared reluctant.

"We really want to make sure you are safe," I added.

"Donald is there," Ronnie said with a smile. "You always have fun with Donald."

"Donald is fun," Emily replied, matching Ronnie's smile. "He will not mind?"

"Not at all, he's always up for a slumber party."

Emily repeated the words slumber party like it was the first time she'd heard them. Ronnie caught it. "Sleep over, Emily. A slumber party is a sleep over." She smiled. "I think it'll be fun."

"Yes," Emily said. "I will pack."

"I'll help," Ronnie offered.

"No, I can do it," Emily said, and got up. "I will be some minutes."

When she left the room, I stood up. "She wasn't this bad when I was talking to her in the shop," I said. "She seems to be struggling."

"She's tired," Ronnie said. "It's harder for her brain to keep up, and for her to make decisions, when she's tired. I'm surprised she's still awake."

I wandered around the room and into the kitchen. More lists. One on the kitchen door and one on the back door. I joined Ronnie again.

"What's with the lists?"

"They make sure she gets things done. Emily ticks off each item once it's done and, at the end of the day, she wipes the lists clean ready for the next day."

"Clever. Where's the toilet?"

"Through the kitchen, and off the laundry," Ronnie said, pointing.

"Thanks."

I found it without too much trouble. As I washed up, I noticed the name across the top of the mirror. Emily Jones. It was right above my head. I wondered how often she forgot her name and had to read it off the mirror. I remembered when I met her, and she said *People call me Emily*. Not, I am Emily. Whatever happened to Emily really screwed her brain. She didn't know who she was anymore. No wonder she wasn't sure about liking coffee and had to write everything down.

I rejoined Ronnie. "What happened to Emily?"

"Car accident," she said. "Four years ago, she was driving home from work, yes, she worked for me then, and a car smashed straight into her."

"Man, that sucks."

"Yep."

"She doesn't know what happened?"

"Nope, she doesn't remember her life at all."

"Did she know she knew you?"

Ronnie shook her head. "She still doesn't. She said to me once she wished someone would walk through the bookshop door and remember her."

"But they do?"

"Yes, of course, they do, but she doesn't remember them. For a long time, we hoped that being in a familiar place would help her recover, but so far, it hasn't."

"When does she think she started working in the bookshop?"

"A year ago," Ronnie replied. "She always says I've been here a year."

Emily walked into the lounge carrying a backpack and a messenger bag. "I have my diary," she said.

"Good," I replied. "Let's go get you settled at Ronnie's."

It didn't take long to get to Ronnie's place. That was a bonus of being in Upper Hutt. She wasn't far away from my place. In fact, it'd be an easy walk even after a couple of beers too many.

Ronnie, Emily, and I went inside. Donald was telling a story to Ben.

When I walked through the door, silence dropped like a ton of cement.

"Sorry, carry on," I said.

"Dave Crocker," Ben said, standing and offering his hand.

I shook it. "The famous Ben Reynolds," I said, "It's a pleasure."

Ronnie spluttered a laugh from nearby. "Two fan boys. Yay."

"And you must be Ronnie's cousin, Donald," I said, reaching for the other out-stretched hand.

"Aren't you a big strapping lad," Donald crooned, using my hand to pull himself to his feet. "What do we ride?"

"A Harley," I replied, extracting my hand from his tight grip.

Donald fanned himself with both hands. "Be still my little black heart."

That was my cue to leave.

"See you later Emily. Ronnie and I have to go to work," I said, patting her on the shoulder.

Ronnie spoke to Ben, "Emily has her diary with her. Sometime over the last few weeks someone left a note in the bookshop. Relevant to our job. That information might be in the diary."

"Okay, I'll see if we can find it," Ben said. "Is that okay, Emily?"

She nodded. "I am tired."

Donald swooped in and put his arm around her narrow shoulders. "Come on precious, let's get you set up in the spare room."

"Good luck," I said to Ben. "Be aware, someone could make a play for Emily's diary or Emily."

"She's safe here," Ben said. "Be careful out there."

Ronnie led the way to the back door.

"What's with the sign on the door? 'Accompany Romeo'," I said.

"He has a habit of taking himself off to patrol the area if he's let out at night by himself," she replied. The door closed behind us.

Chapter 19
[Ronnie: The pub.]

"Let's go have a beer. The atlas is secure for now. Emily is safe. Our current problem is the missing woman no matter who she really is." Okay, not our only problem, but a major part of our paid gig.

There was no sign of Enzo at the pub.

I texted **Ben**: No eyes on Enzo. His motorbike is not in the carpark.

Ben: Emily is asleep, I am going through her diary.

Me: Keep us posted.

Crockett ordered us a beer each while I found a booth that gave us a good vantage point. I wanted to be able to see the kitchen doors and the staff coming and going. Ben rang as Crockett walked over carrying two beers. He placed them on the table and sat opposite me, leaning in the corner so he could see into the room.

"Hey, what's up?" I said into my phone.

"Enzo is back," Ben replied. "Our new mate Enzo is parked up across the road."

"I wonder if it's him who will make a play for the book?"

"If it is, I'll be ready."

"Okay. Keep Donald indoors. You know what he's like when he sees a Harley. Is Romeo inside?"

"Yes. And he's prowling from room to room," Ben said. "He was lying with Emily for a while."

He knows something is up. "See you when I get there. Stay safe."

I hung up and took a sip of the cold beer. It was really good. Panhead. Drink local.

"Everything okay?" Crockett said, taking a swig of his beer, then nodding his head slightly and looking at the bottle. "Upper Hutt makes decent beer."

"Enzo is parked outside my place. Ben has it under control. Emily is asleep. He's going through her diary. The dog and Donald are indoors."

"Let's deal with one thing at a time," Crockett said, and swigged more beer. "Let's find out if Charlie is malicious, or just a fat bastard with no life who drools over ladies who come in alone."

"Now that's something we didn't explore. Is she alone?" I sipped my beer and enjoyed the bite in the hops.

"I think so. There was nothing to indicate she met anyone or has company."

Fair enough.

I still had the feeling Charlie had seen Bateman. A glint in his eye that made no sense when he saw the photo. Not like she was a Bond girl or anything. She was a regular looking woman, and it was damn near a mug shot. Nothing to glint about.

We kept an eye out for Charlie while we talked.

"I really don't see how her vanishing act was, or is, beneficial. She didn't pick up her go-bag," I said, sipping my beer. "She's out there somewhere without anything

..." My mind rolled around the reasons to be out in the middle of nowhere, and kept coming back to dead, or something else lurking on the sinister line.

Crockett shrugged. "Maybe she had another one stashed."

"She left the passport. If she'd gone for another bag, because the location of the bag we found was compromised, she'd have taken the passport or destroyed it ... unless ..."

"Unless she was coming back and something happened," Crockett raised his bottle. "Like Charlie."

"Yes, or an actual accident and she's in the hospital."

I picked up my phone and called Hutt Hospital claiming to have a missing sister and asking if someone fitting Tania Bateman's description was admitted to Accident and Emergency in the last two days. Nope.

"Not an accident?" Crockett asked.

"Probably not an accident," I said. "Still room for error."

"In a ditch somewhere ... over in Whitemans Valley."

"That's cheerful. Not a lot of ditches between here and the river, so maybe." A noise near the entrance attracted my attention. A small group of loud older teen boys entered and made for the bar.

"And you're thinking?" Crockett asked, swallowing another gulp of beer.

"Someone grabbed her. Who else is looking for the files she had?"

"If she's a Russian, then half a chance they are looking

because she didn't hand them over."

"Hmmm." I wasn't convinced. Why did she camp out? She could've holed up in a motel. We weren't looking for her until Tuesday. Did we know for sure she wasn't home between Saturday and early Tuesday morning? No, we did not. "Did she have cameras at the house?" It really wasn't a home, so it was a house. The place she slept. Or maybe she didn't even sleep there. Maybe it was a front and there's a real home somewhere. Except I didn't find one dowsing.

"I don't recall any, but then ..." He downed the last of his beer and smacked his lips together. "I was looking for obvious cameras, not concealed ones."

"We should go back to her place tonight and check."

Crockett nodded, and took the empty bottle from my hand. "Another?" he asked and nodded his head toward the bar. Charlie was talking to a man I'd seen come in behind the group of teenagers.

"Yes, please," I replied. "Charlie's got his phone out. He just put it on the bar. Looks like the opportunity you need to clone his phone."

"I'm going to need a distraction," Crockett said with a grin. "I need to plug his phone into mine, and I need sixty-seconds."

A cringe grew within me. I shuddered. A minute can feel like long time.

"Okay." I took a deep breath, and headed toward Charlie and his friend, with Crockett.

"You good?" Crockett said, just before we reached the

bar.

"Yep, sixty-seconds. That's all you get."

"It's all I need," he whispered. "Do your thing."

Crockett placed the bottles on the bar just past where Charlie and his friend stood. I went right, as close as possible without being weird about it.

"Hey, Charlie, isn't it?" I asked. They both looked at me. "Sorry, didn't mean to interrupt. I thought you might know, are we too late for a meal, and what's good tonight?" I smiled. "The chef gear is a bit of a giveaway."

"Yeah, I'm Charlie. It's not too late. Kitchen is still open. You came in earlier with your … boyfriend."

"Not my boyfriend, we're mates, that's all," I said, with another winning smile. His friend leaned closer to me.

"You came in with him tonight," Charlie said, like it was news.

There were about five people between me and Crockett now. I wasn't sure how he'd get the phone or if he had the phone. Not my problem. I was the distraction.

"We like to go for a beer, we're mates. So, what's good tonight?" Angled away from the friend a little, he moved closer, and I did not want his arm to creep around my waist. Pretty sure he'd think it was a bit strange if he felt the holster or the magazines under my jacket. Better that than him touching me though. I controlled the creeping revulsion I felt inside.

"Depends on what you like," Charlie replied. He'd warmed up a little. "You look like a chicken parma kind of lady, and I do a great parma."

It did sound good. Chicken parma is a hard to beat favourite. "Sounds delicious."

His friend moved closer. "I'm delicious," he said.

Gross. I very much doubt it. Forcing myself not to gag, and making sure I maintained a smile, was hard work. On a positive note, he didn't match the description from the barista either.

"I like the sound of chicken parma. What about dessert? I'm partial to some sugar."

"You don't look like you eat much sugar," Charlie said.

I took it as a compliment. "Big ice-cream fan. What's the best dessert you do?"

"I do an amazing baked Alaska, but it's not on the menu here. You'd have to come to dinner at my place for that."

His friend touched my hand. I pulled away. "Don't be like that," he said.

"I don't know you," I replied. "It's rude to touch people. Didn't your mother teach you manners?"

"The name is Paul. So, now you know me."

"Two chicken parmas and we'll decide on dessert later," I said to Charlie, ignoring Paul for a moment.

"Ditch your friend. I can show you a good time," Paul said. "What's your name?"

For some unfathomable reason I said, "Tania."

Paul grinned. "I like Tanias. They're fun."

"Know a lot of Tanias, do you?"

"A couple," he replied, with a wink at Charlie.

Now what was that about?

"Fun is not a word usually associated with me," I replied, smiling. "Maybe I just haven't met the right guy."

Charlie leaned over the bar toward me. "Tania?"

Shit. Did I introduce myself earlier?

"Isn't your friend looking for his sister called Tania?"

"Yeah." Phew. "Lot of us around. Everyone knows at least two."

He delved into his pocket and pulled my card. Damn. That's right, I gave him a card. He looked at the card and then at me. "There's no name on this card you gave me."

I smiled and breathed a sigh of relief. Smart me gave him the generic card, not my card. "That's our company business card. We can all use it. Cheaper that way," I said. "Small business, you know what it's like." I smiled. "That's the office cell number on there."

Charlie looked from me to the card. "Right." He nodded. "Makes sense. Sure add up if everyone wanted their own cards and everything, I'd imagine."

Whew.

Paul shuffled closer. "What kind of work do you do, beautiful Tania?"

"I'm an investigator," I replied.

"I've got something you can investigate," he said.

"I didn't bring my magnifying glass."

"Very funny," Paul said, taking another half step closer. "See, I was right, you are fun."

Not intentionally. Movement in the corner of my eye told me Crockett was back. I looked at Paul. "What's your phone number, you know, in case I feel like having more fun later?"

He smiled, and it somehow made him more unattractive. Deep inside a part of me shrank away. Paul pulled a pen from his pocket and wrote a phone number on a napkin and handed it to me. His fingers lingered on mine.

Crockett grabbed my elbow. "Something's come up," he said. Then addressed the men. "Sorry."

He escorted me out of the bar and over to the car. Once ensconced safely in the car, Crockett started the engine and drove away. But not far. He parked just around the corner and down a bit from the Fergusson Drive entrance to the retirement village.

"Did you get it?" I asked.

"Yep."

He handed me his phone. "That last app on the screen. Open it and it'll download all the activity on his phone."

I did. And it did. I sifted through a lot of text messages. I pulled the napkin out of my pocket and checked Paul's number with the numbers on the text messages, and any calls. There were a few Paul's as regular contacts, so narrowing it down with a number that belonged to the Paul at the bar, was helpful. And there was quite a bit of back and forth between them over the last few weeks. Paul wanted a job; Charlie didn't have any going. Paul wanted a loan; Charlie was okay with loaning him cash but kept it under five hundred. Paul wanted beer; Charlie said he'd be over with a dozen after work. Paul wanted a job; Charlie had a casual job going on behind the bar

Monday night.

"Get this, Charlie gave him a casual job behind the bar on Monday night."

"And we have a winner," Crockett said. "Perhaps we should've shown him Bateman's picture tonight."

"They're pretty tight," I said. "Charlie and Paul. But there is nothing from Charlie about a woman at all." I scrolled down looking for the most recent communication. "Tuesday morning, Paul calls Charlie. Doesn't look like Charlie picked up. There's a couple of texts from Paul, innocuous blah blah texts, then there is one about a woman he met."

"Okay, and?"

"You saw them. How many women in their right minds would want to spend time with either of them?"

"That's not very nice," Crockett said. "But I see where you're coming from."

"He described her as a hottie." Gross. My skin crawled. "Charlie replied to that text saying he'd like to meet her, and he should bring her into the pub for dinner."

And the next text from Paul said that wasn't a good idea.

"Does he use a name?" Crockett asked.

"Nope."

"We've got nothing much then. Except he was in the pub on Monday night and on Tuesday he's talking about a woman he met," Crockett said. "I think we were right about Charlie knowing something. And the Paul guy could be the reason he knows something."

"Let's set up a trace on the Paul guy's phone, as well as Charlie's, then go check out Bateman's house again." Something felt off. Really off. I passed the phone back to Crockett. "Can you trace phone numbers from your phone?"

He shot me a grin. "I can."

I handed him the napkin. "Go for it."

Chapter 20
[Crockett: Back to Bateman's.]

Ronnie wasn't very talkative on the way to Bateman's house for our second look. Can't say I was either. There were things. No. Not things. There was one thing weighing on me. She didn't know everything about the job, and I didn't like that situation, but orders are orders.

For me, it wasn't just find Bateman and bring her in safely. It was a clean-up mission. Anyone who came in contact with her was a loose end. If Paul and Charlie had something to do with her disappearance, then they were loose ends. Charlie looked like he'd be messy, in a people would miss him kind of way. He'll have to be an accident. Paul could go either way. The reason we got this job is that we are deniable. The agencies involved can walk away with clean hands. Ronnie hasn't mentioned that, but I'm sure she knows. She's been in the game a long time, it's not her first deniable mission. But even though we're off-book, we still have a higher power and orders, or at least I do. Ronnie is a bit different - she's a private contractor. Hence, she wasn't read in to the full scope of my part in the disaster prevention scheme MacKinnon cooked up and called *Witcher*. The whole thing had crap fest written all over it.

I pulled into Bateman's driveway and cut the lights. No point parking on the street. It's not like she's going to complain. Ronnie poked around behind her seat for a moment before we exited the car together and quietly closed the doors.

Ronnie walked ahead of me, using her phone torch to see the way around the house. She had something in her other hand.

"What have you got?" I asked hoping I was whispering.

"RF detector. If she's got hidden cameras and they're sending a signal, then this little toy is the easiest way to find out." She shoved it in her pocket and bent down near the door. She found the key no problem. Good memory.

Once inside, I stopped moving. If she had cameras, she could be remotely monitoring them. Hell, I do, and I bet Ronnie did too.

"What's the matter?" Ronnie whispered from beside me.

"Cameras mean remote monitoring ability."

"And? We're kinda counting on that to be able to detect them. You think she's really going to be sitting somewhere watching us toss the house?"

Yes. I do. I pulled my phone out and turned it off.

Ronnie turned the RF detector on. It lit up and squealed. She grinned at me. "Going dark," she said switching her phone off. The RF handset she held stopped squealing. Ronnie moved in the dark ahead of me. I saw a red light glowing and watched it move across the floor. It went green. A loud squeal followed. She silenced it and came back, bumped into something in the dark, and swore quietly. Probably hit the corner of the bench.

"All right?" I said, keeping my voice low enough so the neighbours wouldn't hear.

"Yeah." She rubbed her thigh. "Something is definitely sending a signal in the living room. Could be hidden in the smoke detector," she said. "I got a good strong signal when I lifted my arm toward the ceiling." She turned her phone back on and shone the torch at me. "What are you worried about?"

"That she could have this place rigged to go bang while we are snooping about looking for the DVR or NVR, or whatever is recording footage from the camera."

"She's going to blow up her house in a suburb of Upper Hutt, and risk collateral damage?" Ronnie's voice held a hint of incredulousness. "That'd cause all kinds of questions and lead to someone uncovering what was going on with her."

I motioned to her to go back out the door. "Just like that time the Americans called in a drone strike on a research facility in Wallaceville a few years ago ..."

"Fake news," Ronnie said, with an evil chuckle. "According to the media that was an accidental explosion."

"Yeah, and I accidentally rolled out of bed this morning still breathing." We were standing outside the house on the path in the dark except for Ronnie's phone torch. "We need to check for explosives."

"Got a sniffer on you or is there an app for that as well?"

"Smarty pants. I'll be back. Don't go anywhere." I ran

back to her car. I'd dumped my bag in the back and in my bag was a sniffer. Once a boy scout, always a boy scout. I grabbed a plastic case from the bag and opened it on the back seat. Inside was a device about the size of a small smartphone. I lifted it up and turned it on. l didn't bother locking the car, and rejoined Ronnie on the path outside the door.

She'd obviously had time to think about the house.

"It didn't occur to either of us to check the house for explosives when we first came here," she said, as I moved into the kitchen.

"If we'd known then ...," I replied, over my shoulder. "Give me a minute." I had my phone in my left hand and the torch on. My right held the sniffer. I checked light switches on the way to the front door. A small rush of air left my body as the display remained neutral. The silence in the house was overshadowed by my thumping heart as I moved from room to room, giving the bedrooms a cursory going over. I was more interested in places that housed electronics, which could potentially be a snuggly little shrapnel shrouded casing for C4. I checked the television, DVD player, fibre modem, and the wi-fi router, even the couch, and chairs. On a deep breath, I moved to the kitchen and double checked the cooker, toaster, and the hot water cupboard, washing machine, dryer, and meter box in the laundry. Nothing.

I turned off the torch and pocketed my phone. My hand paused over the kitchen light switch. The sniffer remained dormant.

I flicked the switch and exhaled. Fuck me.

Ronnie spoke from the doorway. "We good?"

"Yeah."

She stepped inside and shut the door behind her. "You sure?"

"Yep," I said, with a relieved smile, but putting the sniffer away was another story.

"Let's get a look at that smoke detector in the lounge," Ronnie said. "Likely place for a camera."

I figured that was my cue to take the smoke alarm down. I reached up and gave it a twist. Easy enough. What should've been the flashing light saying the alarm was working was a tiny wireless camera.

"How many others, do you think?" Ronnie asked, peering at the smoke alarm in my hand.

"I'm picking the hallway has one."

Ronnie checked out that smoke alarm and sure enough another camera.

"Let's see if we can find a recording device. This is a wireless system. It might not record. It might just send," I said, but didn't believe it. If you have cameras you want to be able to review footage if something goes wrong.

Back to work. I started opening cupboards. We hadn't seen a DVR or NVR anywhere the first time we'd been in, but we weren't looking, either. If it wasn't obvious, then it'd be in cupboard or maybe the ceiling crawl space.

Ronnie wandered off while I checked kitchen cupboards. I opened the last cupboard, and then it dawned on me that Bateman had very little in the way of pantry items and kitchen gear. I had more than she did, and I'm a bloke who doesn't cook unless necessary.

Ronnie called out, her voice loud enough for me to hear, but still controlled. "There's a trapdoor in the ceiling of the main bedroom wardrobe."

Damn, how did I miss it? I hurried to her.

"Back up," I said. "I'll let the sniffer have a look first."

I held my arm up above my head, the sniffer vibrated and beeped. "Fuck me." I looked over my shoulder at Ronnie. "Move."

She took off at a run, I followed. We barrelled through the back door and into the car. Doors slammed shut. I cranked the engine and slammed the car into reverse. Looking over my shoulder, I drove backwards at breakneck speed, jamming the brakes on at the corner. Still facing the house. An explosion ripped through the air, shaking the car, sending flames, smoke, and debris into the air.

"Jesus, someone was watching us for sure."

"We need to get out of here," Ronnie said. "Drive."

I turned the car around. People were starting to emerge from houses, shocked and staring at the leaping flames and billowing smoke in the dark sky.

"Your place?" I asked, before the next intersection.

"Office," she replied, sinking into the passenger seat. A few seconds later she said, "I need to ditch this car."

That was a good call. We didn't know if anyone had seen the car tonight, or us for that matter. We'd been there twice and once in daylight. Different car, same people. I'm a hundred percent sure I stand out more than she does.

"Where?"

"Head toward Stokes Valley," she said.

I turned down Whakatiki Street and onto the River Road, headed south. Multiple sirens wailed behind us into the night.

We crossed the bridge at the Silverstream exit, then went under the rail bridge toward Stokes Valley. "Now where?"

"I have a place on Hutt Road, a garage."

"If anyone got the plates ..."

"My cars aren't registered to me."

"Could they trace it to anything that links to you?"

"If they tried really hard, but it'd take time."

Good to know. Really good to know.

She directed me along Hutt Road to a series of workshops in an industrial area. The door to one slowly slid up as we neared.

"The car is chipped?"

"Yep, all of mine are."

I drove inside, lights flickered on, the door closed behind us. There were two other cars parked. I recognized the Mustang she'd used but hadn't seen the other vehicle before. Ronnie swung her door open and climbed out.

She took everything she had in the car and laid it on the ground by another car. I followed suit. From a shelf at the back of the workshop, she picked up gloves, cloths, and spray cleaner. She chucked gloves to me as well.

"Get cleaning. The quicker this car is fingerprint free, the faster we can get back to Upper Hutt."

Halfway through, my phone pinged. I checked the display.

"Hey, Charlie's mate, Paul is on the move."

"Clean faster," Ronnie replied. "I want to see where he goes."

She wasn't alone.

"Nearly done," I said, closing the back passenger door. "There's a bit of dog hair in here."

"Vacuum is over there," she said, pointing to a cupboard. "It's industrial, make sure you empty it into the furnace when you're done."

"Furnace?"

"Back room."

Covering her tracks well.

"Crockett," Ronnie said, over the top of the car.

"Yeah?"

"Why'd the house explode?"

I grinned. "It was rigged."

"That's not what I mean. Why then, why not before?"

Good point.

"She didn't have cameras then, but someone installed them after she went missing." Someone like my tradies, but this was not one of my jobs.

"Maybe, but they were wi-fi capable, so how would someone know her password?"

"It'd be on the bottom of her router. And very few

people change them."

"She had a key under a bloody flowerpot. That's risky for anyone, let alone someone like her."

"That bugged me too." I'd given brain time to the key under the rock thing a few times since we'd been to her house the first time, and the only thing I came up with was that she didn't have anything worth giving a shit about. Nothing sensitive was kept at the house. "The house was generic. She kept nothing there that mattered."

"Maybe," Ronnie said, and got back to cleaning inside the last door. I grabbed the vacuum cleaner and went to work on the dog hair making sure any human hairs were sucked up as well. It'd be pretty stupid to wipe fingerprints away and leave obvious DNA.

Half an hour raced as we cleaned. I emptied the vacuum cleaner into the furnace. Ronnie threw in her gloves and the cloths she'd used as well. I followed suit, then watched as she set a timer. It would burn for half an hour. All trace of us in the car would sail into the night sky as a smoky vapour.

Chapter 21
[Ronnie: Secrets in the books.]

"Hey Crockett, where did Paul's phone ping from?" I looked at my watch. It was getting late, but Nana would still be up, probably playing poker with the Cronies, or cooking up schemes and planning Mrs White's demise. She was definitely getting rather good at causing trouble.

"About two clicks north from the Quinn's."

"Middle of town ... another bar ..."

"We need to make damn sure that little drive is secure, then we'll go chase Paul and see where he leads us," Crockett said.

"New car should make it a bit harder for your mate Enzo to spot us tonight. That's a bonus," I replied, as we cruised up Fergusson Drive. "Park out the back of the office in the alleyway."

I didn't mind that Crockett liked to drive. I could've thrown a wobbly, but what would be the point? At least this way I could think. I scrabbled through my bag in the footwell and pulled my tablet out. When you ruggedise tech, it becomes bulky and easy to grab. The whole camera thing bugged me. Someone could've put those cameras in after she left, but why? Was it to catch her if she came back and blow her to pieces, or was it intended for us? Either way, it didn't feel very nice. I opened my camera app and checked my house. Donald's car was up the driveway. Ben's car was behind his. Good. I checked each camera; I have eight. Nothing untoward showed. There were no alerts apart from two when Donald and Ben would've arrived home, and the alert marker for when we dropped Emily off to them. Safe. Secure. As I watched, the back door opened, and Romeo wandered down the steps and into the back yard. He walked sedately. That was a very good sign that no one was about. For a change he was unaccompanied by Donald. That was also a good thing; meant he listened to me this time.

I shut the app then opened another. Security is important. The second app showed me four more cameras: the alley way behind my building; the front of the building; the interior of the stairwell; and the main office from the back toward the door.

"You all right?" Crockett asked.

"Yep, just looking at my camera feeds. All okay at home. Now I'm checking the office."

"Don't suppose you have a camera in the bookshop?" he asked.

"Nope. Wish I did. Then we'd be able to see who left that note for Bateman." Maybe I'll add a couple of internal cameras to the bookshop once this is sorted.

"That's what I was thinking."

"I can see along the building past the bookshop door, but we'd never be able to figure out who left the note." One camera flickered, then came right. A person walked north toward the bookshop; I could only see their back. They stopped and peered in the shop window. Browsing.

People do pass that way during the night and there are twinkly fairy lights in the shop that catch people's attention. The person moved off and disappeared around the corner.

I closed the app. Camera watching was addictive.

"What do you want to do once we secure that drive?" Crockett asked.

"Find Paul," I said. "We should've turned that drive over to MacKinnon when we found it." And we didn't. Why didn't we? Well, I didn't want to, because I thought something decidedly strange was going on, especially when I saw the numbers in the files, and now that Bateman's house was toast, I was certain something untoward was going on. But why didn't Crockett insist on handing that drive over to MacKinnon? It all floated uneasily in my stomach.

"We should've," Crockett said. I looked at him, he flashed me a smile and fixed his gaze on the road beyond the windshield. "Thing is Ronnie … no one mentioned that drive to me."

"Didn't tell me about it either. As far as I'm concerned, she's a missing cryptographer and that's it, just missing." I paused. "And yet, we know she isn't just a missing cryptographer. Don't we?"

"Yes. This has turned brown and smelly." He swallowed hard. "Let's sit on the drive until we find her."

Fine by me. If we didn't know about it, then no one is going to ask if we found it. A small smile tweaked the corners of my mouth.

Felt a lot like old times.

Adrenaline, lies, half-truths, and spies.

"We need to put it somewhere safe and inaccessible." We needed to stick it in a post bag and pop it into a post box; it had to be somewhere no one could get it no matter what. Even if they got the location out of one of us, they couldn't get the drive. That thought bounced around my mind. Who were *they*?

"Where to?" Crockett asked, breaking my inner rumblings wide open.

"Turn into the Countdown car park, drive through, take a left, take another left into Princes, and turn into our alley," I instructed, as we neared the roundabout by the gym.

Crockett did as I asked. There was no one in or near the access way to the back of the building. I lead the way to the door on Fergusson Drive. Still, no one around. I locked the door behind us. A long beep resounded as I flicked the light on, and punched my code into the alarm box, listened for the single disarm beep, and then headed upstairs to the offices. I unlocked the main office door and went straight to my desk.

"Shut the door," I said over my shoulder. "We should post the flipping drive, that way it's safe. But first I want you to tell me about the books that you think correspond to the numbers we found."

Crockett's phone buzzed. "The target is still in the CBD. Looks like he's moved one building. Why would someone do that?"

"What street?"

"Kings."

"There are two bars, side by side," I said. "He's in no hurry to go wherever he goes. I guess he lives somewhere. Maybe there is no one to go home to."

My laptop sat dormant on my desk. I lifted the lid, waking it from its slumber. Crockett dragged Steph's chair over. Good choice. It's way more comfortable than the guest chair in front of my desk. "Now, back to those books."

"Why?" he asked.

"Because we have missed something, Crockett." There was a reason I struggled to get a reading on the missing woman, and I didn't know what it was. I considered it was her three names muddying the waters, but it could've been more than that. And the books were really starting to bug me.

He took his notebook from his pocket. I noticed it for the first time. A black Moleskine. Nice.

"These are the books that correspond to the numbers, the ones that made sense."

"I get that you are quite sure it's about one set but humour me. Give me all the options."

Crockett gave me a half smile. "Okay, ready?"

I nodded, fingers poised over the keyboard and an open, blank document file at the ready.

"Digging Deep, Catching the Last Tram, and A Place to Stand."

I typed the names directly underneath each other into

the document. "Next."

"The Strength of Egg Shells, Alexandra the Great, and Shark Harbour."

When I was finished, I looked up. "Okay."

"The Evolution of Sylvia Graves, Styling Wellywood, and A Striking Truth." He waited while I finished typing. "Ethylwyn, Being Shirley, Miranda Bay."

"How many more?"

"We're halfway."

Bugger. "Okay, fire ..."

"A Woman's Sphere, The Disenchanted Soldier, and Winter Duet."

"Go."

"The Thirsty Rooster, Blank Canvas, and Song Shifting."

"Yep." I was getting faster.

"Kindred, Call me Ishmael, and No Sweat."

"Twenty-one books so far, and you only shared one grouping with me to start with."

"I thought I'd figured it out. Reading them out to you, I'm not so sure."

"You might've, but let's finish this and find out?" I said, "There is something here, I can feel it."

"Yeah. A Taste of Blood, Horse Soldiers, Pierced."

"How many more?"

"Three ..." He sighed. "Inside a Black Horse, Shadow of Doubt, and Qubyte."

"Last one again?"

"Qubyte."

I glanced at him. "Got it. Next."

"Nothing Bad Happens Here, then Eraserbyte, and Carlswick Conspiracy."

"Go."

"Political Secret, Mesquite Smoke Dance, then Danger Close."

"Are we done?" I asked, looking at the list running down the page, and not at Crockett. "What drew you to the Carlswick grouping?"

"One of the books was out of place and the note was behind Eraserbyte, or where it should've been."

I sighed. "People move books around all the time. Let's look at the whole list. For now."

We sat in front of the screen and stared at the list. It was something. Not just the Carlswick grouping, but as a whole. It was something.

"See anything?" I asked.

He shook his head, then stopped and nodded. "It's a message."

Yeah, it is.

"Exfil via train to Wellington," I said.

"Alexandra could be Alexander. Russian." He pointed to the line. "Russian is disenchanted or was flipped? Is that her?"

"Could be," I said. "The Thirsty Rooster, I reckon that's a pub reference."

"Is her contact someone called Ishmael?"

Could be. "They know and they're coming for her."

"Danger Close. That makes sense if someone is coming

for her. Intel or data would make sense with the Qubyte reference."

"That's what I think too. And now we want to know who the hell Carlswick is, and why she hid the drive instead of destroying it."

"You think Eraserbyte means destroy it because they were closing in?"

"Unless we find her, we will never know."

"Hold it. You're saying someone knew she was Russian and warned her. The whole bookshop thing isn't about setting up a dead drop to that intel, it's about not getting caught with it, or not handing it over to whomever?"

I think I am. Shit. What the hell is going on here? "Question, how did she get it?"

"The drive?"

"No, a bar of chocolate," I grumbled. "Of course, the drive."

"First thought, she downloaded the intel from TechSynth - but why did they have classified intel on their servers?"

We looked at each other for a blink of an eye.

"They stole it," Crockett said. "They fucking stole it."

"We have a tech company stealing intel on spies as a sideline?" That didn't sit right. "Hang on, I want to check something." I opened a new internet browser window and searched for TechSynth. "Last time I was on their website I was looking at personnel and I didn't spend much time looking at what the company does."

Crockett waited, watching the screen. An ad popped up

when I went to change pages.

"That's interesting. Web hosting," Crockett said, pointing at the ad.

"That puts another spin on things," I clicked a link in the ad. "Secure web hosting for companies and whoever can afford them, by the look of it."

"Bateman might not have stolen that intelligence from TechSynth as such, but from someone who uses their web hosting services," Crockett said.

"But she still stole it, we just don't know who from. And we don't know if it was for the Russians, the North Koreans, or the highest bidder." Stealing stolen intel. Now there's a fun way to make a living. I stared at the screen. "Who the fuck is Ishmael?"

"Language," Crockett said, in a semi-whisper.

"You can talk," I replied. "Maybe it's, *what is* Ishmael?"

I grabbed my keys from where Crockett dropped them on the desk and unlocked my desk drawer. From the very back of the drawer, I wrestled a small box free from the bracket that secured it on the top of the drawer. Out of sight. From inside the box, I took a small key. I stood up and walked over to the computer at the back of the room and turned the screen around. At the back on the right side was a tiny hole. I inserted the key and turned it to release a door. My fingers found the small drive we'd taken from the garden and pulled it out of the compartment. I closed the door and spun the screen back, so it was usable.

I sat back down at my desk and inserted the drive into my laptop. We knew it was safe. There was nothing nasty that would harm my laptop. The encryption cracker icon sprang to life. I dragged the folders from the drive into the program.

"On here as well," Crockett said. He even sounded a bit impressed.

"Just in case," I replied, watching as all the files unpacked.

Crockett laughed. "Bet you were a Girl Guide."

"Never made it that far, became disillusioned at Brownie level."

"What were you, the most cynical nine-year-old in the country?"

My turn to laugh. "I was eight, actually."

The program finished opening the files. I thought a quiet thank you to my long-time computer hacker friend, *Justin Case*. Yeah, that's his real name.

I searched the atlas. No Ishmael.

"Crockett, what am I missing about Ishmael? Who is Ishmael?"

"Depends, if you're talking biblically. In which case, Ishmael is Abraham's first born who was exiled to the desert."

"Or?"

"Or the narrator of Moby Dick who sailed with Ahab."

I tried searching for Abraham, Ahab, and Moby Dick. Nothing. Then I had a thought. "Crockett, what if three, five, twelve is a Bible reference?"

"You're kidding."

"It could be, couldn't it?"

He nodded. "Anything is possible. We don't even know who we're really dealing with, so, yeah."

I did a fast internet search. "The book of Proverbs."

"Okay, King Solomon wrote the book of proverbs, try searching Solomon," he said.

I glanced at him quickly, but he caught my curious look. "I know things," he said. "I went to Bible class."

"Nothing for Solomon or King Solomon."

I brought up an internet search for The Book of Proverbs 3:5-12.

"Have you read this?" I asked. I opened three versions: English Standard, and the New King James, and then the International version. They definitely all said the same thing, just slightly different ways. It wasn't good as far as I was concerned.

"A long time ago."

"It seems to be about trust, but not trusting yourself, oh no, you have to trust God." My eyes rolled. Imagine thinking for yourself. "And you're supposed to give a portion of everything to God, so he'll make sure you have enough. And my favourite bit - don't be afraid when he disciplines you, because shitting on you from a great height means he loves you." I closed the page I read from. "I might've paraphrased a little there."

I looked at the atlas again and typed in Proverbs. Why not? Nothing else was working.

"Ding, ding, ding. We have a winner," I said, as a

highlighted portion of text appeared. "It's a codename. And the intelligence officer it belongs to is none other than James MacKinnon."

Our eyes met.

"That cannot be a coincidence," Crockett said, slowly.

"Her contact was James MacKinnon? Was it him that warned her someone was coming, or was she supposed to hand the drive over to MacKinnon?" I already knew the answer, and I knew how dangerous the game was.

"Fuck knows, but I'm glad we didn't turn this over. What's Proverb working on?"

"An operation called *Genesis.*"

Rivers of cold dread ran through me. I knew what it was. I knew because of Justin. I knew this day would come, and someone would find out what we'd been doing all these years.

"You all right?" Crockett asked.

"Yes, of course," I said, shaking the feeling of doom away and focusing on the files in front of me.

"You sure?"

I nodded. "So, the numbers had two meanings," I said. "A message in the titles and a code name in the atlas." There were three meanings. They used the numbers to identify intelligence officers within *Genesis.* The only person who could know who we all were, was the founder of Genesis.

"Curious about *Genesis,* but I imagine it's above our pay grade," Crockett said. "We have personnel files ... do we do this?"

I nodded, definitely above yours. "In for a penny ..." I found the relevant file and we sat glued to the screen reading. James MacKinnon. the off-spring of Alexandra Major and Richard MacKinnon. He'd worked multiple operations in Eastern Europe, then he spent six months in Finland working out of the consulate. "That's our MacKinnon, right?" I said, touching Richard's name on the screen with my index finger and hoping I sounded normal and not stressed. At the bottom of the last page was the number three-thousand five hundred and twelve.

Crockett blew out air. "Yes. I have a feeling we were never supposed to know any of this."

"That Ishmael is Proverb, and that Proverb is James MacKinnon, your boss's son."

"He's an intelligence operative." I leaned back in my chair. "So, did Bateman steal the intel back for Proverb, or did she steal it for the Russians, or did she steal it for someone else?"

"Let's secure this and find Bateman. She can probably shed light on who Proverb is working for. Who she is working for. And, what the actual fuck these people are doing with intel that could get people killed."

I disconnected the drive and found some bubble wrap and a small mailing bag. Without another word, I wrapped the drive, addressed the bag to Writers Plot Bookshop, using the street address, not the P.O. Box.

The great thing about street addresses and the New Zealand mail service is, there are only three deliveries a week. I knew we had a good three days before this drive would pop back up, via the postal service, because that's how long it took for mail to be processed and delivered. All we needed to do was drop it into the post boxes by the Mall, on our way to locate Paul at whatever bar he was currently enjoying. Once the package was mailed, it was in the system until it was delivered. No one was getting it.

Chapter 22
[Crockett: Follow the leader.]

Ronnie dropped the package into the mailbox near the mall. I saw her shove her hand right in and make sure it wasn't snagged on anything. She didn't want it reachable. That was clever. I was starting to see why MacKinnon wanted us working together. But why didn't he tell us his son was involved with Bateman? There was a chance he didn't know, I suppose. Ronnie jumped back in the car, shut the door, and clicked her seat belt. I checked the mirrors and pulled out.

A buzz emanated from my phone. I pulled it from my jacket pocket and dropped it in Ronnie's lap without looking.

"Can you check, please?" I asked. "My passcode is four-four-two-five-zero-zero." I turned left into King Street and cruised past both bars before parking.

"He's on the move," Ronnie said. She looked around. "There. I think that's him." She pointed behind us to a dark shape walking past a car yard. "Let's watch."

"He didn't walk up here ..." I was thinking out loud. "What's over there?"

"Vet, funeral home, plenty of parking ...," Ronnie replied. "Maybe he likes parking out of the way."

Another buzz came from my phone. Ronnie gave it back.

"Charlie is on the move. He must've finished cooking

at the restaurant for the evening." I watched as another message appeared on the app showing the messages on his phone. "Paul texted him about coming over to his place for the night. Said he has entertainment."

"Sounds awful."

I watched Paul disappear near the corner. "Ronnie, I think it'll be bad for Bateman, if he's the one who has her."

"What if he isn't and this is a wild goose chase?" Ronnie said.

I started the car. The tracker moved faster and came towards us. A car cruised past moving east. Ronnie reached for the phone. Our hands brushed.

"You drive, I'll navigate. He's on Fergusson Drive going south."

I drove down Queens Street, turned up Logan, and then south down Main. My plan was to allow him a bit of space.

"We good on Main?"

"Yep," she said. "He's still on Fergusson."

We followed Paul, keeping to parallel streets where we could, and maintaining a good five car lengths away when we couldn't. Before long, we were snaking along a mountain road.

Chapter Twenty-three: [Ronnie]

I lifted my head. A thumping pain pounded through my temple. That wasn't a good sign. When I tried to move my hands, I discovered I couldn't. Darkness was everywhere. I didn't think I was blinded, just somewhere dark, with a shitty headache. Bits and pieces of the night began to slide into place. We were following Paul, and knew Charlie was somewhere behind us, heading in the same direction. Over Blue Mountains Road and onto Whitemans Valley Road. A car flew out from the Russells Road intersection and hit the front guard. I remembered spinning. It wasn't a car that hit us, it was an SUV with bull bars.

Hands pulled me from the car. I saw a man drag Crockett out. When I tried to thank the stranger there was nothing. Nothing. Between then and now, I had no clue what had happened.

"Crockett?" My voice skipped and croaked. "Crockett?"

"I'm here. You okay?" He sounded close.

"Bit of a headache."

"Yeah. Me too. I think someone hit us or we bashed our heads in the crash."

"Doesn't feel like someone hit me. Feels more like a drug," I said, everything felt a bit sideways and blurry. "I remember the accident, and seeing someone drag you out of the car, and then someone pulled me out."

Crockett fell silent for a while. Felt like hours but was probably less than a minute. Darkness screws with time.

"Could've been drugged," he said. "Who did you see?"

"I think it was Charlie."

"Shit, so was Paul there too, or someone else?"

"I didn't see the man who dragged me from the car." Or did I? I thought about the crash. Crunching metal, car spinning, the sudden sick-making stop. I was looking at Crockett when it all stopped. I undid my seat belt. The door opened, hands grabbed me and pulled me. What did I see? Bright lights in the darkness. Then Boots. Black motorbike boots and black jeans. "Enzo."

"Enzo?"

"Yeah, I think it was Enzo who pulled me out. Paul wasn't wearing black jeans and motorbike boots and he was ahead of us on the road, far enough ahead that he wouldn't even have seen the crash in his rearview mirror."

"Enzo probably drove the truck that hit us," Crockett said. "And Charlie came along after the fact. Bet that was helpful for ol' Enzo."

"Did Charlie come along after the fact or were we set up?"

I heard a slow exhale from Crockett. "Fuck me."

Everyone was playing everyone, and we'd become the filling in the sandwich. I drifted back into my own world and let the silence take over.

Sometime later Crockett spoke, "You okay?"

"Yeah." My mouth felt dry. Thankfully, the headache

had subsided. "You?"

"Yeah. Think you're right about it being drugs and not a smack to the head." His voice sounded a bit croaky. "I'm not hearing any signs of life," Crockett said.

Nor was I. We could've been alone, or our captors could be asleep nearby. Hard to know.

"What's your story Crockett?" It'd taken a while for my eyes to adjust to the complete darkness, but they had. I could see Crockett next to me well enough to know which way he was facing.

"We don't have time."

"Readers Digest version."

"I still don't think we have time."

"We're not going anywhere in a hurry, and it's going to be a while before Jenn and Steph know I'm missing ..." I said, wriggling on the chair and tugging my wrists. "I told them I'd be out all week." I peered into the darkness in front of me.

"Ben will figure it out," Crockett said. "He's smart."

"And if he doesn't?"

"Guess we better save ourselves."

"Best you get on with that. I'm a spy, not GI bloody Jane."

"Ben and Donald will be looking for us ..." He sounded convincing, but I wasn't buying.

"How long did it take us to figure out Paul and Charlie could be holding Bateman in Whitemans Valley? And nobody knows we were following them." Then a thought popped up. "Unless my phone is still on. Donald can trace me. If he thinks of it, that is."

"He'll miss you. He'll think of it."

"He'll text me a couple of times because I haven't checked in, then go to bed and forget about it," I said. Donald is Donald. He'll be wrapped up in taking care of Emily, and wet dreams about Enzo.

"Ben won't let it go that easily. Enzo was outside your place then left, so Ben will be on alert wondering where Enzo went and if he's coming back, and you're not answering your phone." Crockett rocked the chair he sat in. "He'll put it together."

Putting it together is one thing, finding us is a whole other ball game. We didn't tell anyone where we thought Bateman could be. She had no connection to Whitemans Valley. And no one but us knew the aliases she used. Emily knew one of them. I hoped she was still safe with Ben.

I started thinking about the messages Paul and Charlie sent each other, and other phone numbers. I didn't remember anyone called Enzo, or anything similar to Enzo. Was he working on the same job as us? Is that why he was following us around Upper Hutt? Did he piggyback on our investigation and find Bateman?

I watched Crockett work on the restraints. "You worked with Ellie Iverson," I said, determined to use the time to get to know more about Crockett.

"Statement or question," Crockett said.

"I'm not sure," I said. "Were you working with her four years ago? The mission that blew half of Wallaceville sky high, and another three plant explosions around the world?" He didn't reply. "Jeez, Crockett are you the lone survivor?" I said. "I never knew who it was, above my pay grade, and all that. I'd shake your hand but ..." I lifted my bound hands. "Are you planning on a hero move anytime soon?"

"I'm an intelligence officer," he said. "I was undercover with the Inferno Jesters for a number of years. That's it."

"Something tells me that's not the whole story. Takes a bit to get Ben fan-girling like he did when your name came up." I worked at the tape securing my wrists, using the chair arm to stretch it. "Nice of your mate to put me in a chair with arms."

Tape ripped. All of a sudden Crockett bounced to his feet. He reached into his boot then sliced the tape holding my ankles to the chair leg, and the tape on my other wrist.

"He's not my mate," Crockett said, "Come on."

"Where?" I asked, we were in a dark windowless room. Limited vision told me there was one door.

Crockett rattled the doorknob. Locked. "Stand back," he mumbled, and planted a kick just under the handle. Wood splintered and crunched. He shoved it open. It wasn't as dark with the door open. Moonlight. "Stay behind me."

I closed the gap between us. "Put your hand on my back and keep it there," Crockett said.

I placed my hand flat in the middle of his back. Shadows raced across the floor. No sounds. Nothing but deepening grey as clouds scurried across the moon, and a cool breeze.

"Where's the breeze coming from?" I whispered.

"Our way out," Crockett replied, turning toward the moving air. "Keep your hand on my back." I felt his arm move to the back of his jeans. "This is not right," he said, and lifted his weapon from the holster. "He left me armed," Crockett whispered. "Moving."

I did. We inched forward, staying close to the wall on the right.

"Do you think he's around?" I whispered. I checked my waistband. The Glock was there. "I'm armed too," I said, and slid the gun from its holster, seating it comfortably in my right hand, but keeping my left hand on Crockett's back.

"Don't think he's here. He would've heard me open the door."

"Then we could move faster."

"We don't know what we're walking into."

We moved another few metres and found another door. Locked. Crockett inspected the door.

"Can you open it?"

"Yep," he said. "Back up."

Crockett smashed the wood under the lock. I smiled to myself. That wasn't exactly what I meant, but it worked. The door flew open. Crockett reached back and grabbed my hand.

"With me," he said, and ran.

The wood under our feet sounded and vibrated like

decking. Our feet clattered across the timber. Not exactly stealthy.

Birds woke from their dreams and took flight. The clouds moved on and the sky lightened enough for us to see where we were. It wasn't a full moon, but it wasn't far off. Crockett and I stopped running once our footsteps deadened into the earth below and no longer announced our presence.

"Where are we?" Crockett said.

I looked around for familiar landmarks and found none in the moonlit world. "We're not in the main valley. They didn't take us back over the hill. Maybe Whitemans Valley, or we've been taken further north to Mangaroa," I said.

"Do you have your phone?"

I holstered the weapon and checked my pockets, then shook my head.

"Let's find a phone," I said, turning on the spot hoping to see a house or a road. "Where's your mate?"

"No idea."

"The pendulum showed us Bateman is in Whitemans Valley. She could be near here somewhere." Wherever here is.

"Let's move. We need shelter and a view of whatever this place is. Time to think and get a plan together would be helpful," Crockett said. "Stay with me."

We walked over grass, leaving the building behind us. Trees rose like ominous giants, close enough that we stayed in their dark shadows. Once far enough from where we'd started, Crockett pulled me under a tree. "Rest, let's wait for clouds to move again so we can get a clearer view."

Smart move. Better than falling into or over something in the shrinking darkness and tricky shadows. I figured we may as well sit down, so I sat. Something jabbed me. My fingers sought the problem and came up with a handful of pine needles. "Pine trees," I said.

"Could be worse," Crockett replied. "Could be raining."

"Enzo didn't do the best job of frisking us," I replied, as I leaned on a tree trunk and my gun dug into my back. "Why, would he leave us armed?"

"No idea," Crockett replied. "And he left my knife in my boot."

"Just our phones gone."

"That begs the question, who is he working for?" Crockett said, sitting close to me, his back against the same tree trunk. "The Enzo I knew isn't a charitable bloke under normal circumstances."

"Is this related to our missing spy, or is this Enzo situation something else?" I felt his shoulder move. A shrug wasn't reassuring. "I'm sure he drugged us with something like chloroform. But to do that, Charlie had to be in on it. I saw him pull you out and then there was nothing. What did you see?"

Crockett sat quietly before speaking. "Across the roof of the car I saw you facing me. There was someone else, but it was dark, they were dark. Next thing I knew, I was taped to a chair in that room."

Birds settled in the trees as clouds crossed the moon blocking the light again.

"What was your last mission?" Crockett asked a few minutes later.

"Sanctioned or freelance?"

"Sanctioned."

"Algeria."

"How long?"

"Five months in country."

"Doing?"

"Staying alive."

"Why Algeria?"

Moonlight filtered through leaves and peppered us in white light. I could see Crockett's face quite clearly.

"It was my mission," I said with a smile. "There was a scientist who had Novichok in his possession, he was on the run and looking to sell. He fell in with a bad crowd." I gave him a quiet smile.

"Hope you had good people with you."

"I did."

"Why'd you leave?"

"Because there is always going to be another terrorist with Novichok, or whatever they've developed since then." I adjusted my position but couldn't get comfortable. "And Nana is not getting any younger."

Crockett nodded. "I get it."

"That life can eat you up and spit you out. I wanted more from life, and less stress."

"How's that working for you?" Crockett asked, with a

good-natured nudge.

"Mostly it's nine-to-five, easy peasy, home for tea."

"Boring," he said.

"Sometimes."

I stretched my legs out. "Been a bit interesting this week." I could feel the smile on my face as I thought about another interesting week I'd had in the past. Ben and I hunting gnomes and a zombie virus, and how we saved the world. Sometimes I get it right and sometimes I end up miles from home with no phone and no idea what happened. Life. Never truly dull. "Sometimes retirement is more exciting than it should be."

"We've had a busy week and earned a beer or two that's for sure."

"As soon as you magic a plan to get us out of here, I'm buying."

Chapter 23
[Tania: Potential disaster.]

Tania awoke and opened her eyes. She tried to move but couldn't shift her legs or arms. Her head moved. She looked one way, and then the other into the shapeless darkness. She sighed. Her mind scrambled through the bleakness, piecing together what she knew.

She was alive.

She was on a bed.

It was dark.

Her wrists were tied to the headboard of the bed.

Her ankles were tied to something at the bottom. Probably the bed end, she thought.

There were no noises except her beating heart and the blood rushing around her circulatory system. Her head ached.

A musty smell rose from the mattress and irritated her nose. Her eyes felt heavy, and it took effort to keep them open. She tugged her right arm but couldn't pull it free of whatever bound it. She flexed her fingers on both hands and wriggled her toes. A cold dread grew. She felt cool air on her body and shivered. Where were her clothes? What had happened?

She listened for noises that meant people. Beyond the darkness that surrounded her, she heard a low hum and recognised it as voices. Not one voice but at least two. They felt far away, but she couldn't be sure.

Wood scraped and hinges creaked. The door opened.

Light poured across the floor hitting her in the face. She closed her eyes too late and was momentarily blinded by the light. Nothing but white holes filled her mind. She blinked to try and clear them. The white holes covered the owner of a voice. She knew it was the man called Paul.

"Good to see you awake," he said, running his hand along the side of her left leg from her ankle to her hip. His fingers warm against her cool skin. Her body recoiled. "It's time to play."

"I don't feel well," she muttered, as her vision cleared enough for her to see his face hovering near hers.

"I don't care," he replied. "I've bought a couple of friends to meet you. It's party time."

He ran his finger down the side of her face. She turned away. He grabbed her face, his fingers digging into her flesh, and turned her head toward him. "Don't be like that."

Noises beyond the brilliantly lit doorway, filtered through the blood pounding in her ears. He wasn't lying. There were more people out there.

"Where are my clothes?" She struggled against the ties that secured her hands above her head.

"You don't need clothes. It's a come as you are type of party," he said, his face inches from hers. The smell of beer on his breath. "And you'll do fine in what God gave you."

Panic surged within her as the realisation of the fate

that awaited landed squarely on her.

"I thought you were going to ransom me. No one will pay if you hurt me."

He laughed, and ran his finger down her neck, between her breasts, and froze.

"They'll pay. By the time they find out how much fun we had, we'll be long gone with the cash," he said, walking his fingers back up. He stared into her eyes and gave her right nipple a hard pinch before reaching over and pinching her left. "Like that, do you?"

She shook her head and bit her lip. Blood seeped into her mouth. Metallic and hot. "No."

"Let's see?" He plunged his hand between her legs and laughed as she tried to squirm away from his prying fingers. "I knew you'd be fun."

He straightened up and walked to the doorway. "Who's first?"

"Me," said a deep voice.

"Nah," said another man. "Paul told me about her on Tuesday. I've waited longer. Anyway, you got that other woman."

Tania strained to hear what the voices were talking about, as she concentrated on the words said in the next room.

"Her and her boyfriend are going to be trouble," Paul said. "What'd she say her name was, Charlie, when I was at the pub. She said Tania, right?"

"Yeah, she said Tania. And the guy, he was looking for his sister. And that's her in there." Tania picked out his voice as the man Paul called Charlie. She didn't have a brother, so who was it, they had. Obviously, a man and a woman. She'd put money on the woman's name not being Tania.

The deep voice spoke again and sounded closer to the door, "How about I worry about them and you let me go check out the evening entertainment."

"Aw, come on, I knew about her first," Charlie said.

"That's true," Paul said. "But maybe I should be first, I've waited longer than any of you."

"How do we know you haven't already had her," the man with the deep voice said.

"The anticipation is half the fun. You know that." He took a backward step into the room where Tania lay. "Sure, I stripped her off and that got me going a bit. But apart from looking, I haven't done anything, yet. I like 'em awake and interactive." He groaned. "I'm ready."

"Hey, Charlie," the deep voice said.

"Yeah."

Tania heard the crack of a fist hitting someone, followed by a heavy thump that shook the bed.

"What'd you do that for?" Paul said, confusion ringing in his words. "Shit, stop! What are you doing?"

"You're a scum bag, pal," the deep voice said. "On your knees."

"Hold it, you don't need ... this is nuts, just go first then," Paul spluttered.

"On your knees," the voice said.

Tania craned her neck as far as possible to try and see

what was happening. Her heart pounded in her chest so hard it almost deafened her. A shadow fell into the room from the doorway. It was bigger than Paul's shadow.

"You don't need to do that," Paul said. "No!"

A gunshot rang out, shocking her to the core. The shadow stepped backward into the room, then turned.

"Tania Bateman?" the deep voice said, coming closer. "Let's get you out of here."

Confused, Tania said nothing. The man cut the restraints, helped her sit, then searched for her clothes. He found them in the corner of the room. She watched as he gave them a shake and handed them to her.

"Thank you," she said quietly.

"Get dressed. We don't have much time. It's farmland out here, but someone would've heard the gunshot."

She did as she was told.

"You need shoes," he said.

"I had sneakers," she replied, shoving her arms in her hoodie.

The man found her sneakers under the bed and placed them beside her. "You right?"

"Yeah," she said. "Who are you?"

"Enzo."

"What do you want?" she asked, as she shoved her feet into her shoes and tied the laces.

"Let's get you out of here, then worry about that," he said.

"They said you had someone ..."

"Don't worry about that, they're not going anywhere."

He grabbed her by the hand. "We're leaving."

Chapter 24
[Crockett: Lost and found.]

A male voice spluttered curses from somewhere behind us losing strength in the darkness.

A loud crack ripped the silence in half. Birds took to the air. I grabbed Ronnie's forearm. "Behind that tree," I whispered, "Go. Stay down."

Enzo leaving us with fire power was fishy as fuck. I drew my weapon and scanned the area. The sky was lighter without clouds, shadows shrank deepening closer to the trees. Could've been a farmer shooting a possum.

I waited. It was hard to tell which direction the shot came from, but it was a gunshot. It probably didn't originate from the building we were in. If there was someone there, they would've heard me kicking down doors, and come after us. It was dark when we left, could've been other buildings behind where we were.

"Where did that come from?" Ronnie said.

"Don't know."

The next noise gave me a good idea of the direction. "Moving," I whispered to her, "Put your hand on my back and stay behind me."

I heard footsteps deadened by grass and ducked behind another large old pine tree with Ronnie. I held my finger to her lips. She nodded.

The ground trembled slightly. It was just enough to tell me people were out there. Someone approached, moving as fast as the night allowed, but they hadn't reached us yet.

A man spoke, his voice carried in the stillness, "There's a car about a kilometre up the track." He sounded a little familiar.

A woman replied, "What about Paul and the other man? Was his name Charlie?"

I waited for the footsteps and breathing to draw level with our position. One swift move and I was behind the male with my weapon to his head. He stopped walking. The woman glanced over her shoulder, her eyes wide. I probably didn't come across as friendly.

"If you think I won't pull the trigger you have another think coming, pal," I growled, and a dawning occurred. "Enzo, you wanker!"

"Crockett, good of you to join us." He didn't attempt to turn.

"Tania Bateman?" I asked. "Or do you prefer Lissette, or maybe Sharon?"

"Tania will do," she replied, quietly.

Enzo turned. I holstered my weapon. He grinned as Ronnie joined us, weapon in hand. She was obviously unhappy about his presence.

"Veronica Tracey," he said, "Sorry about the whole rendering you unconscious thing earlier, didn't have much choice. No hard feelings."

"I have a plethora of hard feelings." She holstered her weapon. "Just in case I accidentally shoot you if my hard feelings go off."

I bit back a smile. "Seems we're all here on some weird midnight picnic," I said. "Hope you like pine needles and grass. Unless you packed a picnic basket?"

"Sorry, no picnic," Enzo replied.

"You have our missing person," Ronnie said, stepping closer to Enzo. "We'll take it from here."

Enzo laughed. "We need to exfil and argue about who gets what later."

"Charlie and Paul?" I asked.

"Temporarily out of circulation."

"You didn't shoot one of them?"

"Gave Paul a fright, then knocked him out. I doubt they'll be going to the cops considering what they were up to." He grimaced in the moonlight. "I doubt it was the first time Paul has snatched a woman and used her as a toy."

"Charlie?"

"Not sure what his real involvement in Paul's sicko behaviour is. But he dropped like a sack of crap."

I motioned for them to walk on in front of us. "We don't want to draw too much attention," I said. Looking around, it was hardly likely we'd draw any. Who would be out in the middle of the night? Possum hunters and those up to no good. The latter was the category we fell into. I slung my arm around Ronnie's shoulders and dangled my hand in front of her. She wound her fingers through mine. Hopefully, we looked like a couple on the way home from a night out. Instantly that seemed like insanity. Who the hell would be in the back of beyond for a night out?

Enzo looked over his shoulder, then grabbed Tania by the hand.

"Car?" I queried, recalling that he'd mentioned one to Tania. "Or are we walking out of wherever the hell we are?" The car wreck scene came back with vengeance. "Where's our car?"

"Charlie towed it to a barn attached to the place we held you," Enzo said. "It's a bit fucked, sorry about that."

"Sure you are. And how are we getting out of dodge?"

"Paul and Charlie both had cars, they left them about a click east of here," Enzo said. "One each."

"No, we take one and disable one," I said. "You and I need to have a conversation. And we need to talk to Tania or Lissette, or whoever the fuck that sheila is."

Enzo nodded. "Figured it wouldn't be that easy."

"You'll be driving, Enzo. I guess you know how to get to Ronnie's office?"

Ronnie looked up at me. "I've got questions."

"So do I. We'll get answers."

There are a lot of different silences in the world. The one that crept over our party of four was the distrustful kind. I didn't know what Enzo wanted with our target and I didn't know if he was aware of the thumb drive. A growing feeling that there could be others involved that we needed to worry about, brewed.

Variables made me jumpy. A phone buzzed. Enzo stopped walking and pulled something from his pocket.

"Slowly," I said.

He turned and handed the object to Ronnie. "Yours." She let go of my hand and took the phone. A couple of seconds later she showed me the screen. A camera alert for her office. Now who would be in the office at zero dark thirty, or whatever the fuck time it was?

"This isn't good," Ronnie said, opening the camera app.

"Keep walking," I said to Enzo. We walked behind them, as Ronnie and I watched two men ransack her office via the app on her phone. She took a couple of screenshots and managed to get their faces. "Good work."

They either didn't know about the cameras or didn't care. Ronnie stopped watching and sent texts to Steph and Jenn, warning them to stay away from the office. She made a call.

"Sorry to wake you," she said. I couldn't hear the response, just her side of the conversation. "Tap into the office CCTV feed. Two men are trashing the place." She listened. "If they didn't have the alarm code, the security company would've rolled in by now." Another pause. "Where are Donald and Emily?" Another pause. "Romeo?"

Ronnie grabbed my arm. Concern etched into her face. "Find her!" She hung up and stuffed the phone into her jeans pocket.

"What happened?" I asked.

"Emily is gone."

I blew air out of my lungs in a long exhale. Shit. Thoughts scrambled, trying to get purchase.

"Problem shared is a problem halved," Enzo said, over his shoulder. "Two heads and all that."

"Aren't you full of old wives bullshit?" I muttered. "Someone we care about is missing, and a few blokes are snooping around Ronnie's office." My words hung on a hard edge. "Know anything about that?"

He shook his head. "Careless, Crockett. What is it with you losing people?"

"Keep walking, dickhead."

"I was out here all night," Enzo said. "Tania can vouch for me."

"Yeah, great, that works." Jesus.

Ronnie nudged me. "We need to find her."

"I know."

"Who are those arseholes and why are they in my office?" she whispered close to my ear. "Only we knew."

"Unless that thing had a beacon. Something that called home when it hit something that was internet capable?"

"Probably," Ronnie said with a sigh. "That's on me then."

Tania spoke, "You have it?"

"Had," I said. "Had it."

She fell silent and Enzo left it alone.

"When did Emily go missing" I asked Ronnie, sidestepping a hunk of fallen tree branch.

"Don't know. Ben will go over the house footage and look for alerts."

"None on your phone?"

She checked the log in for the house. "No, strange that

there aren't."

"Would a power cut prevent that?"

"Yep."

Her phone rang. "Hey, Ben ..." She listened. "Is he okay?" More listening. "Call the vet."

She jammed her phone in her pocket. "Ben thinks the power was off. The microwave clock is flashing."

"Is Romeo okay?"

"He can't wake him. He found him in the yard."

"Drugged?"

"That would be my guess. He doesn't take food from strangers though."

"Cameras?"

"He's looking, but they probably cut the power before doing anything else. I expect a dart." Her voice broke and crumbled at our feet.

I slung my arm back around her shoulders and gave her a squeeze. "He's a big strong lad."

"He is, but it depends what they used. Greyhounds don't cope well with anaesthetics, or any drug really."

I flipped my other hand out and smacked Enzo in the back of the head to get his attention. "You like drugging people. Drug any dogs last night?"

"I was out here, only drugged you two."

"Dick."

"Just up ahead," Enzo said pointing. "Through those trees we should see the cars."

I got the feeling Ronnie was glad of the interruption, and to know we were going in the right direction. I can't say I blamed her. The trees Enzo pointed out were nothing more than darker clumps on a dark night. I hoped he was right about cars being close.

"Everything all right?" Tania asked.

I chose not the reply. Better to say nothing, than sound like a prick. Neither of them needed to know anything yet, or maybe ever. I wasn't that keen to share intel with someone I knew as a biker with The Inferno Jesters. I doubted he was the biker I thought he was; his presence now indicated he might have been undercover.

Concern mounted for Emily. There were a couple of fuckheads trashing Ronnie's office, and we could only guess that they were after the thumb drive. They wouldn't find it.

Ronnie's silence was deafening. We. *We* were a team. I liked being part of a close team. It was different to life before when I was on the inside and my team were on the outside, trying to keep it all together. Trying to keep me alive. This was a good different. I always thought I didn't mind, even liked being inside, and effectively alone. But this I liked. The interaction, the camaraderie, someone having my back, and me having hers. And the dog and Nana. I liked this whole life she had going. Could be that there is more to life than work.

"Ronnie," I said, stopping her in her tracks.

"We need to get to the car and get out of here," she replied.

"He's going to be okay. We'll find her, we'll find Milo."

"Milo?"

"Emily," I corrected. "Inside joke."

"They're trashing my office looking for something that isn't there ..." She took longer strides, keeping pace with me. While she walked, she sent the screenshots to Ben.

Chapter 25
[Ronnie: Getting out of Dodge.]

"Where to?" Enzo asked, as he drove over Wallaceville hill.

I shot a look at Crockett. He nodded.

"Not the office. We need a safe house." Well, Nana does. This was a dangerous and fluid situation. "Ward Street. Go to the Fergusson drive end. Park in the Quinn's Post carpark."

I looked at the time. Coming up on four-thirty. Hunger gnawed at my stomach. Toast and coffee would help. Waking Nana probably wasn't a good idea. Old people need sleep, but she always says she hardly sleeps any more.

Enzo parked where I asked. I jumped out first. "Tania with me," I said. She climbed out. I grabbed her just above the elbow, and led the way to Nana's apartment. We went through the garden, because I knew the front door would be locked, and the desk unmanned at this ridiculous hour.

Crockett escorted Enzo.

I knocked on the ranch slider. The curtains were open, and I could see Nana in the kitchenette. Awake. She was dressed in a pale blue floral frock and a dark blue cardigan. She waved out and hurried over to unlock the door.

"Veronica, it's very early." Nana slid the door open,

then looked from me to Tania. "You found her," Nana said with delight. "Come inside. Do you need breakfast?"

"Please, Nana, that'd be great. Crock ... I mean Dave ... is right behind us with another guest."

"The more the merrier," Nana said, with a smile. "Good thing I rise early."

Very good thing. Early rising allowed more time to cause mayhem. The early bird catches the worm and all that. I was surprised the *Cronies of Doom* weren't already stationed in the living room. No doubt they'd be along at some stage. They might be late risers, like, seven or something. The thought of seven being late amused me. I was tired.

Crockett tapped my shoulder. "Right behind you."

I crossed the threshold with Tania and pointed her to a chair. She sat down. Crockett shut and locked the door behind him and Enzo.

"Nana, this is Enzo," I said, waving a hand in his direction, while Crockett encouraged him to sit by Tania. "It's been a long night. I'll help you make coffee." I left Crockett to supervise and joined Nana in the kitchenette.

"Donald rang me," Nana said, leaning close as I filled the kettle. "He sounded upset. What's going on, dear?"

"This morning, Nan?" I clicked the lid on the kettle and flicked the switch.

"Yes, about twenty minutes ago. He was quite flustered. Said Emily is missing, and Romeo is sick."

"It's been quite a night, Nana."

"I think you better tell me all about it."

"Nan, remember how I used to go away a lot and I could never talk about it."

"I do. Your grandfather was very proud of you, you know."

I smiled. "Well, it's got a lot to do with the job I used to do."

"Secret business," Nana said, touching the side of her nose with her index finger. "I'm glad you left that life, Veronica, it's no life for a lady."

"Yes, Nana."

The kettle boiled. I spooned coffee grinds into the French Press that sat on the bench, then filled it with boiling water.

"I'll have tea dear," Nana said, and warmed the teapot. "Toast?"

I nodded. "I'll make it."

Being at Nana's felt normal and grounding. I dropped bread into the toaster and pressed the slide down. I could hear Crockett talking in the living room because it was just one big room. His voice was low, and his words careful, as he spoke to Enzo.

I made a pile of toast, buttered it, and placed it all on the plate. Nana loaded a tray with cups, sugar, milk, side plates, and the French press.

"I'll take that, you take the toast," I said, and carried the laden tray to the coffee table. I set it down. Nana placed the toast plate on the table then went back for her teapot. "Eat," I said to Crockett, Tania, and Enzo.

My phone rang. It was Ben.

I walked into the kitchenette for as much privacy as I could get.

"And?"

"We're five minutes out with Romeo. He's doing okay. Revising the time, Donald is driving. Might be another ten minutes out."

I heard Donald grumble, but not what he said.

"Any word from Emily?"

"Not a dicky bird, Ronnie. The cameras were down for twenty minutes from three-fifteen this morning."

The time frame was out.

"If I activated something by accident with a device we had in our possession, related to this job ..." I took a breath. "Why did it take them so long to act?"

"They can't have been nearby."

"So, a couple of thugs flew in from places unknown," I mused.

"Or came from an embassy. The images you sent. They are Russians attached to the embassy."

"In what capacity?"

"According to their very light profiles they are security consultants."

So was I, a few times. Not for the Russians though, obviously. I'm not a traitor.

"I'll show Bateman the images from the cameras and see if she recognises them."

"I went over the office footage while we waited for the vet. There were three people near the bookshop. Two larger that looked male, and one smaller and slimmer, probably female."

"Emily could be in the building. If so, she wasn't in the main office, but there are a lot of other rooms that we don't have cameras in."

"Almost with you. Dropping Donald and Romeo, be ready to roll." Ben hung up.

I pulled the first screenshot off the CCTV up on my phone and walked over to Tania Bateman.

"Do you know this man?"

She looked at the picture and shook her head. I scrolled to the next photo and showed her. She shook her head. "No."

"You're sure?"

"I've never seen them before."

"They're Russian, they're with the embassy, and they seem to be looking for something."

"What does this have to do with me?"

I felt Enzo perk up. His piece of toast froze half-way to his mouth. "You have it," he said, placing the toast back on the plate. "That just cut you out of the equation, Bateman."

Crockett stiffened and shot Enzo a warning look.

Enzo gave a nasty smile. "She's your problem now, Crockett," he said, then turned to look at Tania. "Sorry."

"What does that mean?" Worry creased her face. "What does that mean?" she repeated, as fear radiated from her eyes.

"Eat your breakfast," Crockett said. "You're fine." He looked up at me. I was still standing with my phone in my hand. "What next?"

"Ben is in coming with Donald and Romeo. You're here with them. Ben and I are going to find Emily." I could see the argument brewing on his face. "I am going with Ben. You are here."

The sliding door flew open, and Romeo trotted in. "Bud, you're back," I said, rubbing his head as he wagged his tail at me. "You stay with Nana." Romeo moved to Nana and sat by her feet waiting for her to pat him.

Donald stepped over the threshold. "He's waiting," he said to me, then took in the room. As I levelled with him, he grabbed my arm and whispered in my ear. "Be still my manly heart, is that our holiday friend?" He fanned himself with one hand. "He's even more delicious in person."

"It is, but maybe you should go easy on the manly heart bit, Donald," I whispered back with a laugh. "Take care of Nana."

"Aye aye, Cap-i-tarn," Donald said, with a mock salute.

"Back soon," I called into the room, and closed the ranch slider behind me as I left.

Ben was parked outside the gate, motor running, passenger door open, for me.

It was a five-minute drive to the office. On the way I checked the cameras. They must've worked out where the main office camera was situated, because there was a fuzzy screen of nothing on the internal camera. The outside cameras showed a pre-dawn street view of bookshop frontage, and an empty alleyway behind the building. Ben parked in the empty Countdown carpark. We walked together down the street to the bookshop. I peered inside and saw nothing out of the ordinary. The twinkling lights were off, the main lights were off. The shop interior was shrouded in deep darkness. We moved on to the entrance way to *Wherefore Art Thou.* I tried the front door; it opened. I drew my weapon. The stairs rose to the landing outside the main office. No escape in the stair well. If they were still in the building, we were sitting ducks. I glanced at Ben when I heard a noise, and saw he had his side arm in his hand. Ben shut and locked the front door. If they were still inside, it'd slow down their exit having to unlock the door.

"Moving," I said to Ben. "With me."

I crept up the stairs, Ben three stairs behind me. At the top, I breathed and scanned the hallway. Nothing. I twisted the handle on the main office door and flung it wide open. No noise apart from the door hitting the doorstop. I stepped inside, scanning the room down the site of my weapon. No one.

Computers were on the ground, drawers dumped on the floor, desks flipped. Both filing cabinets were ripped apart, paperwork strewn everywhere.

"Moving," I said, and left the room. Next stop was the kitchen. I paused at the door. It was open. I peered around it and saw no one. The room was a mess. Tea, coffee, sugar were everywhere. I stepped in; the floor crunched under foot. The jug was upended in the sink. And the contents of the fridge spread all over the table.

Ice from the freezer was melting onto the floor.

"Moving," Ben said, from the hallway.

He went ahead to the first meeting room, while I took the storeroom. The door stood open; spare computers were smashed onto the floor. Shit. I walked three paces into the room and knelt on the floor. I reached under the bench and pressed on a panel. It popped open. Pulling the hidden door wider enabled me to punch in the safe code, then open the safe door. I removed two handgun cases and a rifle case, then all the ammunition boxes. Behind me on the floor, I saw one of our black duffel bags. I grabbed it and shoved the weapons and ammo in the bag, then hoisted it over my shoulder. At least they didn't find the weapon stash. I needed them gone from the premises. We had to report the break in and damage for insurance purposes; having police find the safe and its contents would be a mistake I wouldn't come back from in a hurry. I could probably make that mistake go away, but it'd take some big favours that I might need another day. Best to deal with it now, myself.

I closed and locked the safe, then shut the secret panel. Ben emerged from the meeting room across the hall, as I stepped out with the duffel bag.

"Anything?" I said, dropping the bag on the floor by the wall.

"Not yet."

"Moving," Ben said.

There were still two more rooms and a bathroom. I was right behind Ben when he swung the next door open.

Something metallic hit the ground.

Ben yelled, "Grenade."

I dove down the hallway covering my head with my arms with Ben right behind me. An explosion lit the room, smoke billowed from the doorway.

"All right?" I asked, pushing myself to my feet, gun still in my hand. My ears rang. The smoke alarms whined through the smokey air.

Ben scrabbled to his feet and picked his weapon up. "Shit. We need to get out of here."

"Two more rooms," I said, "Let's go."

The sprinkler system activated. Water seemed to flood from everywhere. Just what we needed.

I ducked past the wrecked room. Water poured from the ceiling, dowsing the flames and us. At the door to the next room, my special meeting room, I stopped. The door was ajar. I never leave it unlocked, let alone open. I wiped water off my face and flicked my hair behind me so I could see. I flung the door open and ducked behind the solid hallway wall, just in case. Nothing exploded. I couldn't hear much over the running water.

I stepped into the room and looked around. Nowhere to hide unless someone was under the table. No one was under the table. The credenza was in pieces. Now soggy maps were spread on the table. Maybe they thought I'd left a clue. X marks the spot. I'm not a pirate.

My pendulum box was upended on the floor and the pendulum under a chair. I scooped it up and put it in my pocket. Ben stood watch in the doorway. Everything was saturated. The deluge slowed.

"Moving," he said. "Bathroom."

"Coming," I replied, and fell into step behind him, the carpet squelching under foot. Ben opened the bathroom door with care. I watched the hallway. Water seeped from the carpet, running onto the Lino in the bathroom. There were no sprinklers in the bathroom.

I turned my attention to Ben. He'd stepped into the room and crossed the floor to the shower. We looked at each other for a split second. I nodded. Ben slid the shower curtain back. Nothing. He took a step sideways and tried the toilet door. The handle turned. He opened the door.

"Emily," he said with relief.

I hurried over. Ben stepped aside, and there she was, gagged, and tied up, sitting on the closed toilet seat.

I holstered my weapon and removed the gag. "Are you hurt?"

"No," she said with a smile. "Thank you for finding me."

Ben threw me a knife. I cut the restraints holding her hands and feet and shoved the tape and cable ties into my pocket, then folded the knife and slipped it into the other pocket. "You sure you're okay?"

"Yes," she said with a smile. "I would like to go home."

"How about we go to Nana's?" Ben said, watching the hallway from the bathroom door.

"Okay," Emily said, and stood up.

"Go to Ben," I said to her.

When she reached him, he said, "Put your hand on my back and keep it there." He looked back at me. "Moving."

"Coming to you," I replied, and caught up, then swung back to check the hallway behind us was still clear. When we reached the wet black bag, I scooped it up and hung it over my left shoulder. By the time we cleared the building and were in the car, my heart settled, and the pounding and ringing in my ears subsided. We were soaked. Emily was okay.

Ben drove, I called Steph. "The building is clear, there was a grenade explosion, sprinklers did their job. Going to need police."

"How are we handling this?"

"Turn up to work and call police," I said. "I have the contents of the safe with me."

"Good, I was about to ask. Anything else that suggests you were there this morning?"

"Probably, but the place is a disaster so anything can be explained away by that."

"That bad?"

"Yeah, it's going to take days to sort it. We've lost our computer gear and the spares."

"TV?"

"Smashed, both of them."

"Arseholes," Steph said. "You all okay?"

"Yeah, wet, but unharmed. I'll be at Nana's."

"Jenn left her computer at work yesterday. All her notes on the Mrs White case are on it."

"Damn. She might have back-ups, or even her

notebook might give us a starting point."

"You really want to know what Donald was up to, don't you?" Steph said, with a small laugh.

"Yes, I do. We'll worry about that later. For now, let's get the police report and insurance claim."

"How did they get in?"

"Kidnapped Emily to turn off the alarm."

"Bastards, is she okay?"

"Yeah, we've just arrived at Nana's. I'll get her a milo and some breakfast, pretty sure that'll help."

Chapter 26
[Crockett: Safe, for now.]

The sliding door opened, and Ronnie walked in, disheveled, dripping, and weary.

"You all right?" I asked. She nodded. Behind her I saw Emily. "Milo!"

Emily's smile beamed across the room, and she didn't pause before she said, "Crockett."

June stood up and shuffled a bit before she got going. "Emily, dear, come on in and have a cup of milo. I've some in the kitchen."

"Thank you, Nana," Emily said. "That would be good."

I watched as she followed June to the kitchenette. Ben and Ronnie joined me. Ben carried a bag.

"We'll change and be right back," Ben said, then called out to June. "Is it okay if we use your bathroom to change, June?"

"Yes, dear. There are fresh towels. Try not to drip on the carpet. Put your wet things in the hamper," June called, from the kitchenette where she was making milo. "I'll get them washed for you later."

Ben and Ronnie went into the bathroom. They emerged five minutes later in dry clothes. Ronnie looked like a warmer version of a drowned rat.

I indicated we should speak without eavesdroppers. We moved back to the ranch slider. Donald was busy entertaining Tania and Enzo. He'd been busy since

Ronnie and Ben left on their rescue mission. I didn't know Donald, but even I could tell he liked Enzo, and that it was reciprocal.

"Office is trashed, nothing salvageable," Ronnie said. "Those arseholes had Emily tied up in the toilet. They also rigged a grenade in one of the meeting rooms."

"You look intact," I said, looking from one to the other. Romeo ambled over and nudged Ronnie's hand until she petted his head.

"Luckily," Ben replied.

"Anyone respond to the bang?" I asked, be hard to explain an explosion.

Ronnie shook her head. "No, luckily. Guess no one heard it, or they explained it away to themselves, so they didn't have to act."

"Lucky there," I said. "You sure you're all right?"

"Yes," Ronnie replied with a smile. "Bit wet and smokey and could do with a hot cup of tea."

"They were gone?"

"Yes. We need to talk to Emily in case those men know more than we think. She might've heard them talking," Ronnie said, looking across the room at her Nana. "And we need to make sure nothing happens here."

"At least we know they didn't get the thumb drive ... anything taken?"

"Couldn't tell to be honest. My locked drawer was smashed open, apart from the brief we were sent about Bateman, there was no information on our current job in the office." She tapped her head. "It's all up here or in our notebooks and we carry those."

"Or in the mail," I said, with a smile. "That wasn't a bad idea."

"Wasn't it? Because I have a feeling they're going to keep coming until they find out where it is, and that puts everyone here in danger," Ronnie said, still watching her Nana across the room.

"Time to get hold of MacKinnon and move to a safe house." I glanced at Enzo and Bateman. "We have to do something with them. I need a conversation with Enzo, because he sure as hell isn't who I thought he was."

"What have you been doing since we left?" Ronnie asked, with a smile. "All that time and you haven't got any answers." She shook her head. "Slipping, Crockett."

"My attention was fully snagged by your cousin. He's quite a handful, isn't he?"

"Oh, yeah, Donald is a unique guy," Ben said, grinning widely. "He's come through for us a few times. Not that he knows it, but he has."

"I'll make the MacKinnon call, and then we should be able to move. Everyone," I said.

Nana called across the room, "Veronica, did you want tea?"

"Yes, please," Ronnie called back. "I'll come and help."

She and Ben walked away, leaving me by the door. I flicked the lock down and drew the sheers curtains across to make it harder for anyone coming in the back gate to see us inside. I was tempted to shut the heavy drapes, but then we wouldn't be able to see out. I'd sooner see what's coming.

Took five rings for MacKinnon to answer. No doubt he was asleep.

"We have Bateman," I said. "We need a safe house for eight people and a dog."

"What happened?"

"There is no time for that conversation. Safe house?"

"Contact Art Jeffries. I gave you him for a reason."

"I'll be in touch."

"Deal with Bateman at the first opportunity."

I hung up and rang Art. He answered quickly. Must be an early riser.

"Art speaking."

"It's Crockett, I need a safe house for eight plus a dog."

I heard a page turn. "We have a house in Fendalton Crescent. Back section, big yard, fully fenced. Sending you the door code and street number."

"Cheers, Art."

I hung up, my phone buzzed, and there was the street number and the code. Forty-one Fendalton Crescent. I joined Ronnie.

"We have a house. Let's get ready to move," I said.

"Where?"

"Fendalton Crescent."

"That's Pinehaven, backs onto Witako Scenic Reserve," she said. "Nice up there."

"Glad to hear it, because that's our new base until we resolve the last few issues and wait for the mail."

"I'll help Nana, you sort that lot out," Ronnie said,

waving a hand toward Bateman and Enzo.

Seemed reasonable.

Enzo was still engrossed in conversation with Donald. Bateman listened. None of them took much notice of me until I spoke, "We're moving out in ten minutes."

Enzo's head turned toward me. "Where?"

"Safe house. We don't know how much Emily's kidnappers know."

He nodded. "Two vehicles?"

"Yep. You, me, Bateman here, and Donald in one. Ben, Ronnie, Emily and Nana in the other."

"The old lady is coming?"

"Yes." We're not leaving Ronnie's Nana to whoever trashed the office. In case they know about the retirement home. That's the last thing I wanted on my conscience.

I heard Ronnie and her Nana talking and a door open. I turned in time to see Ronnie take her Nana into the bedroom. Ben sat down on the sofa near Bateman. I joined Emily in the kitchen.

"You all right?" I asked, touching her elbow.

"Yes," she said, with a smile. "Nana made me a Milo."

"Good. Did they hurt you?" I searched her eyes for answers.

"My head hurts a bit," she said, her hand touched the side of her head.

"Did they hit you?"

"I don't know," she said. "Maybe I banged my head on something."

"Did they tell you anything?"

Her eyes moved across mine. "One said, 'this is the building' and the other one said, 'open the door'."

"Anything else?"

She nodded. "They had accents. The first man he made me open the door, and then went in all the rooms, before he tied me up in the bathroom."

"You weren't near them when they were wrecking the place?"

"No. I heard things breaking."

"Either of them say anything else, that you heard?"

"Nezdez. But it is not anything that I know. It sounded funny, so I said it over and over in my head. Nezdez, Nezdez. The man sounded angry when he said it."

"*Ne zdes'.*" Not here. "Guess it does sound funny. It's Russian for 'not here'. Did you hear any other words?"

"Yeah vot," she said. "Definitely angry when he said that."

"*Yebat'.*"

"Yes, that."

"It's a curse word. The *f* one," I said, not willing to say it to her. It sounded better in Russian. "I'd say he was angry, all right. Glad you're okay."

"I am fine," she said with a smile. "What is going to happen now?"

She turned to see Nana appear from the bedroom, with a small suitcase.

"We're going to another house, where it's safer."

"All of us?"

"Yes," I said. Then I paused as a thought emerged.

"Hey, Emily, did they give you anything or put anything in your pockets?"

She frowned. "I don't think so."

"Can you look in your pockets for me?"

That's when I realised, she was dressed. Not wearing pyjamas, or pyjamas and a hoodie, but dressed in jeans and hoodie and shoes.

She stuffed her hand in the pockets on the right side of her jeans and her right hoodie pocket, then did the same on the left. She opened her left hand and showed me a round object about the size and shape of a ten-cent piece. "This is not mine."

"Thanks," I took it, and turned it over. They knew someone would come for her. It was a tracker. Dammit. "How come you are dressed?"

Emily blinked, lines formed on her forehead, her eyebrows drew closer together. "I put my clothes on to take Romeo out, and it was still dark. I did not have my dressing gown. Clothes are better than being cold."

Good answer. I spun around and called out to Ben. "Found a tracker, time to move." I kept it in my hand. The best thing I could think of was a false trail. I gave Ronnie the address and door code for the house and sent her, Ben, Nana, and Emily on their way, with a promise to lock up when we left.

"Enzo, let's go, we're going to lure the Russians away from here." I showed him the tracker in my hand.

"Sounds like fun. Who's driving?"

"You," I replied.

We drove north to Te Marua. I threw the tracker into the bush. We drove south to Pinehaven.

Chapter 27
[Ronnie: The house.]

Dawn broke wide open. Blue sky, and bird song filled the air. The day was lurching toward sunny and warm. Ben and I went into the house and looked around first. An entrance way led in two directions, one up the stairs, and the other beside the stairs toward the back of the house. I took the downstairs, Ben went up. I opened a door beyond the stairs into a hallway. There was another door straight ahead, which I opened and peered around. A very nice bathroom. I closed the bathroom door. On my right was another door. I opened that to reveal a bedroom. I walked through the bedroom and opened another door into a sitting room that had large windows and an external door into the front garden. From the window, when I looked to the right, I could see our car on the drive.

I went back to the hallway and walked straight ahead. Another door, this time into a double garage. Across the garage was a small room. I had a look. An office or storeroom.

Ben called out from the top of the stairs. "All clear."

"Here too," I replied. "I'll go get them."

I went back to the entrance way, closing all the doors behind me, then opened the front door and waved at the car.

Nana, Emily, and Romeo made their way up the stairs

to Ben. I stayed behind them, watchful.

Ben opened double doors on the right into a huge lounge with large leather couches and armchairs. A big TV hung on one wall. Ranch sliders leading to a deck opened off the end of the room, and there was a wooden door on the right. Curious, I opened it. A study. A big window overlooked the driveway, and another window overlooked the stair well.

Through the lounge I walked into a dining room, which turned left into a large well-appointed kitchen and open plan laundry. Another set of ranch sliders opened off the laundry into the back yard. I took Romeo out to explore that part of the yard. Fully fenced. Excellent. Back inside I went through a door in the kitchen and found myself on the landing at the top of the stairs. On my right was a door with glass panels. It opened into a hallway. Off the hallway on the left was a master bedroom, on the right a large bathroom. Past those, there were two more bedrooms, one left and one right. The one on the right had an exterior door to the back yard. I wandered back through the house. There was another door off the landing. I opened it and found a toilet and a shower, and a door into another bathroom containing a bath I'd seen down the hall. Linked bathrooms. Smart. This was a very nice house.

There were a lot of exterior doors to keep an eye on, and a lot of enormous windows. Being a back section helped. I wandered into the living room. Ben had turned the TV on for Nana and Emily.

"Everyone all right?" I asked.

"Yes, dear," Nana said. "This is lovely."

"I'll take your bag down to one of the bedrooms, Nana, if you like?" I picked the bag up from the floor near the armchair she sat in.

"Thank you," Nana said. "What a shame the girls couldn't be part of this adventure. They'd love it."

I didn't doubt it, but I was glad they weren't caught up in this. Three old ladies in a safe house smacked of trouble. So much trouble.

"Coffee?" Ben said, from the dining room doorway.

"Yeah," I replied, "I'll drop this bag down in a bedroom and be right there."

I felt a bit lost. No computer. No real idea what the hell was going on. No Crockett. And bloody MacKinnon not telling us all the information. Back in the kitchen, I rang MacKinnon.

"It's me," I said, when he answered. "Why is Bateman so important?" I wanted to see if he'd tell me something real.

"She's a cryptographer," he replied.

"Good to know you're sticking to the same bullshit story," I said, leaning on the bench while the jug began to boil. Ben opened the double doors to a pantry and surveyed the contents. He found a French press and some ground coffee and put them on the bench.

"She's a cryptographer," MacKinnon said again.

"Yeah, you said. She's a cryptographer with a private company. Who are denying her existence."

"You had to find her, Ronnie," MacKinnon drawled. "Find the woman was your mission. You are working *Witcher*."

"And Crockett's mission?"

"To work with you."

"And Enzo Giuliano?"

"What are you talking about, Ronnie? You, Crockett, and Ben have the mission." I heard the edge in his voice.

"Well, that's not entirely true is it, MacKinnon ... unless you don't know someone sent Giuliano in, because that's something you should know, right?"

"There was a rumour," he said with a sigh.

"A rumour?

"Chandler ..."

"A heads up wouldn't have killed you," I grumbled. "What the hell has Chandler the bastard got to do with this operation? What does he know about *Witcher?*"

"He had a whopping meltdown when Crockett refused his advances is what I heard."

"When was that?"

"Earlier this week. He ordered Crockett to meet with him and did his usual; he wasn't playing, and he got pissed off."

"The time frame is all wrong. Giuliano showed up in photos from last week. Family photos of mine."

"Only know what I've heard, Ronnie. Scuttlebutt is that he turned him down and put him in his place on Tuesday morning."

Tuesday. I met Crockett Tuesday afternoon. A few

things he said fell into place. But it didn't help with the Enzo Giuliano situation.

"You think Chandler set him in motion after that meeting?"

"It makes. Sense. To me," MacKinnon drawled slowly.

"Then why was he all over our family photos the week before?"

"That, I do not know."

"What does Chandler want?" I thought about it for a beat. "Don't say Bateman, he doesn't want her."

"Two choices," MacKinnon said. "He wants to fuck *Witcher* because Crockett hurt his nasty little feelings, or he wants something Bateman has."

That felt more like it. He's a piece of work, and it would give him pleasure to screw us over, despite it damaging an operation.

"What do you think that could be?" I really wasn't keen on telling MacKinnon what we'd found.

He sighed. "We suspect Bateman is a foreign agent."

"Tell me something I don't know." Like whom she works for. "Who does she work for?"

"Maybe the Russians."

"You need to be sure, MacKinnon. This is a very messy situation."

Already my Nana is involved, and after what happened to Emily and Romeo, I'm not keen on what could happen next.

"Crockett will bring her in."

"Great, but meanwhile, we're stuck with her and a

293

situation, and it looks like we have to protect her."

"From whom?"

"Possibly the Russians and maybe Giuliano." Tires crunched on the driveway outside the house. Ben ran through the kitchen and into the lounge. "Get back to me when you know what the hell is going on out here. Meanwhile, we've got company."

"I'll ring you back, Ronnie."

"Make it soon," I grumbled, and hung up. Wouldn't be the first time both ends were playing the middle, but I had no desire to be one of the ends, or have my family caught up in Chandler's lunacy. I hurried down the hallway to the first bedroom and peered out the huge windows that opened onto a deck and overlooked the driveway. There was a car parked next to ours. Crockett exited the vehicle followed by Enzo, Bateman, and Donald. By the time I got to the landing, Ben was at the front door.

He looked up and smiled, then opened the door to greet the newcomers.

"Welcome to castle *Witcher*," he said with a flourish. "Donald, upstairs."

Donald looked up at me waiting at the top for him and smiled.

"Go on through to the door past the stairs and turn right," I called out to everyone else. "I'll be there in a second." I ducked into the lounge, leaving Ben organising the posse downstairs. When I didn't immediately see Donald come in from the stairs, I went back out to the landing. He was longingly watching Enzo walk into the downstairs rooms. "Peel yourself away Donald, he'll be up here soon."

He turned and fanned himself with both hands, caught Nana watching from the doorway, and immediately dropped both hands to his sides. That didn't look guilty at all.

"What's going on?" Donald asked, trying to deflect attention. "Why aren't they coming up here? What's Ben up to?"

"It's work," I said. "Just go in there with Nana and Emily."

"He's glorious," Donald crooned.

I rolled my eyes. He said that every other week about someone.

"You three stay in the lounge. We need a few moments downstairs."

Donald raised his hand. I gave him a look. "Yes, Donald?"

"Can we at least explore upstairs?"

"Yes but stay up here and stay inside."

"And if Romeo needs to go potty?"

"He's been out, but if he needs to go again, use the laundry door. The yard out there is fully fenced, and the fences are over six feet high. Make sure you watch him, Donald."

"So bossy! You're really in your element, Ms Bond."

With a hefty eye roll and a warning look, I left them to it.

Crockett opened the door to the apartment for me. "Let's get this done," he said, as I walked past him and into the bedroom. "They're in the living area."

Ben was sitting in a chair. He smiled at me. Tania sat opposite him. Enzo stood, he looked out the full-length windows into the front garden.

I sat on the arm of Ben's chair.

"They all right up there?" he asked.

"Yep, for now. Let's get on with this."

"Go for it," he said.

"Tania - Sharon - Lissette, any of those names real?" I asked her.

"What do you think?"

"Lissette Markova."

She shrugged. "So?"

"I think I'll just call you Tania. Who do you work for Tania?"

"TechSynth."

"Uh huh. For the last five years they have filed tax returns that stated you were their employee." I paused and made eye-contact with her. "Well, until the weekend that is."

"What do you mean?"

"On Saturday they reported you missing. On Monday they told your workmates your father had a stroke and you left to take care of him." By the expression on her face, that part was news to her. "When I called the office on Tuesday, they said you didn't work there."

"I must've missed the memo where I was fired," she

said, quietly.

"We found your go-bag, under the Moonshine bridge," Crockett said. "Care to explain that?"

"Why? You clearly know more than TechSynth," she said, and attempted a small smile. It fell short.

"Why did TechSynth wait so long to declare you missing?" I asked. "Valuable time slipped away, and even when they did reach out, the information was sketchy."

"You'd have to ask them," she said.

Enzo joined us, sliding into an armchair. "I think it's time we laid all our cards on the table."

"Go right ahead," Crocket muttered. "I'd love to know what your part in this is."

"TechSynth have a web hosting service," he said. "It's used by a lot of people with high security clearances."

Crockett caught my eye. We'd figured that was the case.

"And ..." I said, "Who knew about their client list?"

"SIS," he said.

"Okay, so the SIS monitored their clients, but I bet even they didn't have access to the information stored on the hosting service, and why we were employed?" I said, shifting my position on the arm. Not the most comfortable place to roost.

"They had someone on the inside to try and locate certain information for their own use."

Great, spying on a private company and their clients.

"How long has this been going on?"

"A couple of years. TechSynth have some government

contracts, as in some government departments use their hosting. Which I guess gave the SIS a legitimate reason to keep tabs. A year ago, they discovered someone was trying to access information held on particular servers. So, they beefed up their monitoring to see if that person would show their hand."

"Fantastic, shall we guess who that person is?"

Enzo grimaced. "Turns out the person on the inside managed to access information and got away with it before anyone could stop them." His foot kicked out and smacked into Tania's foot. She jumped. "Want to tell the class what you did?"

She shook her head.

"I think you should," Enzo said. "I really do."

She bit her lip.

"I think we can guess," I said. "And I think the reason we're involved is because someone told MacKinnon all about it." Or he found out through listening devices and other covert means, which wouldn't be a surprise. "And he had a vested interest in locating that intel and making damn sure it never reached a buyer." Yet, he never told us about it. We just had to find the woman.

Crockett spoke, "Tania, you don't have to tell us anything. We're more than happy to turf you out. So whoever else wants you can find you."

Her eyes flashed at me, then Crockett. "No."

I smiled. "No worries at all. We'll hand you over to MacKinnon." His name did not spark any recognition on her face. "Alternatively, we can let Enzo have you."

He looked like he could handle some assisted interrogation.

"Get in line," Crockett said. "I have orders and you probably won't like them."

That was the moment I realised there actually was a kill-order out on Tania Bateman. She really did piss the wrong people off. MacKinnon is the wrong person, every damn time.

"We could flip for her," Enzo said, fishing a coin from his pocket and spinning it in the air. "Heads Crockett gets you, tails I get you."

"You could let me go," she said quietly. "Just let me go. I'll leave the country and you'll never see me again."

Crockett and Enzo laughed.

"How far do you think you'll get without that intel?" I said, smiling sweetly at her. "It's gone. You needed that to bargain your way out." From the corner of my eye, I saw Enzo's reaction and it confirmed for me that he was involved to get the intel.

A single tear ran down Tania's face. She brushed it away. "I know where it is," she said. "I'll get it for you."

"What, in the matchbox under the bushes in the garden?" I asked. "I'm afraid you won't be getting it."

All colour drained from her face. "They were supposed to pick it up from the park near the movie theatre, but I didn't trust them."

"Who is Carlswick?" Crockett asked. "Or what is Carlswick?"

Enzo shifted his foot. "Answer the question," he said.

"Tell us."

"It's a codename maybe."

"Uh huh," I said. "For?"

"I don't know. I tried running internet searches on it, but it keeps coming back to that book." Another tear rolled down her face. "I don't know what it means or who it is. It's the one thing I couldn't work out from the code."

I reached over and took Ben's phone from the arm of his chair and did an internet search for the book in question. I read the blurb. "Super simplifying this story, it's about a woman who is trying to keep ahead of a blackmailer." I looked at Tania. "Was someone blackmailing you?"

She swallowed hard. "No. Yes. They didn't ask for money or anything. Someone left me notes and I had to answer a pay phone every other Friday. They'd tell me what information to get and where to leave it. They knew my codename. So, it had to be someone on the inside."

"Which inside?" Crockett asked. "Russia, or was there another option?"

She shook her head, then changed her mind. "I don't know who it was. I assumed Russia."

Of course, because she's Russian.

"You believing that?" I said to Crockett. "Because I generally know who I'm working for." I smiled. Right now, I was working for the Aussies with a side of Kiwi, but I *knew* that.

"Struggling," Crockett said. "But we have Russians involved, we know that, and Bateman here has a Russian passport. Would be pretty easy to say it was the Russians. We don't know who else is making a play here. Do you, Enzo?"

He tipped his head toward Crockett. "If I had to guess, I'd say an Asian interest."

"If you had to guess," I repeated. "Great." Something still wasn't adding up.

"I never met anyone. A few days ago, someone was supposed to show, we had a live drop set up, and no one showed," added Tania, "The next drop was a dead drop. And by then I didn't trust them, so I hid the device to pick up later."

"About that, we found the coded memo telling you where to leave the device, and it wasn't at the park, like you said, was it, Tania?" Crockett said, with a hint of menace in his voice.

"And?" I asked. "Why didn't you just take it and leave? Why hide it somewhere else?"

"It's not that easy," she said, making eye contact with me, fire shot from the depths. "I got the last message, and it was a piece of paper shoved in my letterbox. It took me a few days to work out what it meant."

"The bookshop," I said.

She nodded. "I went to the bookshop to find the rest of the communication. It was pretty clever. Whoever set that up, spent some time at the shop to know the order of the books."

Yeah, they did. If only we knew who it was or even when. A when would give us a date stamp for the camera outside the Wherefore Art Thou entrance way.

"And then what?" Crockett said. "You were missing according to TechSynth from Saturday, until we know you popped up in the Retirement Village garden at midnight on Monday."

She nodded her head. "I wasn't missing. I was laying low."

"We know, using a credit card with another name so no one could track you," I said. "What'd you do next?"

"I was supposed to use the dead drop then catch the train to Wellington. FSB were after me. They wanted the data to find out who was running something called *Genesis*."

FSB. They are Russian. But so is she; why would her own people be after her? "How do you know that?"

"The person who left the code for me at the bookshop. They warned me they were close, and I should delete the data."

"You didn't delete the data. If you'd tried, they would've found you earlier."

She frowned. Her eyebrows scrunched together. "How could they?"

"I was hoping you'd know," I said. "Where did you get the device?"

"Two weeks ago. It was placed in my letterbox in a blank envelope."

"By whom?"

"I don't know."

"And you mentioned this to who?" Crockett asked. "It's

been my experience that when you're working for someone and they give you something, they let you know they're giving you something, and what it's for."

"Yeah, it's usually not a surprise," I added. "Oh, look here's a funny little USB drive, wonder what I should do with it?" I leaned back in my chair. "I don't know about the rest of you." I looked around the room. "But I wouldn't immediately think, hey, why don't I use this to download data that's classified *top secret special.*" Which got me thinking. "You have to have a Top-Secret Special security clearance to even get within a sniff of that kind of data."

"I see where you're going," Ben said.

"Enlighten us," Crockett said. "Enzo looks as blank as I feel."

"To get our highest security clearance the background check covers a full fifteen years. Fifteen. That's a lot of backstory and I don't know anyone who could sit through filling in that four-to-five-hour questionnaire and provide all the dates and referees and old passports and whatever else they need, if it wasn't actually their life." It'd been a long time since I'd needed to update my security clearance, but I recalled how long those questionnaires took to fill out and that there was more than one. "I guess my question is, what's your clearance, Tania?"

"Confidential," she said, her voice barely audible.

Good luck getting much information with that. "Lowest of the clearances, they only look back five years." The easiest one to fudge. "Someone chose you, with bugger all clearance, to steal data which wasn't just sitting around asking to be stolen, and I doubt it was easy to get to, or to even know what you were looking for. It's a funny old world, isn't it?"

"Who gave it to you, Tania? Who was it?" Enzo leaned closer to her. "Who asked you to get that data?"

"Do you know who?" I said, as I stood up and moved to an empty chair, a little bit closer to Tania.

"No."

"Funny thing, I don't believe you. I believe you're a foreign agent and have accessed information for that foreign power."

Crockett coughed to get my attention. I nodded. We were right about the code in the book titles, and he was pleased, I could tell.

"If you didn't want to do it or changed your mind, why didn't you tell someone?" I asked.

"It's just not that easy. You know that. You're Veronica Tracey. You're a fucking spy."

"How do you know who I am?" My gut roiled. "Why did you choose the retirement home to stash the device?"

Who did she know? Chandler? Could this be one of his screwed-up operations?

I stood and tapped Crockett on the shoulder. "A word." We walked into the bedroom.

"Is she working for someone else or is she working for the Russians? What were you told by MacKinnon?"

"To find her ..." his voice trailed off.

"No mention of the data?"

He slowly shook his head. "Find her, just like you." He blinked slowly. "Not quite like you."

I knew it. He was clean-up. She wasn't walking away. "She's expendable."

"Collateral damage." His expression hardened. "Not the part of the job I like."

Good to know he wasn't a heartless killer. He was a killer with a heart. Not that it made any difference to the outcome. Between Enzo and Crockett, Tania's days were numbered and could actually be counted in hours.

"Enzo is after the data. We were after her. Who hired Enzo?"

"My money is on Chandler," Crockett said. "We'll get to him, but let's sort this Tania thing out first. We need to know more about how she did what she did. That's the key to stopping it happening again."

"What happened to turn her over and finish the job?" Oh, he was scoring points. First big job off his desk assignment.

"We have her. She's going nowhere, won't hurt to talk to her a bit."

"I bet we get nothing more from her. She has to know who warned her and who wanted her to destroy that USB drive," I said. "She's smart enough to figure out that crazy message, but not smart enough to ask for help when she wanted out. What the hell is that about?"

"What did they have on her?" Crockett said, in a hushed tone.

"Exactly what I was wondering. Five years ago, she

pops up fully fledged with this backstory about parents in Marlborough, but not exactly a tight backstory, just enough to get through the most basic of security clearances. Looking at that, she was never going to be in the vicinity of anything worth stealing, and TechSynth probably don't keep tabs on what their clients keep on the servers. She didn't have a high enough clearance to be around anything governmental ...”

“But everything is worth something to someone. We might look at it and go, not a big deal, but to someone else, that snippet of information could be the world,” Crockett said. “And someone was inside TechSynth working for New Zealand, because someone twigged that something was up. What do you bet they didn't know that atlas existed either, or where it was? They probably only saw low level shit, that no one really cared about, but they could follow it to the buyers.”

“Good point. I was more thinking she didn't have a high clearance so wasn't going to be around the kind of intel she got her hands on.”

“That atlas might have been from a private company or a private person.”

“Yeah, but she still would've had to know what to look for.”

“Yes, and clearly, she did. Was she working alone?” It wasn't the first time I considered someone else within the company was involved. And it felt like it could be a thing.

“Something to look into, because if she had a partner in crime then they'd want that intel now, too. Especially if it looked like she was about to sell it, or leave with it, and cut them out altogether."

"What if someone knows her real story and that's where this all stemmed?" I wondered out loud.

"The person who wanted the data to start with is probably not the same one who warned her, unless they wanted it to look like they were different people?"

"To what end?"

"I don't know, just spit balling," Crockett muttered.

"There are definitely other players. I think she had someone inside who helped her access that data or even helped her find it. Now we know what she had, I doubt it was left lying around. Probably didn't have a big sign or neon flashing lights," I said. "But what's to stop whoever else is involved from doing this again, by themselves?"

"Us," he replied.

"How exactly?"

"I don't know yet, I'll figure it out."

"The only way I can see is to blow the whistle. Go public with what we know and the evidence. Catch is, going public would expose all the officers in play and those no longer serving."

"Yeah, we're not doing that," he said.

Good, because going public would fuck *Genesis*.

"The device is proof that Tania Bateman was stealing intelligence from the TechSynth servers," I said. "If I owned that company, I'd want her silenced before my clients found out what had happened, and they all bailed."

"How badly do you want the payday?"

I shrugged. "Insurance will cover the damage to my offices. The payday was a nice little nest egg. I can live without it."

"Then we keep her alive."

"Hey, Crockett ..."

"Yeah?"

"How did MacKinnon and Chandler know she had the device? Because they had to know, to send us after her. Why would they give a flying rat's arse about a lowly cryptographer in the private sector?" I leaned on a dresser near a window that faced into the garden at eye-level, which reminded me we were semi-underground.

"Neither of them mentioned the data or a device ..."

"I know, it was all about the woman, but it was too delayed and the information we were given was her cover story, nothing that would actually help us find her."

"MacKinnon has a lot of faith in your ability. Does he know how you do things?"

I smiled. "No. Imagine explaining that I dowse ... not happening."

"When I saw the lack of information and was told to work with you, I have to admit the thought of two heads working on this was much better than me alone." He grinned. "Can you use that dowsing business to find those Russians?"

The sound of something hitting a window in the other room, and sudden movement, reached us.

"What the hell?" I said, as Crockett opened the door a

crack.

"Gunshot," he replied over his shoulder at me, then turned his attention to the room beyond. "Move. On me!"

He stepped out of the way. Another bullet hit glass. Ben and Tania came through the door first. Enzo last. Crockett shut the door and locked it. Then opened the door into the hallway.

"That glass didn't break," Ben said.

"Bulletproof," I replied, with my weapon in hand. "They must've used bulletproof glass down here." I hoped that extended to the glass panels in the entrance way and the accessible doors upstairs.

Crockett led the way to the stairwell. Glass blew across the floor from next to the huge front door. Bugger.

"Moving," Crockett said. "With me."

I locked the downstairs doors and followed them up. Glancing at the broken pane, I realised that even with that glass shot out they couldn't reach the locks to open the door. Small mercy.

A ruckus in the living room caught my attention. The upstairs was like a fishbowl, with concrete block interludes. So much glass and so many doors. Donald was in full freak out mode.

Crockett gathered everyone into the middle of the lounge. "Hallway by the bedrooms, is the only place without windows," he said.

"Or." I had another idea. "Back downstairs into the garage. Those steel doors won't budge, and we can use part of the apartment, a full bathroom, and the small room out in the garage itself."

Crockett narrowed his eyes. I knew he was thinking. "Good idea, more comfortable than everyone crammed into one hallway."

"Downstairs then." I looked for Ben and spotted him with Emily. "Ben, the black bag?"

"I left it in the laundry," he said. "Be right back."

Ben hurried through the lounge and dining room, keeping as far away from windows as he could. An almost impossible task.

"Downstairs, let's go," I said, taking Nana by the arm. "Too many windows up here and too dangerous for all of us."

There were long narrow frosted windows from ceiling to floor in the front of the entrance way and either side of the huge front door. One pane was already strewn across the terracotta tiles.

"Veronica, what is happening out there?" Nana said, with a hint of glee in her voice. Another round hit concrete. "Ester and Frankie would find this very exciting."

"A little too exciting, for my liking, Nana," I said. "Stay behind me, put your hand on my shoulder, and keep close to the wall. Be careful, there's no banister on the wall side."

"Yes, dear."

Nana's boney hand rested on my shoulder.

Chapter 28
[Crockett: Russian's and a siege.]

The last thing I wanted to happen was a siege situation with an elderly woman in the midst of it, and here we were, exactly that. Fuck me.

With everyone safely in the garage, we had some breathing space. Ronnie suggested that Nana and Emily stay in the apartment bedroom for now. The small window that faced into the garden looked like it was hidden from the outside by plants. She shut the small but heavy curtains across it anyway. Not that they'd protect anyone from bullets, but they would stop the glass exploding into the room if whoever was outside found the window. The door to the apartment living room was closed. Thankfully, it was a solid core door. I guess Art thought of a few things.

"Hey," Ben said from the hallway. "Ammo check."

"Seventeen and one in the pipe," I replied. "Ronnie is the same. How about you, Enzo?"

"Sixteen and one up," he said. Glass crashed over the tiles in the entrance way. "Do you think that's the Russian's out there?"

Ronnie joined me and replied, "No idea, Enzo, but even with silencers this mess is going to draw a police response. Early morning glass shattering is going to echo around the hills. No one wants AOS all over the house."

"True enough," I said. That would cause deniability

from the agency and we'd be flapping in the wind. "We need to get a vantage point, or to come up behind them."

"There's no crawl space in the top storey ceiling, but I bet there's a way we can get up on the roof."

"Ladder?" I asked.

"Yeah, a ladder in the back yard," Ronnie said, with a grin. "Ben has a rifle."

Ben called out from inside the garage, "Got something helpful." We joined him. He'd found a long ladder. "Still have to get it up the stairs and out the back."

"Enzo and Ben, can you lay down some cover fire from the apartment?" I asked.

"Yes," they replied.

Ronnie and Ben were deep in conversation, I couldn't hear, and didn't care. They were obviously dating.

I looked at Tania cowering in the corner near the office with her hands over her ears. "Tania, go into the apartment," I said.

She didn't look up or move.

There was another crash, this time upstairs. Okay, so not all the upstairs glass is bulletproof.

"Tania!" I reached her in four strides, grabbed her arm, and pulled her to her feet. "Move." I gave her an encouraging push toward the hallway. "Go over there."

Donald lurked in the doorway of the garage room. "You all right?" I asked.

"I believe so," he said. He didn't look it.

"Go with Tania. Look after your Nana," I said. When he passed me, I gave him a reassuring pat to his shoulder.

"It'll be all right."

"You don't lie as well as Ronnie," he replied. "That big, rugged biker exterior doesn't fool me."

Enzo and Ben joined me near the door. They'd carried the ladder over and laid it on the ground. Maybe I should take one of them upstairs and leave Ronnie to provide cover fire. The glass downstairs is bulletproof.

"You're going to have to fire from the open door," I said to Enzo and Ben.

"Yes, we are. We're also going to pray that glass can act as our cover, and we can rig some kind of extra cover from the furniture."

"Ronnie, you coming?" She was crouched down by the black duffel bag. On the floor next to her I saw two soft rifle cases and a box of ammunition. She straightened up with a pistol in her hand.

"Give us two minutes," I said to Ben and Enzo, before they went through the apartment.

They opened the interior door to the living area and disappeared inside, closing the door. I heard the sound of furniture dragging across carpet.

Ronnie walked into the apartment. "Emily!" She called, then threw her the handgun she held. I watched from the hallway.

Emily snatched it from midair, dropped the magazine into her left hand, counted rounds, slid it back and performed a press check without missing a beat. Fuck me. That looked a lot like muscle memory. I filed all the questions that jumped around in my head, for later.

Ronnie had the rifle bag slung over her shoulder. I took the other and did the same. Then I tapped Ronnie on the arm and indicated she should grab the end of the ladder.

We moved into the entrance way sticking close to the side of the stairs and waited for the first rounds to fire from the apartment.

I looked over my shoulder. Gunfire erupted. "Moving."

Ladder on the left, guns in right hands. I noted Ronnie carried her handgun in the high ready position. She switched hands, spun around, and walked backwards up the stairs. By the time we reached the top, she'd fired five rounds. We heard one yell of pain. There was more to Ronnie Tracey than I'd been told.

Romeo trotted across the kitchen floor, as we entered through the hall door and manoeuvred the long ladder to the ranch slider. I pulled the door right back. The dog ducked out before I did. He ran across the concrete and onto the grass. I motioned to Ronnie. The best place for the ladder was right by the door, as no one could get around the back without scaling the high fences, and right by the door we couldn't be seen from the other yards at all.

I leaned the long ladder against the gutter and hoped it wouldn't collapse.

"Is the dog okay out here?" I whispered.

"Yeah," she replied, matching my hushed tone. "He'll warn us well before anyone comes over that fence."

With the rifle case on my back and Ronnie right

behind me, we scaled the ladder like a couple of monkeys.

Crouched on the flat roof, I saw a high ridge, and figured it was the steeple looking part of the roof that had more windows in it and was visible from inside the lounge. A roof with cover. Helpful.

The steel creaked as we hunched down and duck walked across the expanse to the ridge. We needed to keep our profile minimal. Below us, trading gunfire, were the attackers and our guys. I crept to the right side where the ridge ended. We were still too far back to get a look at the shooters' positions. Abandoning the ridge, we moved closer to the edge. The roof was steel with an uncomfortable ridge every two hundred millimetres. Not ideal for belly crawling or lying on. No one said this job would be comfortable.

Ronnie was nowhere near me. I spotted her moving on her stomach on the far left. We arrived at the edge, high above the driveway, at the same time. I shrugged the gun case from my shoulder and unzipped it to reveal a Mossberg Patriot, with a suppressor nestled next to it, and a small box of ammunition. I screwed the suppressor to the end of the twenty-inch barrel. The magazine held three rounds. I pulled the bolt back, a round filled the chamber, and now I had one up. I took the magazine out and added another round. Three and one up. I liked that better.

I rang her phone. Didn't even hear the buzz before her voice answered.

"Two tangoes on my side. One behind the fence and

one around the side of the house."

"I got one tango, behind the last car."

"Right, let's do this," she said.

I lay the phone on the roof next to me, wriggled back a bit, and got as comfortable as possible with the rifle.

"Contact." Ronnie's voice came from the phone a split second before a shot fired from her direction.

I sighted my target. Cover fire from Ronnie pulled their attention. I put a round through his shoulder, and he staggered, then dropped. Re-aiming, I put a couple of rounds next to the car. Warning shots. I heard Ronnie fire a few more rounds. Someone yelped. All movement below us ceased. I spoke to Ronnie via my cell phone.

"Think we're good. Let's go." I hung up and called Enzo, while I unscrewed the suppressor using the bottom of my shirt, to avoid burning my fingers, and packed the rifle back into the carry case. "Take Ben, secure the area. Coming to you."

I slithered as best I could across the ridged steel until I was far enough back that it was safe to sit. I pushed myself into a seated position, then crouched. Ronnie did the same on the far side of the roof. Once past the steeple part we both stood and moved quickly to the ladder. From the roof top, I saw Romeo patrolling the edges of the back yard. I slid down the ladder and joined Ronnie at the bottom.

Chapter 29
[Ronnie: Too many secrets.]

I left the men to deal with the injuries outside. There were calls made to MacKinnon and the ambulance. No one called police; that was part of MacKinnon's job, keep the heat off us, while we finished what needed to be done. We might be deniable, but he didn't want to risk losing control of Tania Bateman. He still hadn't mentioned the drive. We all knew he knew about it, but he clearly didn't want to talk about it. We had it as a bargaining chip for later if necessary. I hoped it wouldn't come to that. I wanted the thing destroyed before it did any more damage.

I looked out the main door of the downstairs apartment and watched Enzo and Crockett play rock, paper, scissors. Unbelievable. Enzo stayed with the wounded and cuffed Russian attackers, waiting for the ambulance. Ben excused himself and went to help once Crockett returned.

"Donald," I said, turning to face him. He stood in the doorway of the bedroom.

"Is the madness over?" he asked with a slight smile, and a sigh. I joined him just inside the bedroom door.

"Yes. Can you take Nana and Emily upstairs and make them a cuppa?"

"Of course," he said, with a smile. "Does Emily keep the gun?"

I shook my head. "I'll take it."

Emily smiled at me and handed me the Glock. "I know how to use that?"

"Yes, Emily, you do," I said, returning her smile. "I'm very glad your muscle memory kicked in. I thought it would."

"You did?"

"I did. Sometimes I see you in there, unable to find your way out. And when you held the Glock, for a little while our Emily was back." I touched her arm. "There's hope."

Donald took Nana by the arm and escorted the women out of my view and into the glass covered entrance way.

Just another day in sleepy Upper Hutt.

Tania Bateman sat staring at the wall. I needed to know how much she knew, who she could implicate. I snapped my fingers in front of her. "Hey, get up and go into the other room."

We settled her and ourselves. Crockett and I wanted to talk to Bateman first.

"It's not just the drive they want, is it? It's you," I said.

She attempted a shrug. Crockett picked up the mantle. "They want you, why?"

Nothing.

My turn again. "You're one of them, and they're taking you home, bringing you back in. Guess it doesn't hurt that you're a cryptographer. I have a feeling they'll need someone to crack the encryption on the data."

Her eyes widened. "What data?"

Tiresome.

"The data you stole from TechSynth."

"Who do you work for, Lisette?" Crockett asked.

"TechSynth," she replied.

"Not according to them. When they discovered you stole something from one of their clients, they trotted out a cover story to explain your absence. Pretty much says they don't want you back alive."

She shrugged. "I can't help you."

"You don't get it. You are the one who needs help," I said.

"I was going home when that arse, Paul, grabbed me."

"Really? You'd been living under the bloody bridge for days, just a few streets from your house. Home? I don't think so."

She said nothing.

"No comment?" Crockett said.

"You spend days hiding instead of going home, that's not normal people behaviour," I said.

"You're fishing," Bateman said, making eye contact with me. "You don't know me."

"We have your go-bag."

"You have nothing. Conjecture and wishful thinking, is what you have."

I smiled. "We know enough to place you in a garden where we discovered a matchbox that contained a very small USB drive."

"Anyone could've left that."

I shook my head. "You did."

"You can't prove it."

"Yes, I can, but I don't need to, not to anyone, ever." I leaned over the back of the chair she sat in. "It's time you told the truth."

"There is nothing to tell."

"You're a spy. Who do you work for?"

She smiled up at me. "My name is Tania Bateman, I work for TechSynth."

"Usually when a person buys a house, they live in it, and it's sprinkled with signs of occupation. Usually, it doesn't end up scattered across the neighbourhood in matchstick sized pieces."

"What?"

She seemed genuinely surprised.

"The house you bought and slept in, but didn't live in. Because no one really lived there. It blew up. And I don't think you did that, did you?"

"I have no idea what you are talking about."

"Did you have internal surveillance cameras inside your house?"

She frowned. "No."

Crockett bent down and growled into her face, "Are you sure?"

"There were no cameras, there was nothing worth surveilling in the house."

Yeah, we knew that. It was a shell. A set. A faux house.

"Who would install cameras in your home?"

"I don't know; the same people who were shooting at us?" she suggested.

"The Russians who were bringing you back into the fold? Doesn't seem likely," I said.

"Stand up!" Crockett said, hauling her to her feet. He patted her down and turned out her pockets. Then he carefully checked all the seams of her clothes. Eventually, he tugged at something and held up a tiny GPS tracker. "Could've been worse, could've been fed to her."

"Crush it," I said. "Not that it probably matters. They already found us."

"We don't know if there are others."

"What happened to your phone?" I asked Bateman.

"Paul took it."

Enzo opened the door and came in. "Everything is okay out there. MacKinnon will meet the ambulance at Hutt Hospital and take charge of the Russians before there is a diplomatic incident and threats."

"Thanks," I said. "Hey, Paul had a phone that belonged to Bateman. Do you know what happened to it?"

"Didn't know he had it." He waggled his finger between me, Crockett, and himself. "We left Paul in Whitemans Valley. He's probably not feeling too good and trying to find his way out."

"With the phone ..." Crockett said.

"Sucks to be him then," Tania said, with a small smile. "They must be moving on what they think is my location by now."

"They found your location," Enzo said. "Why would they trace the phone?"

Crockett raised an eyebrow in his direction. "Two

trackers, two teams, fuck me."

Enzo sighed. "Two different sets of players after the same thing."

"Three, if you count us," I interjected. "Hold it, how did she get a physical tracker on her. Where was it, Crockett?"

"In the bottom seam of her hoodie."

"Who were you with?" I said, nudging Bateman's arm. "Who else was physically close to you on Monday night?"

"No one."

I thought about the places she'd been that we knew about. The movies. The barista said someone came in after her and went to the movies.

"The movie. Who was the man who followed you in if it wasn't Paul or Charlie?"

"No one."

"Someone," Crockett said. "It was someone. Someone you trust or someone you don't know."

"There was a man who sat beside me. One seat over. We had a seat between us."

"Did he speak to you?"

I wanted to slap her into the middle of next week to see if she'd talk faster and tell us what the hell was going on.

"Yes, he spoke. He had a soft voice and an accent. Sounded like he was from Sweden or somewhere."

"What did he say?"

"He asked about the movie and," she said with a shrug. "He was just polite. He didn't really say anything."

"Have you seen him before?"

"No."

"Were you wearing that pink hoodie?"

"No, it was too warm. It was on the chair between us."

I walked away and motioned to Crockett and Enzo. We confabbed by the door.

"Sweden?" I asked. "Who do we know who worked or works in that region of Europe?"

Enzo shook his head. Crockett stared at me.

"No one in Sweden, but Finland cropped up, remember? Could he be Finnish, not Swedish?"

"Possibly," I said, recalling the mention of Finland I'd seen in the files. "MacKinnon was in Finland."

"But how does that connect to this?"

"Fuck knows," I said, leaning on the wall near the door, and watching the woman in the chair. "Can't we just shoot her and put her out of our misery. Grab the device when it turns back up, and throw it in the sea?"

Enzo nodded. "Happy to help out."

"Take a run at her," I said. "I need a break."

Chapter 30
[Crockett: Genesis.]

I could not believe she turned Enzo loose on Bateman. But to be fair to Ronnie, I was as sick of Bateman's lack of answers as she was. I could understand the decision on one level, but Enzo's methods of extracting information might be outside the perimeters of interrogation best-practice. I had a feeling he high jumped over lines.

She asked if I wanted to stick around and monitor the situation. I did not. I followed Ronnie up the stairs and into the kitchen.

Donald was mid-sentence when we walked in. He looked past me, and his smile slid away. He didn't need to say anything. We both knew he wanted to see Enzo.

"He's busy," I said. "He won't be long."

"Can you go in the other room, please," Ronnie said to Donald. "And send Ben in."

He nodded. The blonde streak in the front of his hair flopped. For a moment I wondered if we looked as tired as he did.

"Maybe have a nap," I suggested. "Time will go faster."

Donald sparked up. "I'm not ninety, I can handle an early start," he fired at me. "Just do what you do. Some of us have proper jobs to get to." He stalked off.

I'd seen the evidence of his job on Jenn's hair, and vowed never to let him near mine. I'm sure some people like crazy hair colours, but I'd be sticking with the local barber.

I opened cupboards looking for glasses. I found them and ran the cold tap for a second before filling a glass and downing the entire thing. I hadn't realised how thirsty I was. I filled the glass again and drank half before Ben came in.

Ronnie poured herself a glass of water as well.

"What's happening?" Ben asked.

"Enzo is questioning Bateman," Ronnie said.

Ben looked from her to me. "Your idea?" he said to me.

I shook my head. Surprise registered across his face.

"Mine," Ronnie said. "I'm tired and done with her shit. There's a chance someone else is looking for her. Might be a Swede, might be a Finn."

"Call in MacKinnon," Ben said. "We've done our job. We have the woman."

Ronnie nodded. I thought about it for a split second. My part wasn't quite over, but I had no appetite for the last part, even though Bateman was annoying as hell. Good chance whoever was looking for Bateman had found Paul and Charlie and wouldn't have been pleased. I imagined they were no longer my problem.

"It's not quite that simple," I said.

Ronnie and Ben turned to face me. I could see it on their faces, the knowledge. I didn't need to spell it out.

"I'm calling MacKinnon," Ben said, taking his phone from his pocket and making the call. He put it on speaker. No secrets now.

"Ben," MacKinnon said. "Do you have good news?"

"We have Bateman. We're done. Transfer the funds and come get her."

"Good work." MacKinnon's voice fell flat. "Send her in with Crockett."

"That won't work," Ben said, looking at me. "He's got his hands full with this Enzo person."

I shook my head. He wouldn't buy into that.

"Send her in with Crockett. I have some news from your Russians."

"What did they have?"

"They said someone else was looking for Bateman. A man called Kari Paunio, Finnish. The description they gave is, six feet tall with dark blond hair and pale blue eyes. His nose was broken at some point and badly reset. He has a scar on his chin from being hit with an ice skate."

Ronnie and I looked at each other. Finnish. Finland. This smelt like it had something to do with that atlas and James MacKinnon.

"And?" Ben said, warning us to be quiet with a look.

"Be careful. I did some checking and he's a merc."

"And he's in New Zealand for Bateman ... why?"

Ronnie shook her head at him.

MacKinnon spoke quietly, "Tell Crockett to bring her in. It's over. I'll have a team locate Mr Paunio."

Ronnie took a breath. "He's probably in Whitemans Valley dealing with something."

"Ronnie, you all right?" MacKinnon paused, then said, "Am I on speaker?"

"Yes," she said, and warned me to keep quiet with a hand signal. "You want Crockett to bring her in, he'll bring her in. Deal with the Finn, I don't want this coming any closer to my family than it already has."

"Did she have anything with her?" He tried to make it sound like an innocent inquiry, but it didn't.

"A tracker placed on her by an unknown male. We thought it was the Russians, but probably your Finnish friend," Ronnie said. "Best you get a team on him quickly and sort him out."

"How, or why, would he be in Whitemans Valley?"

"Because she had a phone, and it's over there," Ronnie replied.

"Sit tight. I'll dispatch a team now."

"Anything else you'd like to ask us?"

"No. I'll call you when it's clear. Send Crockett and Bateman to me, as soon as possible."

Ben hung up.

Ronnie leaned on the bench. "The merc, if that's what he is, is working with the Russians. They want her and the intel. Guess they can't crack the encryption without her, but how can she do it?"

"What do you mean?" Ben said.

"I mean that it's high-level encryption. Just in case," Ronnie said.

"Right, then she can't crack it like an egg. Not without that program you have."

"Had, it's probably non-existent after the demolition job they did on my office," Ronnie said.

"Everything can be cracked given enough time," I said.

Ronnie shrugged. "I don't think they have the kind of time required especially if this is about *Genesis,* and who is involved. It's information they probably don't want to wait weeks or months for."

"Do we know what *Genesis* is?" Ben asked, pouring himself a glass of water.

"Nope," I said. "We do know MacKinnon's son is involved in it though."

The kitchen door opened, and Enzo walked in. How much did he hear?

"You want to know what *Genesis* is?" he asked.

I shook my head. "Job is done, we don't need to know."

"It's interesting," Enzo said. "You sure?"

"Creation of the world," Ben said, and took a swig of water. "The whole Adam and Eve debacle. Caine and Abel. Noah and his ark. The Tower of Babel. It's a lot."

"I hear his wife turned into a pillar of salt," Ronnie said.

Ben chuckled.

"Never knew Kiwis were so funny." Enzo said, looking at me.

"Laugh a minute around here," I replied with a shrug.

Ronnie placed her glass on the bench. "What is *Genesis,* Enzo?"

"It's a way of connecting various countries. An alliance if you will."

"Okay, the world is full of agreements and alliances. Why is this one secret?"

"It's a pact between agencies rather than countries. Unlike Five-Eyes, which is secret. The five countries involved are represented and information is shared officially, heads of state are briefed. This is more a secret alliance between individual agencies in the spy game, and they don't provide reports back to governments on things discussed during their meetings, and no one knows exactly who is involved in this alliance."

"What the hell? It sounds like you're describing a secret society," Ronnie said. She was right. That's exactly what I thought.

"It might be, and everyone who suspects it exists, but wasn't invited in, wants to be part of it," Enzo said. "Or wants to know who's involved."

Ronnie nodded her head slowly. "Of course, spies and lies, and counter-lies."

"All this, this whole bloody mess, is to protect someone she referred to as Proverb. And to stop whoever is after this information, from getting their hands on the person or persons behind *Genesis*," Enzo said. "She was talkative in the end."

Silence fell across the kitchen as we digested the information.

After a minute or so, I decided to throw the scent away from Ronnie and me. No one ever needed to know that we'd seen those files and knew who was behind *Genesis*.

"The drive that we found, and realised was important, that holds this information?"

"That's the assumption," Enzo said. "Bateman knew it

had something to do with *Genesis,* but not what. She also knew what *Genesis* supposedly is, or had at least heard of it."

Ronnie nudged me. "Take her. Take her to MacKinnon or whatever you have to do. I'm done."

"Ronnie, where is the USB drive?" Enzo asked.

"In the mail," she replied. "It'll turn up in about three days. Guess you're going to have to hang around then?"

He nodded and turned to me. "We are on the same team, you know."

"I figured that out," I said. "We'll talk. Sounds like we'll have time."

Enzo smiled. "Anyone mind if I go see Donald?"

We shook our heads and watched him leave. Ben handed me his tablet. "Latest news," he said.

I scanned the front-page headlines. The lead story was about a courier who had died in his van. He'd apparently been eating cherries intended for a customer and choked to death on the pits. Karma. Way down the bottom of the page was a small mention of a loud bang reported in central Upper Hutt, and a related police presence. Police released a statement saying there was a sprinkler malfunction at the Private Investigation offices of *Wherefore Art Thou.* No injuries reported.

"How'd you get police to say that?" I asked Ben.

Ben shrugged. "Just lucky I guess."

I doubted it was luck and scanned the daily news again. No mention of any car crashes over in Whitemans Valley, or gunshots, or anything that would have people raise questions. There was nothing at all about gunfire in Silverstream, or Pinehaven, or any place we'd been. Unbelievable.

"Ronnie, will you be okay here until I get back?" I asked, handing the tablet back to Ben.

"Yes. We'll be fine. MacKinnon has a team looking for the other guy, the Russians are out of action. You can deal with Bateman. No doubt, Chandler will deal with TechSynth, because he can't ignore it now. And, we're going to re-build our offices," Ronnie said, with a smile. "Tomorrow. We can get on to that tomorrow."

Chapter 31
[Ronnie: That was close.]

I waited until Crockett was gone, and Enzo was fully occupied by my cousin before I motioned to Ben to follow me out the back door.

He followed me to the middle of the back yard.

"What's up?" he asked, drawing me into his arms. Smart enough to know it needed to look like we wanted some personal time, and not that we were talking about anything important.

"That was too close to having *Genesis* compromised."

"Yeah. Way too close."

"We're lucky it was Justin who designed the programs and the encryption, otherwise we'd be screwed about now."

"It's a shame he died trying to keep a virus out of circulation."

Genesis at its finest.

"We need to destroy that USB before anyone else tries opening it."

"It was clever to disguise it as an atlas."

"It was. There were enough names and codenames inside those files to throw most people off and make them think that they were looking at an atlas, but those names, they're part of the code."

"You recognised some of them ..."

"Yeah, mine is there."

"Code?"

"It all works together, the so-called atlas and the *Genesis* files. The key to unlocking *Genesis* is hidden in the names of the atlas and books in the bookshop."

"Crazy clever. And?"

"We really need to destroy that USB. Destroy it. Lost in the mail forever. Well, pulverise it with a sledgehammer."

"Anyone figure out our involvement?" he asked.

"Not yet. Let's keep it that way."

Genesis exists to track WMD's, with the agents and officers involved bringing in intel which is analysed off the books. A plan is presented to a multi-nation strike force. It's their job to go in and destroy the weapons. No mess, no fuss. I paused my thoughts and looked into his eyes. "We're not protecting bad people; we're protecting everyone *from* the bad people."

He nodded.

"If we don't get rid of those files, good people will die."

"Does MacKinnon know what *Genesis* really is?" Ben asked.

"I doubt it. He might suspect, but he wasn't invited inside so he doesn't know. That file, all those files, they weren't stolen from any government or private person, they were stolen from *Genesis*."

"TechSynth?"

"They've got someone stealing from the government, one hundred percent. But they've also let someone get information on the most secret project in the world, through their servers."

"Bateman," Ben said. "Bateman doesn't come across as a real big threat."

I nodded. "I think her insider is James MacKinnon. Somehow it all pings back to James."

"Honey trap?"

"That'd be how I'd play it," I said. "Russians like a good honey-trap as much as the rest of us. Why not, put her in play, make sure she got in nice and cosy with James MacKinnon, until she got the intel she needed, and an idea of what he was involved in ... confirmation that he is inside *Genesis*."

"And what? James figured it out, went to his daddy, and said this woman is a spy and she's using me?"

"He said something, he told his father something to get this reaction, but I doubt it was the truth."

"And you really don't think he knows what his son is involved in?"

I shook my head. If he knew that, he'd know about us. And we'd be taking a one-way drive with Crockett.

"What now?" Ben whispered.

"We wait for the mail and destroy that drive." Half a smile lay on my lips. "I think Donald has a boyfriend."

Ben nodded. "Enzo does seem smitten."

I laughed. "Smitten? Who are you now, Nana?"

"What about Crockett? I think we made him a loose end ..." Ben's tone changed as his voice dropped lower. "What do we do about Crockett?"

"Let's play it by ear. We know where he lives if we discover the need to tie a knot in that loose end."

"Keep your friends close, but your enemies closer."

"I think that's wise, don't you? For all we know, his orders could change, and we could find ourselves the expendable loose ends."

"That's cheerful," Ben said, with a frown. "Do you always have to go to the darkest scenario?"

I smiled, making sure it was the sweetest smile possible. "Never hurts to be prepared. And to be honest I don't see what all the legend business is about regarding Crockett."

Chapter 32
[Crockett: Decision time.]

I dumped Bateman's body into a wheelie bin left for me by MacKinnon's crew, at a farm out near Owhiro Bay. Disposal wasn't my problem.

The long drive home gave me plenty of time to think.

Time to consider my options.

As I saw it, there were a couple of viable courses of action. Carry on with my tradie blokes, get them started on the second job, and forget all about Ronnie Tracey and *Witcher*. Or carry on with my tradies, ask Emily out, and stay in Ronnie's vicinity. I knew what I wanted to do. I also knew that the smart course of action was to get my head down, and just work.

And yet, I pulled up outside the bookshop.

I took a deep breath and let it out slowly. Enzo wasn't who I thought, but that didn't mean someone from my past wouldn't come for me. I could be waiting a while. Ronnie and Ben would be handy people to have around in a sticky situation. Ah, hell, even Enzo would be good to have around.

Emily leaned in the doorway of the bookshop and smiled at me. Time to forget about *Genesis* and my past and take a chance on life.

I flung my door open and hopped out of the car.

"Hey, Milo. Got a minute?"

"Hi, Crockett! I have twenty-seven minutes, starting

now."

"Lock up, and let's go get that hot chocolate," I said with a grin.

"Are you going to stay here?" Emily asked.

I held the door for her at the Mayfair café. "I think I am. That okay with you?"

"I like you," she said, and chose a table near the fire. "I would like you to stay."

"Then, I will."

The End.

Acknowledgments

A big joyful thank you to the usual suspects:
The family - Geoff and Dad; Caleb, Lizzie and Isaac; Rebekah, Deaglan, Caeden and Connaire; Patricia, Tim, Tori, David, Corey and Lily; Josephine, James, and Xanthea; Joshua, Jenna and the bump; Caoilfhionn and Brianna; Chrissy and Mike; Robyn and Duigald; Nicky.
Writers Plot: Ange, Pat, Colleen, Bill, Susan, Robyn, Caro.
Backspacers - our monthly word count threads really got this book happening!
Special thanks to Margot Kinberg who is the most wonderful cheerleader (and author) and to Pete Turner for encouraging this.

Even though writing is a solitary process, writers need people in their corner, whether it be for cheering or commiserating, it's good to know there are people who have my back.
So, thank you!

Writing during a pandemic is not as easy as you'd think. After the shittiest years ever, having this book out there in the world is nothing short of a miracle.

About the author

Coffee addict. Tequila drinker. Irresistible, infectious, addictive. Crime writer. Traveler. Believes music and animals are essential to the writing process. Murderer of perfectly happy characters: don't get too comfortable. Knows where to hide the body. And that thing, you think no one knows ... someone always knows. Cat knows.

Connect with Cat in the following places:
Twitter: @catconnor
Facebook: @cat.connor
Website: www.catconnor.com
Insta: @catconnorauthor

9mm Press

www.ingramcontent.com/pod-product-compliance
Lightning Source LLC
Chambersburg PA
CBHW022349020726
47500CB00002B/192